LOCKED BOX

A Pittsburgh Murder Mystery

LOCKED BOX

A Pittsburgh Murder Mystery

REBECCA A. MILES

 Torchflame Books

ISBN: 978-1-61153-369-9 (paperback)

ISBN: 978-1-61153-304-0 (ebook)

Library of Congress Control Number: 2024905503

Locked Box is published by: Torchflame Books, an imprint of Top Reads Publishing, LLC, USA

For information about special discounts for bulk purchases, please direct emails to: publisher@torchflamebooks.com

Cover design: Jori Hanna

Book interior layout: Jori Hanna

Printed in the United States of America

To my parents,
Stephen R. Stepek and Mary A. Kaelin,
who met and fell in love at the
Westinghouse Air Brake Company
Pittsburgh.

AND

To my brilliant friend,
Gina Bertocci, PhD,
Professor and Endowed Chair of Bioengineering
University of Kentucky,
who started her career at Westinghouse Pittsburgh.

CHAPTER 1

CELINE ARCENEAU WAS MET WITH ENTHUSIASTIC GREETINGS from the group of Pittsburgh friends who had gathered for a bon voyage dinner in her honor. As she was French-Canadian, her friends chose a small bistro situated in the East End of the city; Chef George knew Celine, and so was happy to help plan the gathering, but he was also sad that the attorney had finished her teaching sabbatical at the university law school and was heading back to Montreal.

The group was chatty and boisterous, their mood elevated by the first of many glasses of wine that would accompany the meal and the toe tapping music of Stephane Grappelli. A large table at the back of the railroad-car shaped restaurant had been preset with baskets of rolls and baguettes, dishes of farm-fresh butter, and the open bottles of red wine which would be enjoyed throughout the evening.

The finale of the party included gifts and amusing stories of Celine's time teaching at the law school, along with a selection of feathery, light macarons and rich coffee. The atmosphere was so delightfully congenial that everyone lingered.

André Trembly, Pittsburgh's Canadian consul, noticed that

Celine had become quite pale and was holding her hand to her forehead.

"Are you ill?" he asked, realizing that he himself felt clammy.

"I am. I feel nauseated and very hot. I think I'm going to be sick." Celine pushed back her chair and ran to the ladies' room, where she vomited. Unfortunately, she was just the first of the guests to fall ill; some felt dizzy, others nauseous, and a few, like Celine, bolted to the lavatory to retch.

The servers alerted Chef George, who called an ambulance, privately relieved that the restaurant was closed to anyone but this group. A second ambulance brought additional paramedics to help—eventually everyone was driven the short distance to the university hospital. The EMTs notified the hospital that a group of restaurant goers were about to arrive, probably suffering from food poisoning.

George was given the order to leave every bit of food and drink in place so that the public health experts could take samples of everything. He was grateful that he and his staff were not ill.

In the emergency department, the nurses and physicians triaged the ill diners: some needed their stomachs pumped, others were dehydrated and required intravenous fluids. Celine remained in gastrointestinal distress, and as time passed, she became mentally confused. Her primary care physician was notified that her patient would be admitted for observation.

After Celine had been stabilized and settled in a room, Dr. Ellen Smythe arrived. She leaned over the young woman and placed her cool hand on Celine's forehead.

"It's Dr. Smythe, Celine. How are you feeling?" Dr. Smythe gently took ahold of her patient's arm and put a blood pressure cuff on it. Celine opened her eyes, clearly having trouble focusing them.

"I feel so sick. Is that you, Mummy?" she asked.

"Celine, it's Doctor Smythe. It looks like you, and all of your friends at the party, have a case of food poisoning. Lie back and rest, we will take good care of you."

Dr. Smythe had seen her share of food poisonings, but the severity of Celine Arceneau's symptoms and her altered mental state worried her. In addition to this incident, Dr. Smythe had recently been treating Celine for what she believed was a flare-up of irritable bowel syndrome (IBS), so the poor young woman was already debilitated. Dr. Smythe was anxious for her patient to get home to Montreal where she would be treated by familiar physicians.

The doctors in the emergency department had given Dr. Smythe their report, but the toxin screens had to wait until everyone's stomach contents, bloodwork, and the samples from the restaurant food were acquired; she was informed that the public health experts were already at the bistro.

Kate Chambers and Ellen Smythe were having a breakfast meeting at the university club the morning after the food poisoning incident. These colleagues, one at the beginning of her career and the other a doyen, frequently sat on the same committees together. Ellen respected Kate's profession as an academic advisor, so much so that she had referred her grand-daughter Patricia to her for guidance on medical fellowships. After they had finished with their committee business and talking about Patricia, Ellen shared the news of the incident at the goodbye party.

"One of my patients, whom I won't name, and her colleagues at the law school were hosting a farewell party at that little bistro in the East End, when suddenly everyone became ill. George, the owner, had his wits about him and called an ambulance to take everyone to the hospital."

The only sign that Ellen had been up late with a sick

patient were the dark smudges under her eyes; otherwise she looked pristine in her trademark outfit of matching cashmere sweater and pants, and lightly-tinted, coiffed blonde hair.

Kate, who in certain circles was well-known as an amateur sleuth, perked up. "That restaurant has an immaculate kitchen and the finest quality food—it's hard to imagine that it would be food poisoning. I wonder if someone spiked the wine?"

Ellen grinned at Kate's immediate interest in the puzzle. "The physicians who treated the group felt it was food poisoning, but we have to wait for the results from the lab for confirmation. Everyone was discharged except my patient. You know, I never thought about someone spiking the wine. You deserve your reputation as a good detective!"

"Thanks for the compliment, Ellen. So, your patient became sicker than the others? That's both unfortunate and interesting. Do you know what the guests ate?" Kate asked.

"Everyone ate the same thing: scallops a la bonne femme, broccoli rabe, arugula salad with mustard vinaigrette, cheese plate with figs, and a selection of pastries. There were rolls, baguettes, butter, coffee, cream, and sugar cubes. Also, many bottles of wine," answered Ellen.

Kate's compulsive rolling and unrolling of her napkin gave witness to the fact that she had mentally started to sort through the ingredients for a likely suspect. "Were the red wines sitting uncorked on the table in order to breathe? If they were, any guest would have been able to slip something into them."

"The thing is, this patient has had similar symptoms to food poisoning for a few weeks now. She's had diarrhea, lost some weight, is always tired . . . she has a history of IBS. I worry that the food poisoning will debilitate her to the point that she won't be able to go home." Ellen was interrupted by a code page from the hospital.

"I have to go. My patient is in trouble." Ellen ran out of

the dining room, shouting back over her shoulder for Kate to grab her briefcase.

The hospital was only steps away from the university club, and Dr. Smythe made it to Celine Arceneau's room just as the head of the code team, an anesthesiologist, arrived and took charge of the many staff crowding in. Compressions to Celine's chest had already begun.

"If you don't have to be here, clear out!" ordered the anesthesiologist to numerous residents and nurses who were either in the room or at the doorway. "The airway is secured. I'm starting the epinephrine through the IV."

A nurse, sweaty but focused, called an end to the first two minutes of compressions. The code leader added another dose of epinephrine and watched the monitor. "Go," he ordered. Now three minutes of chest compressions began.

Wrenching life back from death's door was a profoundly emotional and physical experience; no one was ever sanguine about their participation in this most intimate of existential tasks. Celine Arceneau was only forty. Efforts to establish a heartbeat would continue for a long time.

Dr. Smythe verbalized what everyone was thinking. "Come on, Celine, come on! Start that heart! Come on, stay with us."

As the battle to save Celine continued, Ellen and the team leader talked through the medical possibilities that could have generated this situation in an otherwise healthy woman. It had been over forty minutes, and everyone was physically drained, especially Dr. Smythe. She locked eyes with the anesthesiologist, he nodded in the affirmative, then he made the wretched call.

"It's over. The time of death is 11:59."

Ellen slumped into a chair, covering her eyes with her

hands; the nurses and medical residents either leaned against a wall, emotionally spent, or wiped away tears of frustration. Ellen finally stood and confronted the team.

"What the heck happened? The report from morning rounds said Ms. Arceneau was stable and responding to treatment, and now this?" Like the splatter from a paintball, her reproach hit everyone.

"I want an autopsy, and I want Aashi Patel to do it. Get her on the phone for me."

Dr. Smythe turned back to her patient. As the team silently took care of the room and the crash cart, she gently closed Celine's eyelids, her soft demeanor belying her raging thoughts.

Not twenty-four hours ago, bright, talented Celine Arceneau had been enjoying her bon voyage party and looking forward to flying back to Montreal. Now she will be a body on the examining table in the Pittsburgh morgue. I want some answers.

CHAPTER 2

Dr. Aashi Patel, Pittsburgh's medical examiner, sat reading the e-chart Dr. Smythe had sent her on Ms. Arceneau. It documented that Celine had been forty, a good weight for her height, but suffered on and off from IBS; very recently she had complained of gastrointestinal issues accompanied by fatigue.

Dr. Smythe had consulted with Celine's physician in Montreal, who said that the IBS seemed to be active during times of stress or life changes; since she was returning to Montreal after her year sabbatical in Pittsburgh, it made sense that this transition might be a trigger.

Dr. Patel read on: Celine Arceneau had had a bout of COVID-19 twice, fully recovering both times. Gastrointestinal problems weren't usually associated with long COVID, but who really knew? When she was admitted to the hospital for food poisoning, an extensive blood panel was done. Dr. Patel was about to access all of the test results performed in the emergency department.

She swiveled her chair back and forth, continuing to analyze the medical record. *Could she really have died from food poisoning? She was getting better and then just crashed. Something isn't right.*

Dr. Patel and her colleagues were waiting on the report from the health department to see if any of the food had been contaminated. She read through the menu the restaurant had sent her and began to list the possible suspects: in the scallops a la bonne femme, there would be mushrooms —always a suspicious ingredient. The scallops could easily have been contaminated with any number of microbial agents—mercury, sewage dumped from cruise liners, norovirus, vibrio, chemicals present in the water used to clean them.

Like Kate, Aashi's first thoughts went to the open bottles of wine on the table, into which anyone could have injected a contaminate. Bacillus cereus was common on produce, meat, pasta, vegetable, and dairy foods. The cheeses might have had some kind of toxic mold, the wheat used to bake the rolls and baguettes might also have had a dangerous mold.

There are so many ways badly handled food can make a person sick. I just have to wait for the samples to be fully analyzed. Dr. Patel had long ago accepted that being a medical examiner meant being patient.

She moved to the body on her examining table, folded back the sheet, lowered the microphone that hung over the table, and began her autopsy.

Antoine DeVille, Chief Detective Stefan Jablonsky's number one, reported that a patient at the university hospital had unexpectedly died and had been transported to the morgue for Dr. Patel to figure out what had happened.

"About ten people were treated at the hospital after having dinner at a farewell party for a Canadian woman: Celine Arceneau had been in Pittsburgh teaching at the law school for a year. I have the list of names—by the way, Chief, André Trembly was one of the guests."

"Is he okay?" The chief knew both the French and Canadian consuls in Pittsburgh; Trembly represented Canada.

"Yes, he's okay—he went home that evening. Only the guest of honor was admitted to the hospital, everyone else was treated and released. The emergency docs suspect food poisoning."

DeVille, a light-skinned, Creole Black man, whose nickname was Coupe, leaned against the door frame looking quite natty in his navy pants, madras jacket, and pink shirt. He hailed from New Orleans, loved Pittsburgh and his job, and was a known coffee snob.

Jablonsky's thoughts turned to Dr. Patel, whom he took every opportunity to see outside of their frequent working breakfasts at Sophia's Café.

"Has Dr. Patel made a decision about the manner and cause of death yet?" As was his habit, the chief made a steeple with his fingers while he waited for Coupe's answer.

"Not that I know of, Boss."

"When did you start calling me boss? Don't! I'm going to mosey over to the morgue and see what's shaking."

Coupe hid his smile, knowing that the chief had a long-standing crush on Aashi Patel. *And who wouldn't*, he thought. She was an admired medical examiner, close to Jablonsky's age, smart, and someone who didn't put up with any jack-assery—*She's just like my grandmother*, mused Coupe.

The chief pocketed his small paper notebook, took out a pack of cinnamon gum, and offered Coupe a piece. He popped a stick into his own mouth and left for the morgue.

Jablonsky was a Pittsburgher, born and bred. Right after college, he went to the police academy, then began his long tenure in the department. Now in his sixties, he was tall and square-built, expanding in the middle, shrinking in the hair department, but still sporting thick, dark eyebrows. His nickname was the Great Horned Owl because he could spot things no one else did; his metaphorical talons were large and sharp, efficient for gathering criminals. Jablonsky was divorced with one daughter, Carly, a practicing attorney in the city.

The chief was respected and feared at work, but in his private life, he could be turned into a puddle of love around his daughter. In addition to his dedication to justice, Carly gave meaning to his life; someday he hoped to add Aashi Patel to that list. On the days he had business at the morgue, he took care with his outfit and a wipe of Bay Rum, a men's cologne that Dr. Patel liked.

Jablonsky pushed open the double doors leading into the morgue, and as usual, was startled by the bright lights. He waited for his pupils to return to normal before walking over to Aashi, who was sitting at a shelf of microscopes, reading a field guide of some kind.

"Any news about our Canadian national?" he asked, curious as to what had her so engrossed.

"I'm reading the *National Audubon Society's Field Guide to Mushrooms*," she answered grinning, her chocolate-colored eyes filled with humor. "The variety of fungi that exists is really fascinating, and equally fascinating is how many can kill you. Food is fuel, but it can also be a weapon."

"Fuel and a weapon! I like the way you think, Aashi. Any idea how the diners were sickened?" Jablonsky loved an unusual poison as much as Dr. Patel did.

"Not yet. Almost any food can kill you. I mean it can be contaminated anywhere in its production or in the kitchen: bad animal feed, rodent droppings in the field, pesticides or herbicides, molds in grain, food not washed before preparation, food left out too long, they're all common culprits. E. coli, botulism, salmonella, Bacillus cereus—I could go on!" Dr. Patel chuckled over Jablonsky's grimace.

"Are you leaning toward bacteria that wasn't properly

washed off the food or something purposely added?" asked the chief.

"I just don't know yet. All the samples haven't been processed, and even when they are, the answer to your question may be ambiguous," stated Dr. Patel.

"What's bothering you, Aashi?" asked the chief, noticing her frown.

"According to Dr. Smythe's notes, this young woman had been complaining of gastrointestinal problems for maybe eight to ten days. Since the patient already had a diagnosis of IBS, Ellen consulted Celine's physician in Montreal, and the two decided that this was another flare."

"Okay, but irritable bowel usually doesn't kill you, correct? Why would she be the only one to die? Was someone trying to cover up a murder by committing it in the middle of everyone else getting a little sick?" Jablonsky asked the question to no one in particular; he stood up and started to pace.

"It's been done before," remarked Dr. Patel. "Make a lot of people sick so that a single murder goes unnoticed. At this stage, I'm declaring her death to be suspicious."

Jablonsky stopped his pacing, rubbed his hands together, and grinned. He knew better than to ask Aashi if she wanted to make a wager on this ending-up to be a murder—she would have found that offensive; but if the case demanded it, he and DeVille might bet a few dollars.

"See you at Sophia's. If you know something before we meet, call me."

Jablonsky headed over to the bistro. As he drove, he called DeVille.

"Coupe. Get pictures of everyone who was at the farewell party for Ms. Arceneau and begin a search into each person's background. Dr. Patel is ruling the death as suspicious. I'll see you shortly."

The East Liberty area had undergone several attempts at gentrification. The worst, most ill-conceived attempt, took place in the late sixties and early seventies; euphemistically termed a "renewal," it had torn apart a thriving African-American and Jewish community of businesses.

The most recent iteration took place primarily on the edges of the old community: The little bistro was one of a few small, privately owned establishments that people loved and frequented. Parking, of course, was still an issue, but Jablonsky pulled right in front—who would dare question him?

Even though the health department had yet to give the okay to reopen, Chef George was there, along with his sous-chef. Jablonsky greeted George, whom he knew.

"Sorry for all of this trouble, Chef. Everyone knows you run a clean establishment. I just left Dr. Patel at the morgue. She listed a myriad of ways that food can kill you through microbial agents—her words, not mine. Could bacteria have gone unnoticed on the food here?"

"Never! Never would unclean or contaminated food enter my kitchen. It is impossible!" The chef's outrage at the accusation was so strong that his face suddenly resembled a wrinkled red heirloom tomato.

"But yet George, it must have. Let me see all the entrances and exits to the kitchen."

Jablonsky was shown through a double-wide door that led directly into a generous hallway that served as a pantry; either side of the wide hallway was lined with shelving for dry ingredients. At the end of that hallway was a freezer, a cooler, and a small desk. At the other end was the kitchen with doors on either side so that the waitstaff could smoothly enter and exit. The restaurant had a back patio area for use in clement weather; the patio did not open onto an alley or parking lot but rather a steep drop to railway tracks.

Lots of unsupervised access to the kitchen and pantry, thought the chief.

"Have you changed suppliers recently? Could a new vendor have slipped in bad food stuffs without you knowing about it?"

"No. No new vendors, and I, and my sous-chef, Henry, know all about deadly microbes. I was trained at Le Cordon Bleu in Paris!" George crossed his arms and jutted out his chin, as if to indicate that being trained at the Parisian Cordon Blue was tantamount to saying he had been trained by God.

"What about the dishwasher, the bartender, or even your waitstaff?" asked the chief.

"No. Everyone here is a regular, even the dishwasher. I personally train them and know them," George stated.

"Okay. Please email me the names and addresses of everyone who works for you. This is just procedure, nothing personal," reassured Jablonsky.

"When can I reopen?" demanded George. "I'm losing a lot of money. My regular patrons are anxious to come and dine to show their support."

"I have no control over how fast the health department will finish its analysis of the food and drink. Hopefully it will be very soon. I will come and dine as well," declared Jablonsky, firmly grasping George's hand to show his personal support, and to avoid being kissed on both cheeks, a habit the chef had picked up in Paris.

Jablonsky headed back to the precinct. In advance of Dr. Patel's ruling on the manner and cause of death, he wanted to start the murder board.

CHAPTER 3

SINCE THE DEATH OF HER HUSBAND OF ONLY A FEW HOURS, Eddie Fitzroy, Kate dealt with her grief by starting new projects. She had been hoping to continue with her glass blowing classes, but since the murder of her young classmate Eugene Rose, she didn't have the heart to return to the glass center just yet; time had to soften the memory.

The haiku poems that Marco Rossetti—a surgeon and new friend—had been sending her surprisingly helped stem her day-time drifting. She looked forward to the poems, not sure when Marco would return from training surgeons in battlefield techniques; he had been in Poland and Ukraine for quite a while now.

She sipped a strong demitasse of espresso made from Johnny's elaborate Italian coffee machine while he graded his students' final term papers. Kate's office was quite clinical, but Johnny's was like a cozy den filled with shelves of art books, a computer with an oversized screen, comfy, over-stuffed armchairs, warm lighting, and of course, his high-tech coffee machine, accompanied by tiny, fragile cups as a counterpoint.

Kate admired how Johnny had dealt with the murder of his mother; he looked to art for healing, immersing himself in his teaching and his research in art history. He made sense of the bad things that had happened to him as a young gay man, and the recent loss of his dear mum, not through distant gods or pharmacological solutions, but through the artistic expressions of music, painting, and architecture. Johnny was a unique, beautiful soul—Kate loved him like a brother.

Vigorous knocking interrupted the studious atmosphere, startling Kate, who once again was mentally floating. Her grief frequently robbed her of focus.

"Dr. McCarthy?" A young man opened the office door just wide enough to stick his head in. "I just emailed my final paper. Did you get it?"

Kate watched her affable friend morph into a stern professor.

"Yes, James. I see it in my inbox. You know that it is now four days late," replied Johnny.

"Yes, I know it's late. But, see, my grandmother died, and I had to go home to the funeral. I've been so upset; it was hard for me to concentrate on the paper," said James.

"Is this a different grandmother than the one you said died at midterms?" Although Johnny spoke in a matter-of-fact tone, the student's eyes grew large as he attempted to recall which grandparent he had previously knocked off.

"I . . . well . . . yeah. I mean, you're right, this is my other grandmother." The student had the good grace to at least look sheepish at having been caught in his lie.

"Since there was this death in my family, does it still mean I can't get an A on my paper, just because it is late?" asked James.

"Yes, James. A late paper always starts with a B rather than an A. The grade can be a B+, but you can't get an A, those are the rules—the same rules for every semester and for every student. Anything else?" Johnny asked firmly.

"No, sir. Thank you." The student's face disappeared as the door silently closed.

Kate and Johnny waited until the sound of his footsteps faded, indicating that he was out of hearing range, then both howled with laughter.

"Did he really use the 'my grandmother died' story at midterms?" asked Kate.

"Oh, yes. A grandparent's death is the number one excuse students give for delivering a late paper; number two is stomach flu, which, unlike a funeral, is difficult to trace." These two academics had never breached a deadline in all their years of education, so the student excuses were highly amusing to them. When Johnny returned to grading papers, Kate grew silent.

Johnny lifted his eyes from the computer screen. "A penny for your thoughts?"

"Oh, I was thinking that I need to set myself a new challenge."

"You've been reading the Olympic swimming posts much too often. You and Joan are quite the pair—she's obsessed with baseball and you are obsessed with Olympic swimmers—I'm the guy here, but I'm obsessed with art," quipped Johnny.

"In my defense, those women swimmers always send out posts that are inspirational. Look, I want to be serious for a minute. My grandfather taught me that grief lives in the body. After my parents' death, he enrolled me in swim lessons, and for years, I never stopped staring at the black line—well . . . not until senior year, that is. The exertion of the endless lapping really helped me cope with the double loss of my parents."

Kate finished her coffee, setting the delicate cup down on the floor alongside her chair; she unfolded her long legs and leaned forward toward Johnny, hoping to communicate her earnestness.

"One post I just read said, 'I get up, I set a goal, I achieve it.' I operate like that with my academic advisees and my sleuthing, but I want that commitment with my workouts. What would you say to training for the half triathlon? I haven't swam in years, but the yardage involved in the mini triathlon isn't that extensive. We could manage it."

Johnny was her workout partner. They kayaked on the river, they jogged around the Highland Park reservoir, they ran the Pittsburgh Steps, they worked through the Upper Frick obstacle course, but swimming had never been a part of their routines. Kate watched him mentally searching for an out.

"Kate—I don't swim," stated Johnny.

"Is that because of your scars?" Kate knew that Johnny had been the victim of terrible bullying by his father and classmates, so as a teen, he took to cutting himself. Her heart broke every time she saw the scars, which fortunately by now, were very thin lines.

"No, it's not that. A longer bathing suit will cover them. I just never learned how to swim," admitted Johnny.

"You'll get a coach. It will all be freestyle stroke anyway. We can train at the university pool. Come on . . . come on, let's do it," she wheedled. "Your figure will be even more svelte, perfect for attracting a new partner," she said, unabashedly trying to manipulate him through compliments.

"Kate, the physicality of training won't erase your grief over Eddie—you know that. No matter how much I work out, I still miss my mum terribly," Johnny counseled, his expression a mixture of empathy and sternness.

"I *do* know that Johnny, but there is research that posits when you change your physical state, it affects your mental state." She didn't need to articulate the rest of the thought; the emotional pain from loss was understood between them.

Kate could be single-minded, even compulsive, when it came to achieving goals; she knew Johnny understood that if he agreed to train with her, there would be no bowing out later. She counted on his unconditional love to make it hard for him to say no to her.

He finally responded. "I'll think about it. Do you have a coach in mind?"

"Well, Ellen mentioned to me that her physician assistant is a triathlete. Maybe he would be willing to advise us. Ellen really likes and respects him—he would know a lot about how to safely train older athletes, like us," said Kate.

"Anything in it for me? I mean, does he cha-cha?" Johnny hadn't been involved with anyone since his former partner had moved to Europe for work; a little romance would be nice.

"No, my dear professor, he doesn't cha-cha. He's straight. I think? Oh! That reminds me. I can't believe I forgot to ask you if you heard about the food poisoning incident that happened at our favorite bistro?" Kate asked with macabre excitement.

"I did hear about it. If everyone got sick from eating the same foods, something must have been tainted," offered Johnny.

Kate responded to his common-sense formulation with a "maybe not" expression.

"Yes . . . perhaps it was an accident. I was at breakfast with Ellen when she got the code alert—one of the diners was a patient of hers. I don't know the upshot of the situation, but my intuition is nudging me toward the possibility that the food poisoning was not an accident. That bistro's kitchen is always shiny clean, and so is the food. Chef George wouldn't have it any other way. I think someone added a poison."

I'll call Joan and see what she knows about Ellen's patient, thought Kate.

Kate was possessed of a suspicious mind. She often saw the possibility of foul play where others didn't—it made her a good sleuth but an eccentric friend. When she looked around the world, she saw disconnections and irrationalities rather than orderly coherence. Since Jablonsky had that same mind-set, she knew he would look at Ellen Smythe as a possible suspect.

"I'm really fond of Dr. Smythe. I hope there is nothing in the situation that would hurt her," Kate said aloud but mostly to herself.

It was almost evening, so Kate and Johnny decided to walk to her Fifth Avenue condominium, Johnny's home away from home. On their stroll, he nagged at her about how many of her patio lights weren't working.

"Get them fixed, Kate. You can barely see Bourbon Ball when he's out there doing his business."

Kate distracted herself from his carping by noticing how the spring air was perfumed with the blooming ornamental pear and crabapple trees that dotted the lawns along the way. She found herself watching the shape-shifting cloud formations that doted the sky, appreciating the painterly quality of its blue and pink light.

Her meditative state was shattered when a bicyclist came out of nowhere, cutting between her and Johnny, knocking her down.

"Hey, watch it buddy!" yelled Johnny. "Are you okay, Kate? He did that on purpose."

"You bet it was on purpose. I seem to be having numerous run-ins with student bicyclists these days. That one was particularly bad," said Kate.

Kate didn't respond to Johnny's worried expression, but it confirmed what she had been feeling for the last year— someone was watching her.

CHAPTER 4

"Dr. Patel has declared Celine Arceneau's death to be suspicious; she and forensics are working on which bacteria was used on what food, or placed in the wine," announced Jablonsky as he stood in front of the sparse murder board, unwrapping a stick of cinnamon gum. Coupe and Annie Lemon already had photos of the dinner attendees tacked in a row at the bottom of the board.

"Chief. Here's the consul's picture," said Detective DeVille, pointing to André Trembly's official photo.

"He might be useful to us. Poor guy. I hope he didn't have his stomach pumped. I want to interview him." The chief placed a picture of Celine Arceneau in the middle of the board, and out to one side, he tacked photos of Chef George, Dr. Ellen Smythe, and under her, a few small pictures of the staff at her private office.

"Detective Lemon, set up an interview with Dr Smythe. I'll go to her office—arrange that for today. Make sure the other staff are also around," ordered Jablonsky.

Lemon handed him a photo of the hospital code leader, an anesthesiologist, Dr. Neil James. "Let's check into this physician. It's a long shot, but he was there at a critical time."

Jablonsky quietly chewed on his gum as he wrote out several questions: Is there a hidden connection between Chef George and Celine Arceneau? (Both French Canadian.) Exactly who had access to the bistro the day before and the day of the farewell dinner? Aside from the doctor-patient relationship, is there another connection between Dr. Smythe and Celine? Is someone setting up Chef George or Dr. Smythe? What about Dr. James, did he know Celine outside of the hospital?

"Coupe. Look over the email that George was supposed to send listing his bistro staff and the restaurant suppliers. I want you to walk the scene with George, who is very cooperative, then interview the others. Be *thorough*," advised the chief.

Detective DeVille had dropped the ball on a few details in the Eugene Rose case. He knew he was under Jablonsky's microscope.

Detective Lemon pointed to Dr. Smythe's picture. "I've been looking at Ellen Smythe's university bio, and the one for Peter, her deceased husband. Here are some facts: She was born and raised in Pittsburgh, stayed for college, then attended medical school here. The dead husband, Peter Smythe, was a founding partner in the law firm C&S—for Cooper and Smythe—LLC.

"They specialize in international business, so he traveled extensively. Peter came from old money, but his law firm made him wealthy in his own right. He was almost twenty years older than Ellen, and he, um, died in his seventies from leukemia. They have one daughter, Rose Delaney, who doesn't work; lots of photos of her in the society pages though." Lemon paused at Jablonsky's open-hand stop signal.

"Focus on Dr. Smythe's private life—who might have it in for her to the point they would frame her for murder." Lemon and DeVille knew that Jablonsky believed individuals on a pedestal were like piñatas: someone always wanted to take a whack at them.

"Lots of attorneys in this situation. There were all the law professors at her good-bye party, Celine Arceneau herself, and then the deceased Peter Smythe," said Jablonsky.

At the board, the chief repeatedly tapped his pen on Ellen's picture, while thinking, *Had some of these local attorneys previously known Celine, and if so, how would it relate to this case? How did she come to have a teaching sabbatical in Pittsburgh?*

"What about Chef George? Everyone likes him, including me." Jablonsky rarely offered that kind of comment on a potential person of interest—Lemon and Coupe took note.

Coupe added what he knew about George. "Our Chef George was born and raised in Montreal, Canada. After high school he went to the Cordon Bleu in Paris, then came home to work at various fine dining establishments in and around Montreal, until he met his wife, a Pittsburgher. They moved here to start the bistro. He is now an American citizen. No criminal history that I could find."

"He was from Montreal and so was Celine Arceneau. Could they have met?" remarked the chief.

"Henry, the sous-chef, also hails from Montreal. He has a green card, no criminal history that I could find, either here or in Canada. That's about it, Boss—oops, sorry, I meant Chief." DeVille's grin was devilish, even Jablonsky cracked a smile.

Detective Lemon looked at a text on her phone. "Ellen Smythe will see you today, at your convenience. Also, André Trembly will come to the station."

"Good. Get me more details on Dr. Smythe's private life and her daughter, Rose Delaney. I'm heading into Oakland," stated Jablonsky.

Forbes Avenue in Oakland was hood-to-trunk traffic. Jablonsky, a patient man, settled back and chewed a fresh stick of cinnamon gum. When he entered Dr. Smythe's office suite, he announced himself and was led down a long corridor to her private office.

Ellen Smythe was standing with her back to the door staring out the window, appearing to watch the large groups of students moving back and forth across busy Forbes Avenue trying not to be late for their classes. She seemed unaware of the chief.

Jablonsky took advantage of her preoccupation to look around at the attractively furnished office. Everything seemed to be in its place: No papers or files strewn on her desk, her spring jacket was hung on a coat tree, an umbrella rested on one of the hooks, and walking shoes were placed on a boot tray under it. The numerous bookcases were filled, and a graceful white phalaenopsis orchid sat on one of the windowsills. It was a calm and studious space. He coughed to alert her to his presence.

"Dr. Smythe, I am Chief Detective Stefan Jablonsky. I'm here to ask you some questions about the death of your patient Celine Arceneau."

"Of course, Chief Jablonsky. Since I had asked for an autopsy, I was expecting you."

Dr. Smythe turned from the window, seated herself behind her desk, folded her hands, and leveled an unwavering gaze at him. Her immaculate white physician's coat covered an aquamarine sweater and matching pants.

Jablonsky noted that her eyes were a startling color of warm gray. She wore neither a wedding band nor a diamond engagement ring, her fingernails were clean and cut short. There was something in her posture and expression that made him think, *This is a woman who is used to authority and control.*

"Would you please recount the events leading up to and surrounding the death of Celine Arceneau?" he asked, placing his small paper notebook on the knee of his crossed leg.

"Of course. The night before Ms. Arceneau died, I received a page from the emergency department (ED) that she was one of the diners who had suffered food poisoning at her farewell party. I spoke with the ED and agreed that she should be admitted. I was already in the hospital checking on another patient, so I stopped to see her. Since the chart stated that she was stable, I talked with the nurses, then went home.

"The next morning I was at a breakfast meeting at the university club when I received a code text from the hospital. Since the club is so close to the hospital, I simply ran over—the leader of the code team, Dr. James, was already supervising chest compressions and had added epinephrine to her IV. Unfortunately, none of our technologies nor any of our skills saved her life. It's a terribly sad and surprising story," said Dr. Smythe.

Jablonsky watched her, waiting to see what she would spontaneously offer, but she added nothing—she sat waiting for his next question.

"You said her death was . . . surprising?" Jablonsky prodded.

"Yes, it was surprising. The symptoms from the food poisoning were abating and Ms. Arceneau was only in her early forties." Dr. Smythe's expression remained impassive.

"She had no other medical problems then?" asked the chief.

"Well, none of the big three—heart disease, obesity, or cancer. Her Canadian physician, however, had diagnosed her with IBS. In these last few weeks before heading home, Celine reported suffering some gastrointestinal problems along with fatigue. I spoke with her physician, and we both felt it was a flare of IBS. It was a stressful time for her; she had just finished a year of teaching here and was heading home to Montreal. While going home is wonderful, transitions can be trying," remarked Dr. Smythe.

"Was your physician assistant with you in the room? That would be a Jake Albert?" the chief prompted, checking his notes for the name.

"No. He remained with another patient's family, and only later came to the nurses' station. I don't think he ever saw Celine. He called Dr. Patel for me," said Dr. Smythe.

"I'll speak with him after we finish. Tell me about Ms. Arceneau." Jablonsky didn't give the doctor any chance to take control of the interview.

Dr. Smythe opened her computer, found the e-chart, and began to read the same facts that Dr. Patel had offered.

The chief interrupted. "I know the medical details. I want your impressions of her. Was she likable, easy to deal with? Was there anything that struck you as odd or made you uneasy about her?"

Dr. Smythe pursed her lips and wrinkled her brow. "Well, she was only my patient for twelve months. Before the last several weeks, she had no substantial medical problems. Jake typically saw her, then reported to me if there was any change in her status—such as the gastrointestinal issues to which I referred. Um, if I'm forced to answer such an open-ended question, I'd say Ms. Arceneau was a pleasure to deal with."

In the manner of Aashi Patel, Dr. Smythe started to slowly rotate her chair.

"I just have a few more questions. How was she referred to you in the first place?" asked Jablonsky.

"The request came through Pittsburgh's Canadian consul, André Trembly. He often refers Canadian nationals who are at the university to me. Why? Is it important?" Curiosity lit her gray eyes.

"It might be. Did you personally know this patient? Perhaps attend a dinner with Trembly where Celine was also a guest?" asked Jablonsky.

"No. I don't socialize with my patients," Dr. Smythe tersely replied.

"Who was with you at your breakfast meeting, the meeting that you left to go to the hospital?"

"A colleague, Dr. Kate Chambers," answered Dr. Smythe.

Jablonsky smiled at hearing Kate's name. *Oh no, Kate's proximity to Smythe might mean she'll want to be involved.*

"Is Kate Chambers a patient of yours?" asked the chief.

"Well, she's a colleague and a patient," offered Dr. Smythe.

"Then you *do* sometimes see patients outside of the office," Jablonsky pointed out, smiling.

Ellen Smythe rolled her eyes and shrugged. "Match point to you, Chief Detective."

Jablonsky moved to shock the controlled Dr. Smythe with his next question. "Do you know anyone who would want to frame you for murder?"

"Frame me for murder? What are you talking about?" asked Dr. Smythe.

"I'm talking about the fact that Dr. Patel has ruled Celine Arceneau's death to be suspicious. She and the public health techs are looking at various forms of food poisoning. Why would only your patient die from food poisoning when the others didn't?" Jablonsky's delivery was neutral, but he was watchful of her reaction.

"You believe that Celine Arceneau was murdered? I didn't expect that."

Dr. Smythe's reaction to the news seemed genuine. "This is a murder investigation then. If it is not prohibited, I'd like to talk with Aashi Patel about the autopsy results—after all, Celine was my patient. I'd like to go through the blood panel that was ordered in the hospital with her."

"At this juncture, I don't see any problem with you and Dr. Patel speaking." The chief paused. "You did not know Celine Arceneau before she came to Pittsburgh: is that your story?"

"It's not a story. It is the truth." Dr. Smythe remained unflappable.

Jablonsky flipped his small paper notebook closed. "I'd like to interview Jake Albert and your primary nurse now."

"You can see them in our conference room." Ellen walked

with him down the corridor; before she opened the door to it, she asked, "Am I a suspect?"

"Our investigation has just begun. I may want to come back to you with more questions—just don't leave town," said Jablonsky.

———

The interview with Jake Albert and Dr. Smythe's primary nurse, Kathleen, did not yield any new information about Celine Arceneau but did reveal their loyalty to their boss.

Jake Albert was a young man in his late thirties with dark, close-clipped hair and eyes that had the unnerving intensity of a raptor. Similar to Dr. Smythe's white coat, Jake's hospital greens were immaculately clean; the pants had a sharp crease, indicating they had been starched and ironed. His arms were muscular, and through the light material of the pants, the chief could see the outline of strongly developed quadriceps. Jablonsky quietly sighed; he was still a vital man but would never again be that young and strong.

"Do you socialize with Dr. Smythe outside of the office? Maybe catch a drink or dinner to talk over a difficult case?" asked the chief.

"No. When you interview to work in her practice, she makes it clear that there will be a boundary between our professional relationship with her and her private life. She does not encourage fraternization between employees," answered Jake.

Since Jake's expression gave no hint of what he thought of the rule, Jablonsky persisted. "Do some of the staff resent the rules?"

"Not that I know of. It is a privilege to work with such a good physician. She treats her patients and staff with respect —and she pays well." Jake finally cracked a half-smile, the first genuine affect he exhibited.

"Glad to hear it." He turned to Nurse Kathleen, who was in her fifties, more zoftig than fit, and less reserved than Jake. "Has Dr. Smythe's rule about employees keeping their private lives and their work lives separate caused any resentments in you or your staff?"

"The rules are fine with me. Some of the other nurses and desk staff would like to celebrate birthdays at work, maybe be allowed to have more personal photos on their desks—those are the only complaints. I personally like to completely focus on work when I'm here," stated Kathleen. Jake nodded his agreement.

"Was there anything about Celine Arceneau that struck either of you as odd?" asked Jablonsky.

Jake repeated the question before answering. "Struck me as odd? The only thing that comes to mind is that she asked personal questions. American patients will only do that once they have been with a physician for a long time."

"What did she want to know?" asked the chief.

"It's hard for me to remember. . . ." Nothing about Jake's expression or posture changed as he lied to the chief.

"Try," pushed Jablonsky.

"Okay, well, she asked what it was like to work with Dr. Smythe, questions similar to yours. I just redirected her," said Jake.

Jablonsky leaned forward in his chair, eyeballing Jake like he was an ant about to be sizzled under a magnifying glass. "You redirected her. . . . Redirected into what?"

Jake's pupils dilated; he got the message that he had better answer. "I redirected her by asking a medical question—like a question about how she was feeling."

"You never gave her personal information about yourself or Dr. Smythe?" Jablonsky kept after him.

"Not that I can remember," Jake stated.

"How about you, Kathleen? Did you give Ms. Arceneau

any personal information about yourself or Dr. Smythe?" Jablonsky queried.

Kathleen was a mature woman and the senior nurse; she wasn't intimidated by the chief. "No. I didn't give any personal information to this patient, and no, I didn't think there was anything odd or unusual about Ms. Arceneau."

Kathleen continued to school the chief. "Canadians are friendly, nice people—she was like that—chatty. I didn't treat her in the hospital, however, just here in the office."

Jablonsky turned back to Jake. "Were you in Celine Arceneau's hospital room the morning she died?"

"By the time I came onto the floor, she was already dead; I stayed at the nurses' station talking to the code team—I called Dr. Patel for Dr. Smythe," Jake answered.

"I'd like a list of everyone you spoke to about Ms. Arceneau while you were at the nurses' station. Email it to Detective DeVille at this number." Jablonsky stood, handed out two cards, then stared down at the young man and the nurse.

"Celine Arceneau's death has been ruled suspicious. I'm looking for someone who may have murdered her—don't leave the city."

The chief left the two shocked employees, which is what he wanted. Neither Jake's restraint in the interview nor that of Nurse Kathleen did either any favors; in Jablonsky's experience with interviewees, restraint was often one of the masks that liars wore.

Chief Jablonsky left the building. Outside, the university area was alive with student pedestrians, workers having lunch, and bicyclists preforming death-defying antics maneuvering through traffic. As he headed to his car, he passed several boutique coffee shops where students were downing cups of coffee, clearly needing the caffeine. Deciding to do the same, Jablonsky stepped into one of the shops and ordered a regular coffee with a double shot of espresso.

He perched at one of the high-top tables, his mind

enlivened by the energy around him and the caffeine bump. The chief had graduated from this university—like a worn pair of jeans, the atmosphere was a comfortable fit.

Jablonsky's impression of Dr. Smythe was that she was one cool customer—but, did that make her a murderer? What would be her motive? He also had noted that she could look and sound sincere—was that genuine on her part, or had she become practiced in that posture from dealing with patients and their families? It certainly gave her the ability to effectively hide something important.

He had to consider that she either personally knew Celine Arceneau or knew something significant about her, or that someone wanted her to take the fall for the murder—but again, what would be the motive? He tossed back the rest of his coffee and called DeVille.

"I'm heading back to the precinct now. I'll expect your full report on Ellen Smythe and Rose Delaney."

CHAPTER 5

ONE LENTEN TRADITION IN PITTSBURGH IS THE FRIDAY FISH Fry. You didn't have to be of any particular religious affiliation to have an opinion about which parish consistently served the yummiest fried fish sandwich. Strongly held opinions about the delectable sandwich had coalesced around the following rules: The fish had to be New England cod, very lightly breaded, and quickly fried. The tartar sauce must include a small amount of finely chopped sweet pickle or relish; tomato catsup as a condiment was frowned upon. The bun could be lightly toasted or plain. No sliced tomato or lettuce should be included—the fish was the star.

Since it was already three Fridays into Lent, Kate wasn't surprised when she received a call from Dr. Joan Weisner, a self-proclaimed fried fish sandwich aficionado.

"Hi, Kate! Are you up for a fish sandwich as early dinner? The parish on Shady Avenue is serving—it's close to your condo. What do you say?" asked Joan.

Joan often helped Kate when she was involved in a murder investigation; most recently, it had been the Eugene Rose case. Joan's relationship with the Rose family had provided Kate an entry into the family, and through that relationship, she discovered important clues that were essential to solving the case.

Joan had an encyclopedic knowledge about almost everything; she was a Scripps Spelling Bee Finalist and a talented general surgeon. Joan was also a fanatic about the Pittsburgh Pirates, especially their new pitcher, Cheeks Malouskas. Since their graduate residencies, Kate in her doctoral program and Joan in surgery, they had remained close friends.

"I have gossip about two medical colleagues," was Joan's inducement to Kate to go to the fish fry. Since she sometimes relied on Joan's knowledge of the "who's who" in the university hospitals, the offer of gossip was a significant carrot.

"Sounds good to me. Since that church is so close—let's walk," Kate suggested.

Before Joan arrived, Kate fed, exercised, and played with Bourbon Ball, her chocolate Labrador. He followed her around as she changed into jeans and a spring sweater, hoping for, and getting, pets and ear massages; she always marveled at how his thick coat was as soft as a bunny's. Just before the doorbell rang, Bourbon Ball let out with a deep-throated woof. After greeting Joan, an official member of BB's pack, he stretched out on the dining room rug, settling into his after-dinner nap.

Once seated in the church hall, Kate didn't stand on ceremony. "What's the new gossip?"

"So, you've already heard about the mass food poisoning at the bistro, but what you didn't know is that the guest of honor unexpectedly died the next morning. And not only that, Dr. Patel has ruled the death suspicious, which is one step toward calling it murder. Imagine a patient of Ellen Smythe's murdered—it's all over the hospital." Joan paused, enjoying the drama of the situation.

"Was it food poisoning or toxins in the wine? Since everyone was sick—it must have been something they all ate or drank." Kate wasn't at all surprised to hear about Dr. Patel's ruling; what else could it be but murder?

"Of course food poisoning is what everyone speculates, but the health department hasn't finished testing yet. There are a million ways food can kill ya." Joan obviously suffered no such worries as she slathered more tartar sauce on her sandwich.

"I found out that Jablonsky already interviewed Dr. Smythe and Jake Albert, her physician assistant, and Kathleen, her head nurse, who has been with her forever. Are you going to eat that last piece?" asked Joan, sliding Kate's paper plate over to her side of the table.

"It would be pro forma that Jablonsky would interview her because it was her patient, but, knowing him, he might be considering her as a strong suspect. But why? Just because a patient dies doesn't mean the physician had malicious intent toward that person. Have you ever been questioned by the police over a patient unexpectedly dying?" asked Kate.

"I've only lost one patient during surgery—the patient suffered a cardiac arrest on the table—the medical examiner was not involved." Having finished the last of her own and Kate's sandwiches, Joan offered more on Ellen's situation.

"Because this patient died unexpectedly and within twenty-four hours of being admitted, they would automatically be taken to the medical examiner. I hear that Dr. Smythe asked specifically for Aashi Patel. Ellen sure as heck would want to know what happened—this unexplained death would be very upsetting to her."

"I'm going to call Ellen and see if she needs anything." Kate pushed back her chair, ready to leave.

"Kate, you want in on the investigation because it's Ellen, and you don't want her unjustly accused of something this serious. Am I correct?" Joan fixed her surgeon's gaze on Kate.

"Well, yes. You think it's wrong to want to get involved?"

"Not wrong for you, my little pretty. Ellen Smythe is important to many women in the hospital, and I too want to help in any way I can. I forgot to tell you that André Trembly was one of the diners who was poisoned. According to my source in the ED, he was released that evening," Joan stated.

"Really, he was there? Do you know him?" asked Kate.

"Not really. I've had patients come here from Canada for specialty surgeries—he sometimes facilitates their entry into our hospital system. Nice guy. I don't know him well enough to introduce you, let alone have you question him!" Joan declared.

"I wasn't going to ask you for an introduction." Kate pretended to look shocked, but Joan had in fact correctly surmised where her questions were leading.

"There is more gossip. Did you know that The Leopard is back in town? His mother died. He just flew in and has been making the funeral arrangements," said Joan.

"It's such a ridiculous nickname, The Leopard," snapped Kate. "Just because he lives alone. I'm sorry to hear about his mom. She attended this parish—her death notice should be in the bulletin. Let's find a copy, that is, if they still print a paper one."

The two women left the hall and went around to the front of the church, only to find the doors were locked—after the synagogue massacre, very few houses of worship in Pittsburgh were open for prayer at all hours.

"I'll look online," said Joan, pulling out her phone.

"He's lost every member of his immediate family—his mom was the last. Now he's an orphan, just like me," Kate whispered, almost to herself.

Joan heard the sentiment but didn't respond to it. "Will you attend the funeral?" Despite his fame, and the brilliance which made him a bit odd, Joan liked surgeon Marco Rossetti. She particularly liked him for Kate.

"You should go," Joan urged.

"Why? So I can flirt with him at his mother's funeral? Come on Joan, let's observe some proprieties," admonished Kate.

"Look, my mother always told me that a funeral is like a wedding: both are vehicles to meet someone. Not that I have followed her advice," she quipped. The process of dating was empty calories for Joan—nowhere near as satisfying as surgery and baseball.

Marco's recent switch from sending postcards with pictures of opera houses on them to copying poems, peaked Kate's interest in him even more. Kate knew that *he* knew she would understand the point of the haiku form; she immediately grasped that in the midst of the brutality of war, those tiny poems could pause time, create stillness, and refresh the human spirit.

Kate hadn't mentioned the poems to Joan or Johnny; as sure as night follows day, they would tease her endlessly about it. She could hear Johnny's sing-song: "Katie has a boyfriend, he's sending her poems." Sometimes it was hard to believe he was a respected art history professor.

"Kate to Earth," prompted Joan, trying to regain her attention. "I'm going to attend the funeral with some fellow surgeons. I'm sure there will be some kind of luncheon. Come on, let's go together."

"I have advisees scheduled every day. I'll text you tomorrow and let you know what my schedule permits." Kate was wise to Joan's pushiness; she often had to employ delaying tactics with her.

CHAPTER 6

D<small>ETECTIVE</small> D<small>E</small>V<small>ILLE WAS TAKING PICTURES IN THE SMALL</small> alley behind the bistro while he went over the details of deliveries with Chef George, whose huffy demeanor bespoke of his frustration at having to repeat what he had already told the chief.

"Was there anything unusual about that day or the several days before Celine Arceneau's party?" The two men walked inside to the kitchen, where Coupe looked longingly at the coffee machine. Being Creole, he appreciated French-inspired cuisine and robust coffee. George took note and quickly made a beautifully steamed cup of cappuccino for the detective.

"Like I told Jablonsky, I don't remember anything that happened that was out of the daily routine." George opened the question to his kitchen staff; his sous-chef Henry responded.

"The only thing that was different was that we have been holding classes on how to prepare the bistro favorites. There've been three classes: the last one was the day before the farewell party. I didn't mention it before because I didn't think it mattered." Prompted by the mention of the classes,

George walked to his cubby-hole of an office and came back with a list of the students.

"Only five students. Three men and two women, all loyal patrons. The cost of the classes was a bit steep." Chef George grinned—he was an astute businessman as well as a talented chef. Coupe took a picture of the list, then stuffed the paper copy into his jacket pocket; he didn't want any hiccups in collecting details for the chief.

"Do you know the students personally?" he asked, quizzing Henry further.

"No. I mean, I'm friendly with them all, but I don't see any of them outside of the restaurant," answered Henry.

"You haven't had a drink with any of the ladies?" Coupe prodded.

"No," was the firm reply.

"Okay. Thanks, man." Coupe bought a packet of home-made macarons and left for the precinct.

As he started his car, a loud clap of thunder announced a rainstorm. Detective DeVille broke out in a drenching sweat, his arms tingled, and breathing became difficult. He knew this reaction would pass, so he waited before starting to drive. Even though he had been just a small boy and safe with his family when Katrina devastated New Orleans, sudden storms still unnerved him. He thought of it as a kind of post-traumatic stress reaction, and he was right.

Detective Lemon smiled as Coupe delicately placed the sleeve of macarons in his desk drawer for a late afternoon snack. She took note of the new information he wrote on the murder board: Five people attended a cooking class. The last class was the day before the incident. Then he listed the names.

The chief walked over to view the new data. "Wait a minute, look at this name." He leafed through the pages of his paper notebook. "Here it is: Rose Delaney. That's Ellen Smythe's daughter." He pulled out a stick of cinnamon gum and began to vigorously work the chew.

"The daughter was in the restaurant—in the kitchen—one day before the dinner. We have to interview her," remarked Lemon.

"Not just yet. I want to know more about Celine Arceneau's personal history—it might give us some inkling of a relationship between her, Pittsburgh, and Dr. Smythe," cautioned Jablonsky. "Is Trembly here yet? He's the man who might be able to help us connect the dots."

Dr. Patel had initially notified Pittsburgh's Canadian consul of Celine Arceneau's death, then later informed him that her death was being viewed as suspicious. As consul, Trembly's primary duty was to protect the rights of Canadian citizens who were living in Pittsburgh. While his job was interesting and varied, this was the first time it included a suspicious death.

"André, thanks for coming in," said Jablonsky, shaking the consul's hand, then indicating one of the chairs. Trembly looked around at the chief's office. A streamline computer and printer sat on top of an old wooden desk. Other than a picture of his daughter at her law school graduation, there were no personal items. Due to his rank, Jablonsky's office was, however, graced with a much-coveted window, which currently only offered a view of white headlights beaming through the vigorous rain.

The consul did notice Jablonsky's blue window-pane suit and thin red-striped white shirt, nicely matched with a yellow-patterned tie. He pulled down the corners of his mouth in a grudging gesture of approbation.

"You knew Celine Arceneau," Jablonsky stated as he flipped open his notebook.

Trembly replied, "Yes, in a way. When she first arrived here, she sought me out to introduce herself—to let me know why she was in Pittsburgh—it was a registration of sorts. Since her work papers were in order, we focused on her need for healthcare during her stay."

"You referred her to Dr. Ellen Smythe for that care, correct?" Jablonsky unobtrusively checked his notes from the Smythe interview.

"Yes, that's correct. Dr. Smythe has such a good reputation, and even though her practice is always full, she accommodates my requests. Usually they are like Celine, who was only here for a prescribed period of time. Ellen has a soft spot for Canadians," answered Trembly.

"Do you know why that is? No? Okay. Is there anything that you found unusual, odd, or even disturbing about Ms. Arceneau?" Jablonsky wanted to probe into the area of cultural differences. As a Quebecois, Trembly would instinctively understand Celine Arceneau's behaviors and manner, thereby providing insight that no American interviewee could.

Taking his time to answer, Trembly gazed out the window at the sheets of rain moving across the streets like the panels of a tall vertical blind rippling in a breeze.

"She was born and educated in Montreal. Her career in energy and international law took her to many countries, and because of that, she could be a charming dinner companion. Her mother, Adele, had also been an attorney. The one personal thing she *did* say was that she and her mother had been close, and that since her death, there was a great hole in her life. Otherwise, I found her to be superficially friendly, asking more questions than she answered," said Trembly.

"Anything else strike you, André?" asked the chief.

"I found it odd that there were no living relatives to contact about her death, just a close woman colleague. At the several dinners we both attended, it was my impression that she was at times . . . preoccupied. Yes, preoccupied and guarded would be my two impressions. Do you link her line of work to her death?" asked Trembly.

Jablonsky nodded. "It is one line of inquiry that we are developing. Did she say why she was teaching in Pittsburgh? Why not Georgetown or Columbia—law schools with more international faculties?" Jablonsky's daughter, Carly, often provided him an insider perspective on law schools.

Trembly shrugged. "She mentioned that the teaching sabbatical was a kind of award. You'd have to ask the law school about it, that is outside my knowledge."

Jablonsky opened the door to the bullpen and called out. "Lemon! Find out why Arceneau was chosen for the sabbatical at the law school. Thanks." Closing the door, he continued his questions.

"Would you be able to facilitate our access into Ms. Arceneau's financial affairs? Details from her official Canadian records and work history would give me a broader context in which to view her and this case," stated Jablonsky.

"Of course I can do that for you, Stefan, *bien sûr*. Anything to help in this dreadful situation," offered Trembly.

"Let's move on to Celine's farewell dinner. Did you know everyone there?" Jablonsky was looking for any detail that would be the thread that tied the people involved.

"No. Celine had invited me as a courtesy, and I was happy to attend because I know Chef George quite well. It was a congenial group, but everything was cut short by the food poisoning. Celine was the first to say she was sick, then others followed—myself included." Trembly grimaced at the memory of the nausea.

"Before the entrée was served, did you notice anyone who was out of place going into the kitchen?" The chief threw a Hail Mary pass.

"No. As I recall, there were two servers, both of whom have been with the restaurant for quite a while. This isn't Le Bernardin in New York, where there are a cadre of servers— it's a little bistro in Pittsburgh," said Trembly.

"Were the bottles of wine already open and sitting on the

table?" Jablonsky, like Kate, was curious about that possible delivery mode of a toxin.

"The red wine was open in order to breathe; the white was kept cool in the kitchen." Trembly cut to the heart of the matter. "You think someone made all of us sick in order to murder Celine? *Incroyable.*"

"It is unbelievable, but very smart. One theory is that the victim was actually poisoned with more of the toxin that made everyone else just sick, or even poisoned with something else in the midst of the group being taken to the emergency room. Mind you, that's just supposition," said Jablonsky.

"Since Ellen Smythe and I are two of the few people that knew Celine Arceneau during her time here in Pittsburgh, does that make us suspects?" Trembly looked like a child who suddenly understood the multiplication tables. Jablonsky offered no response, so Trembly continued.

"I like and trust Ellen. If there is anything I can do to help her, I'm willing and available." The consul's tone made it clear he was on Ellen's side, just like her office staff, just like Aashi Patel.

This woman garners loyalty across life situations. It's unusual, thought Jablonsky, who understood that that kind of loyalty can blind a person to what is in front of them—it is a blindness criminals count on.

"If you think of anything else later on, please don't dismiss it as unimportant. On a personal note, whenever you and Jean-Luc are baking for another brunch, I'm always happy to be a guest!" said Jablonsky.

Jean-Luc Bernard was the French consul in Pittsburgh, who, along with André Trembly, had a reputation as a superb baker; in the name of community relations, Jablonsky had attended a brunch at the consul's home and still salivated when remembering the pastries. The two men shook hands and Trembly left, bracing himself against the rain outside, wishing he had brought his umbrella.

The chief swiveled his chair around to face the window. Looking out, he didn't see the rainstorm but rather was thinking about the information André Trembly had given him.

A picture of the killer is emerging: Someone with knowledge of toxins easily placed into food or wine. Someone who has nerve. Someone who is a careful planner. Someone who knew the restaurant and what was being prepared for the farewell party. Perhaps there's more than one perp? But, what is the motive?

Jablonsky groaned as he leaned forward to get out of his chair and then started to laugh at himself. *Forget those pastries. I need to get to my basement gym.*

He walked into the bullpen and wrote his questions on the murder board, then gave DeVille and Lemon their additional assignments: aside from the details of Smythe's life, and those of her daughter, check into the conditions of Arceneau's sabbatical, and work through the list of people associated with the bistro.

CHAPTER 7

DR. SMYTHE AND KATHLEEN FINISHED REVIEWING PATIENT charts for the day. The two women had worked together for a long time—they weren't exactly friends, rather colleagues who respected and liked each other.

"Rose stopped in to see you today. I told her you were with patients. She was so perturbed that when Jake came to collect a patient, she made some snide comment that if he worked harder, her mother could step back. I felt sorry for the poor patient who had to overhear it. Have you told her about your retirement?" Kathleen knew how Rose hated any change in her mother's life.

"No. Since nothing is settled yet, I don't want to take the heat!" Dr. Smythe laughed at her own avoidance of the situation.

Kathleen, who also had a daughter, laughed along with her but didn't offer any comment; luckily, her daughter had her own life—a life that didn't depend on her.

Ellen knew that Kathleen was glad to have limited contact with Rose, who clearly disliked the nurse's comfortable relationship with her mother. Rose was often just plain snotty to Kathleen. She long ago stopped apologizing for her daughter's behavior to her or to Jake Albert. The two mothers shrugged their shoulders in the universal sign of "What can you do?" They finished their conversation, closed the office, and left for home.

Ellen lived in the area of Oakland called Schenley Farms. It was a historic neighborhood tucked in the middle of the university proper. Stately homes sat on large city lots, each house different in design. The streets were wide, shaded in the summer by either tall sugar maples or mature oak trees. Many professors and physicians lived in this community because of its proximity to the hospitals, university classrooms, libraries, and research laboratories.

Ellen Smythe typically used the walk home as a chance to decompress from her busy schedule, but today she found herself angrily ruminating over her husband's deathbed request concerning Rose. If she believed in such superstitions, she would have cursed him for the chaos his request had let into her otherwise orderly life.

Ellen's internal ranting was interrupted by her daughter, who had swerved her Jaguar over to the sidewalk, calling out to her mother through the open window.

"Mum! I just had to see you to make sure everything is okay. You look tired. Get in the car, and I'll drive you the rest of the way. Please, Mummy, let me take you home. Your patient's death has scared me—what if something happens to you? I want to stay the night." Rose's voice held an all-too-familiar mixture of whining and wheedling, which at this stage of her life only served to set Ellen's nerves on edge.

"Rose, I told you on the telephone that I'm okay. A little dinner and a good night's sleep is all I need. There is no reason for you to stay the night," Ellen stated firmly.

"Come on, Mummy, why won't you let me? You are avoiding me. Again!" Rose whined.

"No, I'm just tired. I'll call you later to say good night. I appreciate your concern, dear, but please, please go home," Ellen pleaded.

"What time will you call? You say you will, and then you don't, so what exact time will you call?" Rose didn't respond to the annoyed beeping from the cars around her.

"It will be after dinner. Get going. You are holding up traffic!" When Rose shot out into the rush hour traffic, Ellen breathed a deep sigh of relief.

The porch light was on, indicating that Maria, her housekeeper and companion, was still there. Ellen called out to her as she hung her Burberry jacket in the hall closet before walking back to the kitchen.

Maria had been Rose's nanny, then stayed on as a live-in housekeeper. Even now, she continued to do some cooking and light housework; the heavy cleaning had long been delegated to young workers with good knees. Ellen cared deeply about Maria and had arranged a generous pension for her old age—which, at seventy-eight, was now.

Maria made up a dinner tray and took it to the sitting room off the main living area. Ellen followed her, kicked off her shoes, and sank into the comfy couch. For Maria's sake, Ellen pushed the food around the plate, taking a nibble here and there, while she told her the details of Celine Arceneau's death. Maria made the sign of the cross, quietly remarking, "I'll light a candle for her soul at St. Paul's."

After the two finished talking, Ellen went upstairs to her bedroom, undressed, took a quick shower, and then ran a hot tub. From the small office off of her bedroom, she grabbed a crystal snifter, poured a generous serving of Martell XO, and eased herself into the tub for a long soak. As her tense muscles relaxed, her mind floated free, ruminating on the subject of Rose.

I never really understood how she looks at the world or even how she lives her life, thought Ellen.

After Rose married and Patricia was born, she hoped her

daughter's life had finally found its center. But it wasn't to last: Josh Delaney, her husband, had unceremoniously and without explanation divorced Rose, then left for Silicon Valley. He barely kept in touch with Rose, but every summer, Patricia happily lived with him for several months. Ellen came to admire how he fathered Patricia and was glad for their closeness.

Rose spent her time engaged with various fundraising events, signing checks for the latest good cause. Ellen appreciated her daughter's generosity but didn't understand her lack of interest in an actual career. Rose had been a good student, intellectually capable of entering any line of work, but she never evidenced the capacity to stick with the training necessary for a profession.

Mothers rarely admit to their most secret thoughts about their children—Ellen loved Rose, but she didn't respect her.

Her ruminations were interrupted when she heard the bathroom door open. A man's voice whispered, "Care for a bath partner?" Ellen giggled as a tall man slipped out of his clothes and eased into the soapy, bubbly water.

"I'll take some of that cognac, my little fish," he said.

Once she and her lover Daniel were in bed and had talked through the situation with Celine Arceneau, he fell asleep. Ellen, however, found herself thinking about Kate Chambers.

Now there is a young colleague I respect. I wonder how open I can be with her?

On the hill above Schenley Farms sat the university's Olympic-sized pool. Johnny was meeting a triathlon partner of Jake Alberts, who had agreed to be his stroke coach, and Kate was about to get wet after a ten-year hiatus.

The world of a training pool was so familiar to Kate that it felt imprinted on her: the smell of chlorine, the sound of a

Masters swimming club (groups of competitive swimmers over the age of twenty-five) kicking and stroking in their lanes, a coach encouraging a swimmer to lengthen her stroke, the extraterrestrial appearance of heads encased in tight swim caps with small goggles covering the eyes—everything was always orderly and predictable at the swimming pool.

Kate eased herself into the chilly, burbling water. The experience of weightlessness in the water stopped time in the same way a still life painting or even a haiku did. *Why have I waited so long to do this? This is my natural element,* she thought.

Kate stretched out into her freestyle, turned, and pushed off the wall. Back and forth she stroked, forgetting everything except the rhythmic motion.

Suddenly, someone roughly kicked her in her side. Kate stopped swimming and looked around for the culprit.

Was this an accident? Since the Masters swimmers in the lane next to hers were practicing the breast stroke, a stroke in which a side kick-out is performed, it was possible someone just got to close to her lane line. She allowed herself to believe this line of reasoning, shook it off, and resumed swimming.

While Johnny was finishing his lesson, Kate sat on the side of the pool, remembering what had prompted her grandfather to start her in swimming lessons.

It had been the day of the annual mother-daughter luncheon; Kate was ten years old and, as usual, at home, excused from school for the afternoon. Driven by her anger and agitation, she slipped out of the house and peddled her bicycle to the riverside park, furious at still being teased over having no mummy and daddy: "How were you even born?" or "You're a freak!" With slow deliberation, she took off her little jacket and boots, folded them neatly beside her, and started to wade in the water, seeking relief from her emotions. Two joggers passed by: "Get that girl!" they yelled, running to reach Kate before she submerged. They grabbed, then dragged her onto the riverbank. She tried to wiggle out of their arms, finally giving up, weeping in frustration.

It was Kate's only suicide attempt; even now, she could remember the rage that had prompted her actions. Her grandfather knew that his precious little girl still suffered from grief, but she never let him, or anyone else, see the depth of her pain. Under the auspices of wanting her to know how to swim, he started her in lessons at the local pool.

Johnny's voice pulled her back to the present—she shook her head, dismissing the unsettling memories. Over the years, Kate had developed the ability to seal off the many desperations of her child self.

The two friends left the aquatic center, brainstorming about where to get dinner. "The bistro reopened, let's go there and support Chef George," urged Kate.

"That's fine with me, but I know you Kate, you want to ask about the food poisoning. If it ends up a murder investigation, have you decided to get involved?" Johnny stopped and faced Kate, giving her his sternest look.

"Maybe. Well, actually, yes. Ellen Smythe is important to me. I want to support her any way I can. Going through a Jablonsky interview is difficult—the very act of the interview implies suspicion. The way Ellen talked about Celine Arceneau gave me the impression that she barely knew her . . . but, maybe Jablonsky suspects that there's more to it than a doctor-patient relationship."

Johnny knew that Kate was possessed of a loyal nature. He had been on the receiving end of that loyalty. It was one of Kate's sterling traits that endeared her to him.

They arrived at the bistro happy to see that business was brisk. Chef George greeted them and immediately proposed entrees: For Kate, he suggested a light dinner of mixed baby greens with a Dijon mustard vinaigrette and a bowl of *moules marinières* with croutons. For Johnny, he suggested a poutine, a dish from Quebec—heavy in both calories and deliciousness.

After the staff served their meal, George returned to sit with them.

"How are you?" asked Kate, who was fond of the chef.

"Well, the community has been great. Chief Jablonsky and his detectives have questioned me and Henry several times." He threw up his hands in frustration.

"No one remembers anything unusual?" Kate asked, reiterating the standard police question. Johnny was so hungry after his swim lesson that he didn't even try to focus on anything other than attacking the French fries and cheese curds covered with gravy.

"Well, the only thing that was out of the routine were the cooking classes we offer." George rattled off the five names of the participants. After he left the table, Kate pulled Johnny's arm, almost shaking the fork out of his hand in her excitement.

"One of those cooking students was *Rose Delaney*. That's Ellen's daughter!" Kate exclaimed.

"I know that fact is exciting to you, but I'm exhausted, so let's finish and get out of here. I need rest," Johnny stated.

Even though it was settled science that swimmers burn the most calories of any other sport, watching Johnny, who had had only one swim lesson, consume the seven hundred calories in the poutine dish, made her feel slightly nauseous.

As they drove along Fifth Avenue to her condo, Kate told Johnny about the incident in the water.

"Okay. This is the *third* time something menacing has happened to you. I'm concerned, Kate. These incidents are stacking up. I want you to talk to Chief Jablonsky about them," urged Johnny.

"I'll see. But thanks for your concern, my sweet boy!" Kate knew that the chief respected her insights into cases, but he made no bones about the fact that he also thought of her as a nebby, intrusive amateur. Would he take these occurrences seriously?

The chief already knew a little about her grandfather, a bit more about Eddie Fitzroy, but nothing about her childhood. Kate thoughts drifted to Marco, then to his lost siblings, her lost parents, and Eddie.

CHAPTER 8

THE NEXT MORNING, THE CHIEF PACED IN FRONT OF THE murder board, silently chewing his stick of cinnamon gum. Finally he stopped and addressed Detective Lemon.

"Annie, did you get ahold of the dean of the law school and ask about Arceneau's sabbatical?"

"Yes, I did. As he remembers it, one of the people on the board of the law school recommended her. The guy is a senior partner at the same law firm where Peter Smythe was a founding member. Coincidence?" she wryly added.

"We seem to be knee deep in attorney's specializing in international business—I feel like I'm in a July cornfield." Neither Lemon nor Coupe caught the musical reference— Jablonsky moved on.

"Aside from being Dr. Smythe's patient, is there any connection between her and Ms. Arceneau? Give me some ideas."

Lemon stood to weave her theory. "Because Peter specialized in international business law, especially related to the energy industry, he was in Montreal, Paris, the Hague, and Switzerland quite often—at least once a month." Lemon added, "Ellen Smythe's husband was never home."

"So your point is that Peter Smythe routinely visited Montreal, and Celine Arceneau grew up in, and then remained in, Montreal." Jablonsky unwrapped another stick of gum, this time offering one to Coupe, who accepted it.

"Lemon, when you talked with the dean, aside from the recommendation from C&S, did he say exactly what it was about Celine Arceneau that made her their pick for visiting professor?" Jablonsky queried further.

"Well, he said that the sabbatical was 'awarded' to Celine Arceneau because she is—or was—the daughter of Adele Arceneau. Adele worked for the government in the area of nuclear energy policy—she was something of a trail-blazer. The mother is dead, so to honor her, I guess they gave it to the daughter. Apparently the position is awarded to a different attorney from a different country every few years.

"I asked him if he personally knew Celine and he said no, but he *had* met her mother, and so had several other attorneys from the firm of that generation. The law school approached the nuclear energy sector of the Canadian government about Ms. Arceneau, and she was awarded the post. That's the public story." Lemon stuck out her hip, placed her laptop on it, and listened as Jablonsky gave her and Coupe a Pittsburgh history lesson.

"The nuclear energy division of the Canadian government? Interesting. Many Pittsburghers don't realize that before and after the collapse of the steel industry, a thriving nuclear energy business existed in our city. Before the spectacularly 'Ignorant Group of Suits,' which I think is their official name, ruined the Westinghouse Corporation, it housed a large nuclear division. Pittsburgh had, and continues to have, a presence on the world stage in the nuclear arena—I suspect Peter Smythe must have personally known Adele Arceneau, the mother."

Jablonsky wrote Adele Arceneau's name above Celine's,

then drew a triangle. Adele-Peter-Celine. "This is a plausible link. Good work, Lemon." He then changed the subject.

"I want to interview Rose Delaney—Ellen's daughter. Set it up for me."

"Yes, Dr. Smythe, what can I do for you?" Jablonsky was about to leave to interview Rose when Ellen called.

"Rose just telephoned and said that you are going to interview her . . . she wants me to be there. Rose can be . . . unsure of herself. Would my presence be a problem?" asked Dr. Smythe.

I'll bet it's unusual for Ellen to ask for someone's permission, thought the amused chief.

"Yes, it would be a problem. Rose is not a minor. She can have counsel with her, but I want to speak to her on her own. Dr. Smythe, this is routine. I'm interviewing everyone who took the cooking classes at the bistro. An officer will be taking an oral DNA swab, just as we will do for every other participant." Jablonsky abruptly ended the call before Dr. Smythe had a chance to manipulate the situation.

Rose's house, like many others in the Squirrel Hill neighborhood, had been affordable in the 1920s and 30s, but now only those with deep pockets could buy there.

The disarray of poverty doesn't leave its footprint on this side of town, thought Jablonsky as he made his way along the lengthy walkway that cut through the groomed lawn and mature rhododendrons.

In response to the panic in her face when Rose opened the door, Jablonsky chose a soothing and fatherly tone of voice. "Thank you for seeing me, Mrs. Delaney. I just have a few questions." He stepped into the entry and stood smiling at her as he took her hand in both of his.

Still holding her hand, he said, "As was mentioned on the

telephone, Detective Lemon will take a quick oral swab for DNA. Is there a quiet place we can sit and talk?"

"Of course. We can talk in here." She gestured toward an open pocket door. All three moved into a traditional wood-paneled library with a vaulted ceiling and a bank of floor-to-beam leaded glass windows. The chief observed that Rose was from a thoroughly Anglo-Saxon gene pool, small-boned, a natural blonde, and had her mother's gray eyes and a flawless pale pink complexion.

They settled into supple leather club chairs, two arranged across a coffee table from two more. Books and papers were stacked on a large desk behind them, and a laptop lay on the arm of one of the chairs. Sun streamed in through the windows, bathing the room in a creamy, soft light.

Jablonsky tried to catch the image on her laptop screen, but she unobtrusively closed it, so instead, he let his eye rove around the room. Rose perched on the edge of the chair across from him, too nervous to fully sit. Detective Lemon was good with Rose; she expertly swabbed her check and then left. Jablonsky discretely took out his small paper notebook.

"That's a beautiful painting. Is it your father?" Jablonsky wanted to ease Rose into the interview, so he opened with a benign question about the large oil painting hanging over the fireplace mantel.

"Yes, yes it is. He was so handsome, don't you agree? You can see that he was older than my mother. He started the successful law firm, Cooper and Smythe." Rose's eyes glowed with pride as she talked about her father.

Jablonsky remarked, "You were close to him."

"Oh, yes. I went everywhere with him. We had the habit of picking up chocolates and fresh-roasted nuts every Sunday morning after church. All the shop ladies knew him and would tease him because he ordered so many candies. He would lift me up so I could see into the cases. They called me his little bonbon. 'What does the little bonbon want today?' they would ask."

Rose's voice quivered at the memory; she stopped, then added, "I miss him every day."

The chief could see that Rose was lost in the scenes of her childhood—he waited before offering a remark.

"I have a daughter. I feel the same way about her that it sounds like your dad felt about you." That simple, personal admission caught Rose off guard—for the first time, she really looked at the chief.

"How sweet," she said. "Fathers and daughters, that's the strongest bond."

Jablonsky jotted "daddy's girl" in his notebook and then began the interview. "Mrs. Delaney, what I want to know is if there is anything you remember about your cooking classes at Chef George's restaurant that stands out—especially the class that was right before the food poisoning episode. We are speaking with your classmates in order to ascertain if there was someone in the kitchen that day who didn't belong there." Jablonsky spoke very calmly and slowly, as if talking to a child.

"I love that bistro, don't you?" Rose began to twist a small bit of her skirt as she talked.

"Why yes, yes I do. What time did you and the others arrive at the cooking class?" Rose looked down at the pattern the sun made on the oak floor, seeming to have disconnected from the conversation.

"Rose?" Jablonsky prompted.

"Oh. Yes . . . um, it was around ten in the morning. Henry, the sous-chef, was teaching the class—he's so darling, I swear I'd take that class just to look at him!" Rose said emphatically.

"Do you see Henry outside of the restaurant? I mean, is he sweet on you?" asked Jablonsky.

Rose picked imaginary lint off the sleeve of her twin set, then, in an annoyed tone, responded. "Sweet on me? I guess he is, but he's a cook—he and I run in different social circles. I mean, the people at the bistro are nice, but not my—well, you understand." She swept one arm wide to indicate the wealth and grandeur of her home.

"This kitten has claws," wrote the chief in his notebook.

"I do see what you mean, Rose, but it's all right to have some fun dating people who come from different back-grounds, don't you agree?" asked Jablonsky.

Rose blushed, her face suffused with the color of her namesake. "You are so wise, Chief Jablonsky! Sometimes a girl just has to go slumming."

"Do you remember if anyone in the cooking class mentioned the party that was being held for Celine Arce-neau?" he continued.

"No, I don't remember anything like that. We just make food, drink a little wine, and have a good time. No one talks about what is going on at the bistro otherwise." Unexpectedly, Rose stopped giggling and spoke with clarity about the police investigation.

"You are trying to figure out how a toxin got into the food without anyone seeing who put it there. I can't help you with that. Perhaps one of the other students can," Rose suggested.

"Just one more question and then we are finished, for now. Were you carrying a purse that day?" asked the chief.

"Of course I was," Rose answered, with a grimace that implied he had lost his mind. "No woman is ever without her purse and the things in it."

As the chief stood up and pocketed his notebook he said, "With your permission, I'd like to take the purse with me to the forensics lab. I will return it, and I promise it will not be damaged."

"That is a really strange request. Did you take the other woman's purse?" accused Rose.

"Yes, we did. It's just procedure," stated Jablonsky.

"I can't imagine how all of this is important, but I'll get the purse," said Rose.

For the second time during the interview, Jablonsky thought he smelled a man's cologne—something modern and spicy.

Rose slowly walked back down the central stairway and handed him the purse. "You know the way out, Chief Detective," she said, going back into the library, quietly sliding the pocket doors closed. Jablonsky gave her kudos for having enough self-control not to slam them together.

A picture of an adult woman who still needed her mother and frequently lived in childhood memories that featured her father was emerging; he felt an unexpected rush of empathy for Dr. Smythe and pride that his daughter Carly was independent.

I'll bet she is calling her mother right now. Neediness and nastiness —quite a combo. Is it a deadly combo?

Jablonsky telephoned the office as he walked down the front sidewalk to his car. "Coupe. Got anything for me?"

"The other cooking class students mentioned that the sous-chef always flirted with Rose, but he denies seeing her outside of class—I'm not sure if that is true. No one remembers anyone unfamiliar in the kitchen or around the class before the poisoning. And, no one mentioned the party."

"Okay, Coupe. I'm bringing Rose's purse in. We are looking for any trace of common food toxins. I want the report on Dr. Smythe's private life when I get back," ordered Jablonsky.

Kate sat across from Patricia Delaney, Ellen Smythe's granddaughter and Rose's daughter, for her academic advising appointment. Patricia was coming to the end of her residency in anesthesiology and was trying to decide whether or not to pursue a fellowship before sitting for her medical boards; their sessions focused on the pros and cons of the extra year of training.

Kate knew that several programs, including the one she was in, saw Patricia as an attractive candidate. If she accepted the offer from the university hospital, she would remain in Pittsburgh for another year.

Knowing firsthand the closeness of their relationship, Kate asked, "Has your grandmother weighed in on this decision?"

Patricia let out a hearty whoop. "Are you joking? Of course she has! I can recite her advice verbatim, because it's the same advice she gives me every time there is an academic decision to be made. Here it is:

"'Education gives women independence. It equalizes power between men and women. Without education and the benefits of human dignity and freedom of choice it confers, women are easy prey for victimization of all kinds.'

"Grandma is always so sincere when she says these things that I have to stop myself from saying an amen at the end of her lecture."

Me too, thought Kate, who was in total agreement with Ellen's point of view. "Has your mother given any advice to you about the fellowship?"

"Not really. She defers to Grandma." Patricia rarely mentioned her mother and when she did, she referred to her as "a lady who lunches." Today, she went further, giving a few details about her mother's life.

"My mother was a graduate of Bryn Mawr in Philadelphia; right after graduation, she married my father—then they had me, then he divorced her. Mom had a hard time with the divorce, so Grandma moved us in with her for a few years. My mother is very close to Grandma and her housekeeper, Maria."

"She might like it if you took the fellowship here in Pittsburgh—it keeps the family close together. Is she worried about your grandmother going through this investigation?" Kate asked, trying to sound casual.

"My mother is extremely worried about Grandma. She relies on her. I mean, *really* relies on her," Patricia answered.

That kind of dependency always results in bad choices. If Dr. Smythe was being threatened by someone, what would Rose do to eliminate that threat? wondered Kate to herself.

"Had you ever met the patient who died at your grandmother's office?" asked Kate.

"No. Grandma never talks about her patients, and I rarely have time to pop in on her at work," answered Patricia.

Patricia scheduled her next appointment and left; Kate immediately called Ellen.

"Ellen, we have a bit of committee work to catch up on. I was wondering if you'd like to meet at either my house or yours, just to have privacy. Your place? Perfect. It's close to my office. See you soon."

Kate was thrilled that they were meeting at Ellen's. Most people are more relaxed in their own surroundings where there are family photos and doodads that prompt conversation. Kate was committed to helping Ellen stay clear of any suspicions by Jablonsky's people.

CHAPTER 9

"THANKS FOR COMING. I KNOW WE NEED TO GET THESE documents back to the committee." Ellen, like Kate, wasn't someone who let things slide.

"No problem at all." Kate seated herself on the living room sofa and looked around. It was a warm room, decorated with pictures of Ellen's parents, Peter, Rose, Patricia, and also a few photos of a young Ellen with friends from her graduating class.

"This is the first time I've seen pictures of your husband. He was handsome, but Rose really has your genes," Kate casually remarked.

"I don't keep personal photos at my practice. I like a firm boundary between the professional and personal. Oh, here is Maria, my friend and housekeeper."

Maria placed a pretty Meissen tea set on the coffee table; the pot was covered with a quilted cozy to keep it warm. After the housekeeper said her hellos and left, Ellen immediately asked about Patricia.

Kate reassured her that her granddaughter was just fine— smart, respected by the attending physicians, and liked by her peers. Ellen visibly relaxed, then surprised Kate by remarking that she hoped Patricia would seriously consider a fellowship outside of Pittsburgh. Kate wondered if Ellen thought it might be emotionally easier for Patricia to be away from Rose, but she decided not to ask.

After their committee tasks were completed, Kate set her laptop aside and poured herself another cup of tea.

"Is anything new in the inquiry?" Kate asked.

"Not that the police are telling me. The truth is, for a while now, I have been considering turning the practice over to someone else—this situation might push me to finally do it."

Kate noticed how deftly Ellen had changed the subject.

"Oh really? Joan mentioned that you might be thinking about retiring. Would you continue on in some capacity at the medical school? Speaking for myself, I so enjoy working with you—like today. You have been a guiding force in shaping which university activities would interest me," Kate admitted.

The compliments were authentic, but the motivation was to maneuver Ellen into a confiding state of mind. It still wasn't clear to Kate why the police would continue to look at Ellen as a person of interest in Celine's death; she needed more information.

"I don't know what type of affiliation I'd keep with the medical school—thanks for the compliments, though." She leaned back in the armchair, sipping her tea, her mood contemplative; this was the state Kate was hoping would lead to sharing personal details that might help explain what Jablonsky was looking for.

"You have many beautifully framed photographs, Ellen." Kate left the sofa and moved to the bookcase, picking up a group photo, which included a young Ellen in cap and gown.

"Are these your friends from medical school?"

Ellen pulled one of the sofa pillows over onto her lap and fiddled with its sheered edges. Was the pillow a barrier against further personal revelations?

Before Ellen could answer Kate's question, Maria came with more hot tea, this time carrying a tray of small sandwiches. Kate immediately sampled one. "Yum! These are tasty. What are they?"

Ellen, who didn't cook, looked relieved as Maria talked about the unusual but refreshing pickled radish and smoked salmon combination.

With one hand toting her sandwich, Kate pointed again to the graduation picture. "I've seen some of these people around campus. This man looks familiar." She indicated a tall, dark-haired man standing at the back of the group. "How nice to keep in touch with friends from your youth."

It looked as though Ellen was about to share something, then changed her mind; instead, she offered a vanilla comment about how interesting it has been to watch her fellow graduates build their careers. Always suspicious, Kate wondered if Ellen regretted the decision to meet at her home —were there too many things to explain away, or hide?

"Peter was in international law? He must have frequently been overseas. Did you travel with him?" Kate decided to test for gas.

"No. I was building my practice and getting involved with developing curriculum for the medical school." Ellen suddenly became animated.

"I love my hometown. Pittsburgh was a great place to grow up and raise a family. My mother babysat Rose every day—they were close. I was happy that she knew my mother and father— Rose was surrounded by people who loved and cared for her."

This was the first time Kate ever heard Ellen speak so openly about her parents and Rose; she decided to share her own experience.

"I adored my grandfather—after my parents were killed, he was my whole world. I think it was so smart to keep Rose close to your parents."

Kate returned to her seat, then asked, "How often did Peter travel?"

"He was gone a week or two out of every month. Needs must—he was growing the firm—I understood that. His work and his reputation were important to him." Ellen expressed no regrets about Peter's absences.

"My Eddie could be away at an archeological dig for years at a time. We kept in touch by writing letters—real letters, remember those?" Uncharacteristically, Kate decided to reveal more.

"When he came back to the States, it was as if we had never been apart; we just picked up where our letters left off. Whenever he was in town, I felt like I was connected to my early life in Boston and my grandfather. We had been an unorthodox kind of family trio."

"Peter and Rose were like that—they were each other's home," said Ellen.

That she didn't include herself wasn't lost on Kate. *So it was Rose who was close to Peter, not Ellen.*

"Well, to be frank, I was at the point with Eddie where I wanted to break up because of the length of his absences. Before he was killed, he suggested that I give up my career and move with him to his latest project. Imagine!" Kate shook her head.

"For someone as talented as you are, I can't imagine that he even thought you would agree to such a thing." Ellen looked surprised.

"Our separations were longer than yours were with Peter, but you seem to have managed the time apart better than I did," Kate coaxed gently.

"I'm not sure about that. You know, I've never thought about it until right now, but Peter was on the edge of my real life; he wasn't interested in my work and never pretended to be. We didn't easily reconnect when he returned home from traveling." Ellen fiddled with her teacup, perhaps afraid she had said too much.

Kate wasn't used to speaking so honestly about her last years with Eddie Fitzroy, but this exchange emboldened her.

"I knew Eddie from the time I was a teenager. He was my grandfather's graduate assistant, so he was always around. At first, he was like a brother to me, then when I went to college, it became more. When you said that Peter was on the edge of your real life—if I'm being honest, it was like that for me as well. Eddie loved me, but he had no real interest in my work or my life here in Pittsburgh. That lack would have been the end of us over the long haul—but, he will always be my first love," said Kate.

Ellen tilted her head, taking in Kate's words. "I know about first love. All that serotonin bathing the brain—it's so intoxicating—but it doesn't mean they will be together. Life events intrude, we make marriages and have children with other people, but, for some, there is always that one who lives in the secret part of the heart."

The two women sat quietly, sipping their tea, and thinking about first love. Kate wondered, *If Peter had had a hard time reconnecting with Ellen after his traveling, to whom did he turn?*

"Did Peter ever take Rose with him on business? I mean, once she was old enough?" asked Kate.

"Yes. I had forgotten about that. When she was in college she traveled with him in the summers. Peter was often in Montreal because one of the firm's clients was a Pittsburgh company that manufactured parts for nuclear plants." Ellen stood and picked up a photograph of Peter and Rose.

"Peter's family still owns property in Montreal, a section of town called Summit Park; they went there in the summer to hike, ride, and fish. Rose often stayed with Peter at that estate." Ellen lifted her eyebrows at the world the Smythes still lived in. "Here they are together at Summit Park."

Kate took the offered photo and scrutinized the picture of

a laughing Peter and Rose, outfitted in their riding clothes, obviously comfortable on their horses, looking tan and outdoorsy.

"I can only imagine how hard Rose must have taken Peter's death." Kate was genuinely interested because, without having been raised by a mother, she rarely heard older women talk honestly about their lives.

"Rose was devastated when Peter died. I moved her and Patricia in with me until her grief was more manageable. Peter was almost twenty years older than me. In the last decade of his life, he was diagnosed with leukemia and died from its complications. In the end, he needed hospice care—those physicians and nurses took wonderful care of him.

"Rose went every day to sit with him." Ellen shook her head—was it disapproval of a dependency or approval of a loving daughter's attention?

"That's a type of devotion, isn't it? I moved my grandfather from Boston to Pittsburgh—he was in one of those progressive care communities. I didn't get to see him every day —like you, I . . . had . . . commitments." Those last drawn-out words were a statement about the complexity of a regular person's life—juggling the demands of work, elderly parents, children, friends.

"I definitely wasn't able to see Peter every day. But Rose doesn't really work. Through the Smythe family trusts, my daughter's a wealthy woman—her work is writing checks."

Kate smiled at Ellen's inability to keep disapproval out of her voice—her amusement bubbled over into outright laughter, sparking Ellen to do the same. The atmosphere lightened.

To no one in particular, Kate said, "After the paper printed a small story about Celine's death, I looked at her online biography. Now that we're talking, it strikes me that here are two daughters who experienced the death of a parent at a relatively early age—Celine Arceneau lost her mother just like Rose lost her father."

"I hadn't thought of it that way, but you're right. My parents lived into their late eighties. I had decades of the security they provided. Perhaps that loss is why Rose is often so anxious." Ellen caught herself before going further in describing Rose's difficulties.

"Even though I lost my parents, my grandfather's love was like the center of a wheel, holding strong in the face of our mutual losses. His pet name for me was 'my precious gift.'"

Ellen smiled broadly. "He did a good job with you, my young friend."

Dr. Smythe rarely gave those kinds of personal compliments; Kate would treasure it.

Ellen's warmth gave Kate even more determination to understand why Jablonsky was looking at her as a possible suspect. Once again, she changed the subject, giving Ellen some psychological space after speaking so personally.

"Ellen, I'm thinking about training for the mini triathlon. Your Jake recommended a swim coach for my training partner, Johnny—they have already connected and started lessons."

"He is a smart and conscientious physician assistant. I couldn't run my practice without him. I don't know much about his private life, but I do know that he competes as a top-level athlete. Don't mention Rose to him, they dislike each other. I think she's jealous of my relationship with Jake, as she is with some of my other staff—like Kathleen, whom you've met. She's bitchy with Kathleen. Rose is, well, Rose." Ellen shrugged.

As Kate walked back to her campus office, she reviewed what she had learned: Peter traveled extensively for business, sometimes he took Rose along. Was there something peculiar about the closeness of Peter and his daughter's relationship?

Ellen clearly wasn't referring to Peter when they were talking about love—is there someone else? Since Peter's death, who has she been seeing? If Rose is a jealous daughter, would she have ferreted out her mother's secret lover?

———————

When Ellen crawled into her bed later that evening, her mind returned to her conversation with Kate. Before Morpheus encircled her in his arms, she thought about her early love life.

Ellen and Peter first met long before they dated. Her parents had insisted that she go with them to a fundraiser at the Carnegie Museum of Natural History, where Peter, a benefactor, was present.

At the time of the event, Ellen was nineteen and Peter was forty, with a reputation as the "bachelor with a black book." Amidst a few hundred people who were having drinks and canapés, Peter noticed Ellen, a slender blonde with stunning gray eyes, engaged in animated talk with a few friends.

Peter made his move by initiating conversation about the importance of researching the world's natural history. Ellen remembered thinking of him as a peer of her father so wasn't really interested in him, but for Peter, there was something about the intelligence of her comments and those luminous eyes that stayed with him. She wasn't like any of the women he usually dated.

Several years later at the same Carnegie fundraiser, they ran into each other again. He joked with her about their previous meeting, which she pretended she remembered, but didn't. Peter asked her for a date.

Because Ellen was dedicated to her medical studies, she kept their relationship to a slow burn. Peter was smart and interesting, traveled and sophisticated; the Smythe Foundation was extremely generous to the city, underwriting cultural organizations like the ballet and the symphony or endowing some of the medical school's research projects. Peter's generosity and interest in their hometown were attractive qualities to Ellen.

There were also glimpses of a kind of emotional distance —a distance with which Ellen felt surprisingly comfortable. They dated on and off throughout her medical training, and when she graduated, Peter began to frequently propose marriage.

"Marry me! You know I love you and will provide for you. Marry me! Your parents approve of me, my friends like you, and I don't care that you will continue to practice medicine. Come on . . . marry me! We will make a great team. We will be a power couple!" he had insisted.

His declarations ranged from passionate to begging, even sometimes demanding, but for a long time they fell on deaf ears. There was something about that phrase, *I don't care if you continue to practice medicine*, that pinged around her brain like a pinball marble.

On the one hand, the comment evidenced a generational disconnect, but on the other hand, it also indicated that he wouldn't interfere with her career. His potential lack of interference in her real life was very, very attractive to Ellen.

Her mother had weighed in on the subject of Peter: "Marry him or move on, it's not fair keeping him in limbo. He's not a young man. He wants a family."

She knew her mother was right about the timing, but she didn't confide the full truth to her; she didn't share that his proposals felt like he wanted to close the deal rather than join his life to hers. She also didn't mention his idea of being a power couple—her parents would have found that ludicrous.

In the end it was his persistence, her mother's insistence, and his stance of non-interference that tipped the scales in his favor. It was the young woman distracted by her studies and still under the influence of her mother who said yes to Peter— a truth she only recognized years later.

CHAPTER 10

Jablonsky and Dr. Aashi Patel were having breakfast at Sophia's Café in the Strip District. Aashi seemed unusually animated—she quickly ordered, then impatiently waited for Jablonsky to make up his mind. Jeanne, their usual waitress, rolled her eyes at Aashi in sympathy; she kept her pen poised over the order pad.

"What will it be, Chief?" she asked, trying to nudge him along.

"Um. I think today I will have two eggs in a nest, with a side of Black Forest ham, orange juice, and coffee. Make sure the yolks are runny."

"Will do." *As if the cook doesn't know your every food whim,* thought Jeanne.

"Now that we have sorted that out," remarked Aashi with a tinge of sarcasm, "I have some news . . . surprising news."

Jablonsky rarely saw her this excited. "Is this about Celine Arceneau?"

"Yes, it is. I made a call to my friends in London," said Dr. Patel.

"London? That means Scotland Yard. Come on then,

Aashi, what gives? Do you have manner and cause?" Jablonsky was starting to get irritated.

Dr. Patel was not going to be hurried; she wanted the pleasure of unfolding her story step by step. "Let me start at the beginning. Celine had recently been suffering from gastrointestinal symptoms and fatigue. Since she was winding up her sabbatical and heading back to Montreal, Dr. Smythe reasonably assumed it was a flare of her IBS. When she consulted Celine's Canadian physician, she confirmed Ellen's diagnosis —all perfectly reasonable, but all perfectly *wrong*."

The food arrived, and Jablonsky squirted his beloved Heinz tomato catsup over his ham.

"During the autopsy, the thing that I noticed was that this pre-menopausal woman's hair was unusually thin, perhaps even bordering on alopecia. That may be a side effect of thyroid disease, but not of IBS. Additionally, there were small dark spots around some of the hair follicles, and that is a dead giveaway for . . . drum roll please . . . thallium poisoning." Aashi clinked her fork and knife together, accentuating the "ta-da" of her statement.

"Thallium? You mean like radiation poisoning?" Jablonsky was so shocked that he stopped eating, and he could eat through most anything.

"That's exactly what I mean. I had everyone suit up and called forensics to make sure no one in the morgue was in danger; we followed all the safety protocols for working on and storing the body. Thallium poisoning requires a specific type of blood test on the plasma, done by the mass spec, that's mass spectrometer to you, so I ordered it. While thallium doesn't stay long in urine, hair, or blood, we did find minute traces in her blood."

"No kidding. What did Bill Reeves say?" asked Jablonsky.

"Reeves sent his people to her office and her townhome to find out if there was a discernible level of radiation present— which there wasn't," answered Dr. Patel.

Jablonsky was always impressed with Aashi, and now even more so. She couldn't stop herself from giving him a brief lecture.

"Thallium is an element. You may remember from science class that when neutrons become unstable, they are considered to be radioactive. Certain forms of thallium are tasteless and odorless, and can be absorbed through inhalation, the skin, or the gut. Thallium has been used to poison political dissidents in Russia and Britain but has not been used for that purpose here in the States—that we know of, I'd have to add."

"I can't believe it. Where would a murderer get ahold of the stuff? This is so, well, James Bond spy-ish." The chief still hadn't resumed eating.

"Radioactive isotopes are used every day in nuclear medicine to treat a whole host of diseases: thyroid cancer, arthritis, liver tumors, just to name a few. In answer to your question, most hospitals and many science laboratories keep radioactive material on hand," stated Dr. Patel.

"But, isn't handling it dangerous? I don't pretend to remember most of high school chemistry, but I do remember that exposure to anything radioactive is bad—the person handling it has to know what they're doing. I have a picture in mind of an old-fashioned Geiger counter clicking away, or even Superman faced with Kryptonite."

Jablonsky was so sincere in his Superman analogy that Dr. Patel didn't laugh, although she wanted to.

"Well, Kryptonite aside, I believe that Celine had ingested the thallium over a short period of time in food or drink, most likely in powder form. What were her daily habits? Did she stop at the same place every day for a coffee? Where did she eat lunch? Did she bring her own or order from a restaurant near the law school? This is for your detectives to determine, Chief Detective."

"What about the food poisoning at the bistro? Was it related?" asked Jablonsky.

"No. That was Bacillus cereus—and plenty of it—sprinkled on the arugula lettuce. Sometimes it can take a few days to become ill from this bacterium, but there was so much of it, everyone reacted quickly," explained Dr. Patel.

Jablonsky was amused by Aashi scoffing at the Bacillus cereus; who could blame her when Queen Thallium appeared on the chess board of poisons.

"So, Dr. Smythe missed the thallium," Jablonsky stated, as he cut into his eggs in a nest, sopping up the yolky goodness with the grilled, buttery bread.

"She wouldn't have thought to look for thallium poisoning. Hardly any primary care physician in the States would have considered radiation poisoning when other common diagnoses fit the symptoms," Dr. Patel stated.

"Medical examiners, however, have to cast a wider net. As you know, in my diagnoses, I always consider the whole range from most likely to most unlikely." She leaned back in the booth, smiling the smile of a champion.

"I know that you would like to believe that Ellen Smythe is innocent in this scenario, but here are the facts: The perpetrator had to have access to some form of thallium, which means they had knowledge of the forms of radioactive isotopes. That person needed access to both the thallium and to the food at the party. They also knew about dosing of the bacterium and where to procure it. Plus, the murderer was somewhere in the orbit of Celine Arceneau's life. All of that could easily describe Ellen Smythe—she had opportunity and means—just not motive—yet."

Jablonsky jotted a few notes in his small paper notebook—radioactive isotopes weren't typically his beat—he wanted to remember everything Aashi had said.

"I'm declaring the manner of Celine Arceneau's death to be murder and the cause to be thallium poisoning." Dr. Patel shot Jablonsky a self-satisfied smile.

"Now, I have to get back to the morgue. All of the regulatory agencies must be notified." With a flourish, she gathered her things, leaving Jablonsky to finish his breakfast and pay the check.

When Jablonsky returned to the precinct, he grabbed Lemon and DeVille, gave them the update, and put a call through to Dr. Patel, whom he put on speaker.

"Aashi, one thing we didn't cover was how you would go about getting ahold of Bacillus cereus? You didn't mention it earlier."

"Labs that research microbial agents and pathogenic microorganisms is where I would start. The university has several such laboratories. Also, private food laboratories have them. There were plenty when Heinz Foods was still in Pittsburgh. Bill Reeves could tell you more," suggested Dr. Patel.

"Thanks, Aashi." The chief turned to his number one and two.

"We have to do the usual work of uncovering the victim's patterns of living. What do you have?"

Coupe flipped open his own paper notebook and began. "I've talked to her colleagues at the law school. Celine followed the same routine everyday: She walked from her Forbes Avenue townhome to the law school. There is a coffee shop in the lobby of her building where she purchased a regular coffee at precisely the same time each morning. She taught two classes and one tutorial. The classroom was the same for each course, and the tutorial was held in one of the conference rooms of the same building where her office was. Celine always ordered a salad for lunch from a little restaurant across the way called The Back Yard. She had a mid-afternoon espresso, then walked home. Her evenings were varied—sometimes she stayed in and worked, sometimes she went out for dinner with a colleague, mostly to different restaurants in

Squirrel Hill—sometimes they went to George's bistro. That's the gist so far."

Jablonsky was glad to see Coupe being thorough about the details—he tried to pound into the detective's head that cases are solved by deep dives into the victim's daily activities and routines.

"Good job. Interview the coffee people, the people from her lunch spot, plus the custodial and security folks from the classroom. Was there a particular student who was known to have an issue with Celine—someone who was angry over grades?" asked the chief.

"Not that any of her colleagues knew of—they mentioned that law students have no trouble raising a fuss if they think they are not being treated fairly." Coupe raised his eyebrows at the power a legal education confers on students.

"Lemon, connect with Bill Reeves and his techs—see if they know which university labs have Bacillus cereus, and also which labs produce or keep thallium." Even the usually nonplussed Jablonsky raised his eyebrows over the word thallium.

Since the same forensic techs reported that there was no discernible level of radiation at Celine Arceneau's townhome, Jablonsky asked André Trembly to meet him there.

"As Ms. Arceneau's countryman, a personal item may have a meaning for you that it wouldn't hold for me," he remarked, giving the reason for inviting the Canadian consul into the investigation.

Jablonsky's people reported that they had found nothing of interest at Ms. Arceneau's place, but he wasn't satisfied. He also wanted to follow up with the consul concerning any additional information he had gathered about her family in Canada.

Celine Arceneau's townhome sat back from Forbes

Avenue, one of the main arteries running through Squirrel Hill; Trembly was waiting for him on the small front porch.

"This was good timing. I was hoping to send her things back to Montreal soon," Trembly announced as Jablonsky opened the front door.

They walked into the living room. Both men silently looked around at the sparsely furnished space. There were no personal photos nor artwork on the walls. The same was true for the small dining area and the kitchen. The rooms were painted off-white; the absence of color in her surroundings mirrored the lack of any hint of Celine's personality in her home. They headed upstairs to the master bedroom, which contained a queen bed and two dressers. The faint scent of perfume lingered, along with the bottle—Chanel's COCO.

Both men raised their eyebrows at a drawer filled with delicate lingerie; the chief carefully deposited them into an evidence bag, surprised Reeves' men had missed them. He also bagged the perfume bottle.

Ms. Arceneau had arranged a workspace in the small second bedroom. The police had possession of her laptop, but the printer and fax machines remained lined up on a long folding table. A cheap office chair sat in front of the makeshift desk. Four bookcases were half full, and on the floor lay several articles about small Canadian reactors primarily used for producing the radiopharmaceuticals used in nuclear medicine.

As Trembly picked up one of the articles, he said, "I wanted to talk with you about what I found in regard to her law practice. I thought we might have a coffee?"

"I'd be grateful for your insights," answered Jablonsky, still looking around the small office.

"Our forensics people didn't find much on her computer, the legal files were encrypted—there was hardly anything personal. Just files of her lectures at the law school and current emails to her colleagues, especially to one friend in Montreal

—perhaps you can tell me more about her life in Canada?" Jablonsky locked the front door behind them.

After obtaining two steaming cups of French roast, they sought out a table in the back of a specialty coffee shop. Jablonsky took out his notebook as Trembly began to recite the facts that he learned from his friends in the Canadian government.

"During her mother's treatment for cancer, Celine didn't travel much for business. It was after her mother's death that she returned to handling issues related to Canada's nuclear plants. You probably already know that an international group had taken over the old Westinghouse manufacturing factories in East Pittsburgh. They fabricate items destined for nuclear plants—heat exchangers, storage casks, spacer grids, things like that.

"Adele, her mother, who also worked for the government in nuclear energy, had been tasked with making the best deals for Canada's nuclear power," stated Trembly.

Jablonsky wrote rapidly in his idiosyncratic shorthand. Then he added what he knew about Pittsburgh's nuclear history.

"Those factories underneath the Westinghouse Bridge are as famous as the bridge itself. The structures used to house WABCO, or the Westinghouse Air Brake Company, and then the Westinghouse Electric Company. That company was world renowned for the quality of its engineering and employed generations of Pittsburghers. Westinghouse was as important to Pittsburgh as the steel industry was. There used to be a museum on site that housed George Westinghouse's original office—I think it's in the Heinz History Center now."

Jablonsky paused—he was lost in memories of the zenith of Westinghouse's engineering influence. His father had worked in the steel mills, but many of his friend's fathers and grandfathers had worked at those Westinghouse plants.

George Westinghouse was more famous worldwide than almost all of the owners of the steel mills.

"So, Adele and her daughter were involved in the nuclear business for the Canadian government. André, what else did you find out?" This was the part of his job that Jablonsky loved—always learning something new.

"During her mother's work travels, Celine stayed with one of Adele's friends, who had a daughter the same age named Isabelle. Isabelle and Celine became like sisters," said Trembly.

"I saw many emails to an Isabelle. Nothing suspicious, just work talk and girl talk—if it is still permissible to say girl talk," laughed the chief.

"Isabelle is the executrix of Celine's will; she sent me a copy of it. There is also a bank box, the contents of which are unknown to me. Here is a copy of the will." Trembly retrieved a document from his briefcase and laid it on the table.

"It's in French," joked Jablonsky. "Anything that might help us with this murder inquiry in it? Is there a version in English?" Trembly started turning the pages, translating certain sections of the will for the chief.

Jablonsky returned to his note taking—he wanted to accurately reproduce the central components of the will for the murder board, even though Trembly assured him that he would send over a copy in English; "You can never be too sure" was the chief's motto.

CHAPTER 11

THE SIDES OF THE MURDER BOARD WERE CROWDED WITH ALL the pictures of people DeVille and Lemon had interviewed: the hospital staff who had had access to Ms. Arceneau's room, the medical staff who had directly treated her, law school colleagues, the cooking class students, the diners at the bon voyage party. Aside from Isabelle, there seemed to be no one else with whom she had been especially close; the professors at the law school were social acquaintances who taught with her, but they hardly knew anything about her private life, either in Montreal or in Pittsburgh.

Out of a rare show of frustration, the chief started yanking down some of the photos and stacking them on Lemon's desk. When he came to Dr. James, he stopped.

"Anything pertinent from the code leader? Did he know Celine Arceneau or anything about her before he led the resuscitation efforts? No?" The chief fired his picture on the pile.

"Okay, Detective Lemon. Tell me why this Canadian national, only in Pittsburgh for twelve months, was murdered," ordered the chief.

Annie Lemon moved alongside of Jablonsky, not intimidated by his mood. "I think this a story about love."

A surprised Coupe inhaled his coffee too quickly and started to choke.

"Go on," said Jablonsky, throwing Coupe the hairy eyeball.

"We know that Peter Smythe pursued Ellen when she was in medical school. And I mean *pursued*—his colleagues at C&S all seemed to know that she repeatedly rejected his marriage proposals before eventually saying yes. Within the law firm, Peter had a reputation for aggressively going after what his clients wanted. I think he took the same tack in pursuit of Ellen." Lemon drew an empty outline right next to Ellen and then continued.

"Peter has been dead a long time now. I believe there is someone else in her life, a man we don't know about." Before she could go on, Jablonsky inserted himself in her theory.

"Dr. Patel said that a fellow student had been in love with Ellen in medical school. Rumor is that person has been back in her life for a while now." He pointed to the empty outline Lemon had drawn next to Ellen's photo.

"Who is this person and why don't we know about him yet?" the chief asked angrily, his accusation drifting through the bullpen like a bad odor.

"I see relational triangles here." Lemon wrote the possible configurations: Peter-Ellen-Celine, Rose-Ellen-Celine, Peter-Rose-Celine, or Ellen-mystery man-Celine, then asked a question. "Is one of the people in these triangles a murderer?"

"Coupe, you and Lemon remain tasked with finding this mystery man. Get after it. I'm headed to Mrs. Rossetti's funeral."

Kate sat next to Joan at the funeral Mass. She found herself whispering one of the haikus that Marco had sent her. Joan shushed her, then returned to looking around to see which of her colleagues had come to pay their respects to Marco over the death of his mother.

There were plenty of physicians in attendance, including Dr. Smythe, who sat in the pew right behind Marco, occasionally resting her hands on his shoulders. Without turning, he would place his hands over hers. Kate was moved by the empathy of the exchange.

"There's Jablonsky." She nodded toward the side aisle where the broad-shouldered chief stood leaning against the wall.

Observing him like this, Kate understood why he was nicknamed The Great Horned Owl. Like his namesake, the chief could hoot sweetly but also relentlessly pursue his prey. Being part canine herself, Kate admired the latter quality. She knew he was here on the hunt.

Johnny squeezed himself into the pew next to Kate and Joan. Renata and Andrea, two elderly friends of Mrs. Rossetti, had stopped him in the vestibule, regaling him with stories about Rosalie's Bakery and his mother, who had worked there. He sighed with relief at making his escape.

Pittsburgh was a large small town; people knew each other, their children, and their grandchildren—there are pluses and minuses to that kind of generational familiarity, as Johnny well knew. Today it had been just annoying.

The ceremony was short and the hymns were surprisingly Protestant: Marco, who didn't believe there was a ghost in the machine, had chosen simple songs—there wasn't an "Ave Maria" in the group.

The hymns reflected his mother's innocent relationship with her God. Kate watched this very Catholic group wiping their eyes at the uncomplicated sentiment of the recessional hymn.

. . .

And he walks with me and he talks with me
And he tells me I am his own
And the joy we share as we tarry there
None other has ever known.

As he walked behind his mother's coffin, Marco caught sight of Kate. For a second, their eyes locked, then he continued his journey down the long aisle. Kate, Joan, and Johnny did not follow him to the cemetery but chose instead to drive right to the luncheon, which Marco had arranged to be held at the university club.

"He looked exhausted," remarked Johnny once they were seated at the club. "I remember how much it took out of me to arrange my mother's funeral and I wasn't flying in from overseas. I give him credit. The Mass was perfect, and this club is centrally located—Mrs. Rossetti's South Oakland friends didn't have to drive far. He's been thoughtful about the funeral."

Joan suddenly rose from her seat to stop an older, dark-haired man who was walking by.

"Daniel! I haven't seen you in quite a while. It's great to see you again." Joan smoothly turned toward the table to make introductions.

"Dr. Daniel Grusin, this is my friend Dr. Kate Chambers, and here is Professor Johnny McCarthy. Johnny's mother worked at Rosalie's Bakery, so he grew up around Marco. Johnny stood and shook Dr. Grusin's hand—his mother had raised a mannerly boy.

"Would you like to join us? I'd love to catch up," urged Joan."

"No. I'm only here briefly and then have to check on a

patient in the hospital. We'll get together soon. Good to see you, Joan," said Dr. Grusin before turning to leave.

"Something we said?" asked Kate as Daniel hurried away. "That was certainly a blow off. But . . . he looks familiar."

Joan kept silent as the servers began filing the water glasses; she watched to make sure Daniel had left the room before she started to gossip.

"He practiced in San Francisco for a long time, then about ten years ago returned to Pittsburgh; he's a respected internist. I like him because he was always a supporter of women going into surgery." Joan downed her cup of hot coffee like it was water, then continued with her story.

"Rumor among the older physicians was that he and Ellen Smythe had been an item in medical school; *hot and heavy* were the adjectives everyone used. After Peter died, Daniel was suddenly back in Pittsburgh, and everyone believes they started up again. Curiously, no one sees them together—they don't sit together at lectures or travel with each other to conferences. If they are lovers, it is very hush-hush." A waitress refilled Joan's cup.

Kate suddenly remembered the graduation picture of a young Daniel from one of the photographs at Ellen's home.

"But why would their relationship need to be hush-hush? Peter Smythe is long dead, Ellen's daughter is grown. Why would they keep the relationship a secret?" asked Kate.

Johnny held up his hand, indicating he wanted to weigh in on the matter. "I think I can answer that. When I found out my mom had had a lover, I was . . . jealous, and very angry. After my dad died, I was supposed to be her number one guy. Immature, I know, but those were my feelings. Maybe Dr. Smythe knows something about Rose's potential reaction that we don't—maybe she would feel jealous and make trouble."

"Ellen said that Rose can be jealous. . . . I don't know Rose. Do you?" Kate asked, turning to Joan.

"No. I don't move in the circles she does. I work and go to

baseball games, she . . . well, I'm not sure what she does," Joan admitted.

The three friends rose together to peruse the buffet. As Kate was picking through cherry tomatoes, cucumbers, and red leaf butter lettuce, Marco, looking funereal in his all-black suit and shirt, suddenly appeared out of nowhere and touched her elbow.

"Thanks for coming, Kate. It was so good to see your face in the crowd at the church. Let's step over here." Marco guided her out of the line—Kate realized that if they had stayed where they were, there would have been a constant stream of offered condolences.

"I'm sorry I haven't called you. I just got back and had to arrange all of this." Marco gestured around the room.

"How are you, Marco?" Kate's expression was solemn, although she was amused by the black shirt and tie. *Too many operas,* she thought.

"I'm really fine. When I decided to take my team to Poland, I knew that she might die while I was gone. Her friends Renata and Andrea, whom you met at Phipps Conservatory, helped her FaceTime with me. Her death was quick and painless—it's all any of us can ask for, don't you agree?" Marco assumed that Kate's understanding of death would mirror his, which it did.

"I do agree. In fact, I believe that the date of our death is tattooed on the bottom of one of our feet—in invisible ink." Kate paused, realizing her light tone might be inappropriate.

"Will you be staying in town or going back?" It was a question that Kate had routinely asked Eddie. As if the sun had suddenly become too bright, she pulled down an emotional window shade, shielding herself from the impact of his answer.

"I think I'm going to stay home for a while. I have to clean out my mother's place and probate the will. And I'm hoping that the war will end soon." He stood awkwardly, appearing unsure as to how to further engage Kate, so she did it for him.

"When I went through my grandfather's things, I found hundred-dollar bills tucked in his books—it added up to a couple thousand dollars. I'd check your mother's books before you pack them away, especially her prayer books."

Marco's surprise over her story turned into laughter. "I'll be sure to look. It sounds like the kind of thing both she and my father would have done."

"I know it's frivolous to say at a funeral luncheon, but I've really enjoyed the postcards and the poetry. Those haiku provide a few moments that take me out of my day-to-day routines and . . . grieving Eddie." Kate lightly touched his arm.

"They do the same for me—the war rages and there are so many mangled young bodies—so much uncertainty." As if he had said too much, Marco changed the subject.

"Speaking of uncertainty, I heard about Dr. Smythe's situation. Jablonsky was at the Mass today, but I don't see him here. I was going to ask about it. She's such a great physician —and person. I'd like to help if I can."

"I'll let her know you asked about her. By the way, do you know Dr. Daniel Grusin? Joan just introduced him to me. She said something to the effect that he and Ellen were a couple?" asked Kate.

Marco chuckled, provoking a head-bob from an embarrassed Kate.

"You caught me. I guess I'm fishing for gossip," she admitted with a guilty smile.

"I don't know Dr. Grusin well, but he's around the hospital. I *have* heard that they are in a relationship, one that isn't very public." Marco stood quietly, then finally asked the question he really wanted to.

"Kate, may I call you?"

"I'd like that. I'm training for the mini triathlon, so we

might have to get together in the pool or on a long run!" she suggested.

"Any time spent with you is okay by me, Kate. Right now I'd better make the rounds." As he walked away, he turned to look at her over his shoulder, twice—blushing the second time.

She returned to the table, wanting to share confirmation of the Grusin-Smythe connection right away; she had the feeling it was important. Just as Johnny and Joan were leaving, Kate caught sight of the chief.

"I'm going to talk with Jablonsky for a minute. You two go on." She approached the chief in the buffet line, then followed him to a table.

"There are a few things I wanted to tell you related to Ellen Smythe. Is it all right if we speak now?" she asked, hoping her respectful attitude would lead to his acceptance.

"Sure, if you don't mind that I eat my lunch while we talk." Jablonsky placed a napkin in his lap, took up his knife and fork, and artfully arranged and separated the food on his plate.

"Joan and Marco Rossetti both said that Dr. Smythe has a man in her life. His name is Dr. Daniel Grusin." Kate detailed what she knew about the relationship.

"Also, Ellen told me that the Smythe family owns a home in an area outside of Montreal called Summit Park. Peter took Rose there in the summers and also when he was on business in Canada."

"Okay, good tip. Anything else, Kate?" asked the chief.

"When I researched Celine Arceneau's biography, it struck me that she must have been very close to her mother. It was just the two of them, they practiced in the same area of law, and Celine never married or moved away. There is something about daughters too close to their mothers—Rose and Ellen, Celine and Adele," Kate said.

"Okay. Are you making a random point about family therapy,or trying to tie those relationships to Ms. Arceneau's murder?" asked Jablonsky impatiently.

"Stay with me, Chief. If an unnaturally close relationship is challenged, bad things can happen. I would even say *dangerous* things can happen," said Kate.

"For example?" Jablonsky asked, spooning up a large mound of couscous spiced with cinnamon and cardamon.

"Dangerous, for example, by provoking a state of rage—not anger, mind you—but rage, which by its very nature is irrational." Kate, who knew the experience of rage, caught her breath, then simply stopped talking.

"So you're saying there is, or was, a connection between the Smythe family and Celine Arceneau, am I correct?" This type of insight was the reason Jablonsky rarely resisted Kate's involvement in a case.

"Yes. The Smythe family . . . but it might not be Ellen." Kate offered.

Jablonsky watched Kate's face as he quietly chewed his food. So far, she was the only person who didn't think he was off base in suspecting that someone close to Ellen Smythe could be setting her up or had done the deed itself. To his chagrin, Kate and he often thought alike.

"I want to help Ellen in any way I can, and so does Marco. Joan Weisner has weighed in as well. You can count on me, on all of us." Kate stood, pushed in her chair, and added one final warning.

"In the natural world, a vine that wraps itself around even the mightiest oak, in the end, suffocates it."

CHAPTER 12

ELLEN SMYTHE SAT ACROSS FROM HER ATTORNEY TALKING about future plans. "I've decided to retire from my practice. As you can imagine, the insinuation that I might have been involved in the death of a patient has devastated my remaining patients—some have gone to other physicians, which I completely understand. Whether or not it makes me look more guilty, it is time for me to step away. I've been exploring other uses for my medical talents."

Elise Rosen listened intently. At their first meeting, Dr. Smythe had declared that she was absolutely innocent of the Arceneau murder, but she never put much stock in initial declarations. Whether Dr. Smythe was guilty or innocent, she deserved the best defense the law could provide.

So far, the only connections between Celine Arceneau and Ellen Smythe were that Celine had been a patient and the notion that Ellen would know how to lay her hands on the toxins used to poison Celine—Bacillus cereus and thallium. There was no motive. Returning to Ellen's question about retirement, Elise offered her point of view.

"From a legal standpoint, I'm not sure it makes a difference one way or another. But, you talk like you really want to retire, and I can see the toll all of this has taken on you. You look thin and tired—sorry to be so blunt," responded the attorney, who had never lost her appetite for any reason in her entire life.

"Have you seen your own physician? It takes stamina to go through this process, even when you are innocent," Ms. Rosen added.

"Thanks for the advice—I'm usually the one giving it! I'm okay, but I did want to mention that I sometimes have the feeling that someone is following me. Could that be the police?" Ellen really had no idea what the police did or didn't do in an investigation.

"Maybe. Be careful when you are out—look around you, look in your car before you get in, and don't walk around after dark or park in a lot at night. If you see someone that looks suspicious, please tell Detective Jablonsky immediately." Those admonitions concluded their congenial meeting.

As Ellen stepped out of the lobby, she began searching in her purse for her car keys and ran headlong in to her daughter.

"Mummy! What are you doing here? This isn't your stomping ground." Rose linked arms with her mother, and they started to walk. Ellen turned her head toward her daughter and sniffed.

"You are wearing your father's aftershave again. Creed Aventus."

Rose teared up, responding defensively. "You know I still miss Daddy. Wearing his cologne helps me."

"I know, it reminds me of him as well. Why are you in the Strip?" asked Ellen, changing the subject.

"Oh, no reason really. I promised Maria I would pick up a few things for her from the restaurant-supply store—I have to drop them off. . . . I was hoping to stay for dinner." Rose hurriedly added, "Patricia may come as well."

Ellen noticed that Rose wasn't carrying a bag from the

kitchen store but didn't comment on it; Rose usually took her questions as criticism.

"I'd love to see Patricia! As long as making dinner for all of us is okay with Maria, it's okay with me. I'm going to head home now . . . maybe take a nap."

"That's unusual, Mummy. Did Elise Rosen have something new to say that I don't know about?" There was that familiar edge of hysteria in Rose's voice as she stopped and confrontationally faced her mother.

"Calm down, Rose. There is no legal case against me. I hired Elise Rosen because everyone told me I needed an attorney, you included. I'm going to the car. I'll see you later," Ellen said.

"No. You are not getting out of this that easily. You are never available when I call, when I stop at the house you are mysteriously out somewhere, Maria never knows what's going on, and you never talk to me about anything other than Patricia—I think you are purposely avoiding me!" By this time, Rose was yelling and pointing her finger at her mother in the middle of the busy sidewalk.

"This kind of behavior—shouting accusations at me that I do not deserve—is more than I can handle. I just can't cope with these kinds of scenes right now. And furthermore, this business with the cologne has been going on far too long! Your father has been dead for *years*. Move on, get past it, or get back into therapy." Ellen's frustration with Rose pushed her past the embarrassment of creating a public scene.

"You just don't understand. Before he died, I was with him every single day—he needed to see me, and I wanted to see him. He was the center of my universe. Wearing his cologne helps me remember all of our good times together. You never loved him the way I did!" Like a tantrumming child, Rose stomped her foot.

"Maybe that is true. Maybe you did love him more than I did, but he's dead. Think about Patricia for a change. Think what a relief it would be for her to know that you had met someone and were making a happy life for yourself. How many times do we have to have this conversation?" Ellen reached out and took hold of her daughter.

"Rose, you could live another forty years. Find someone you can love as much as you loved your father. He would want that for you. I want that for you."

Her mother's intensity brought tears to Rose's eyes. As much as she adored her father, it was her mother she relied upon. But Ellen didn't need her as much as her father had needed her, and like her father, Rose confused need with love.

Ellen kissed her daughter, held her tight, then left to go home. She laughed at herself for being party to such a scene in the middle of the street.

What's happening to me? All my calm reserve is flying out the window with this situation. Damn Celine Arceneau.

When she opened the door to her house, a wave of fatigue washed over her—Maria came running down the hall-way, reaching for her, saying, "I thought you were going to fall! Are you all right? Let me get your jacket." Maria continued her soothing chatter while they walked to the kitchen.

"Rose just called and said that she and Patricia will be over for dinner. Are you sure you are up to it?" Maria placed a glass of water in front of Ellen, then leaned against the kitchen counter, arms firmly folded under her bosom, a concerned grandmother expression crinkled her forehead.

Ellen sipped some water. "I'm going upstairs to change clothes. What will you cook, Maria?"

"I'm not sure. Any requests?" asked Maria.

"You decide." As Ellen rose to leave the kitchen, the phone rang, and Maria answered.

"It's Mr. Daniel. He wants to know if it is okay to come over. I can tell him it's no good," said Maria, protective of Ellen.

"I'll take the call." Maria handed the landline telephone to Ellen, who talked openly in front of her.

"Hi, Daniel. Patricia and Rose are coming for dinner tonight. You could stop over around eleven. Yes? Okay. Just let yourself in the kitchen door."

Daniel ended his call to Ellen as he stood across the street from one of the condominium buildings along the riverfront on Penn Avenue, watching as Rose exited one of them.

With all the foot traffic, he blended in with the crowd, sometimes leaning against a wall or walking a block, then turning and retracing his steps. Ellen had mentioned that she sometimes felt someone was following her, so he had taken it upon himself to trail Rose, whom he considered to be the likely candidate. When Rose drove out of one of the parking lots, Daniel discreetly tailed her.

It was the second time that day that he had followed Rose. The first time was when he tracked her to that condo building. He had no idea who she knew there or even if she owned one of the apartments in the building. It was entirely possible that she kept a place to overnight after staying late at an event in the city; he knew that Rose certainly had the money to own several homes.

Right now, he figured she was headed to Ellen's place for dinner. He parked down the street from the house, turned off his lights, and waited to see what Rose was up to.

A classic James Taylor song, "Fire and Ice," came on the seventies channel of Sirius radio. When Taylor sang, it evoked a vivid memory of how he and Ellen had reconciled after Peter's death.

It was at a medical conference in Orlando, Florida, that he approached her. Ellen was standing in the lobby of the Ritz-Carlton looking out at the single line of palm trees edging the swimming pool. Daniel came up behind her and touched her shoulder, softly saying her name; she turned around and they spontaneously reached for each other.

Like particles in an accelerator, the past and the present collided, breaking apart old hurts and resentments. They talked for hours that night—he spewed out his anger, and she spoke about her youthful lack of self-knowledge.

"I never regretted Peter, but I never loved him the way I loved you. It took me years to understand my own heart," she had admitted.

They extended their stay in Florida, drifting through the days awash in the special charms of a subtropical climate. The future they had once talked about sharing now opened up before them.

Ellen told no one about Daniel except Maria, who gave her commonsense blessing: "Your husband was an old man, and now he is dead. Have some affection and warmth in your life!"

Daniel bought a place close to Ellen's so he could walk to see her instead of parking a car—a car about which the neighbors might wonder. For years, he had expressed how ridiculous he thought her need for privacy was, but it fell on deaf ears. Keeping their relationship private created a growing tension between them—increasingly, Daniel forced the topic.

"Ellen, you are a widow, I'm divorced, our children are grown; why not just get married? No one cares what we do."

"Rose would care," was her stock answer, and so they continued to meet later in the evenings or on the weekends for dinner, walks, romance, and good conversation—all of which mirrored how their relationship had begun.

Daniel was yanked out of his reverie when Rose appeared on the street.

She had parked at the top of the hill and sat in the car looking like she was either blowing her nose or sniffing something. He wondered if she was snorting cocaine. Now she slowly walked toward Ellen's house, visibly rubbernecking to look at the surrounds.

Daniel slouched down in his seat and watched her pace back and forth for almost ten minutes before Patricia arrived. Rose pretended she had just pulled up, and the two went in for dinner.

Returning to his condominium, Daniel changed, microwaved a piece of day-old pizza, and read the paper, killing time before he walked over to Ellen's home. He let himself in the back kitchen door.

"Hello, sweetie," Ellen called out from the living room, where she was lounging on the sofa reading a medical journal. They kissed, and he sat down close to her.

"Did you say that you ran into Rose after the meeting with Elise Rosen?" asked Daniel, immediately steering the conversation to where he wanted it to go. He breathed a sigh of relief that he hadn't been seen by Ellen when he was stalking Rose along Penn Avenue.

"Yes. I literally ran into her. She said she had been shopping, but she didn't have any bags—it struck me as odd that she would lie about it. Then she created a scene in the street, accusing me of avoiding her lately—which I have been." Ellen wearily shrugged.

"Speaking of running into people, after you left the church and went back to your office, I ran into Joan Weisner," said Daniel.

Daniel enjoyed making Ellen laugh, so he told some amusing stories about how Joan handled the male surgical residents when they would harass her during training. The two remained nestled on the couch, but instead of feeling relaxed, his mind wandered to the disturbing image of Rose pacing outside of Ellen's house.

Would Rose ever hurt her mother? Daniel wondered, and not for the first time.

It was an evening for confidences. After Kate and Johnny had finished a run in her neighborhood, she ordered some takeout. Bourbon Ball positioned himself under the dining room table, recognizing all the signs that food was about to arrive.

"Have you made up your mind about training for the mini triathlon?" asked Kate, setting out plates and flatware.

"I've been enjoying learning how to swim, but the amount of running and cycling necessary to really go for it takes too much time. I was actually hoping to travel before the fall semester begins," Johnny admitted.

Kate appreciated his honesty but hated that he didn't want to participate with her. Perhaps more coaxing might tip the scales in her favor, but tonight, she just wasn't in the mood. She poured coffee for them both, then made circles on her placemat with her spoon.

"What's up, Kate?" asked Johnny.

"Something happened to me in high school that I never told you about. I was on the swim team and—actually, I was a pretty good swimmer. I held a few state records in the freestyle. We were at the Massachusetts Interscholastic Athletic Association, and as I walked out with the team, someone pushed me, and I fell and fractured my shoulder." Kate cooly took a sip of her coffee, not wanting a big emotional reaction from Johnny.

"Kate, you never told me! And how did I not know that you were a competitive swimmer in high school? More importantly, did they find the guy?" asked Johnny.

"No. They tried to track down the person, but no one was ever able to come up with any real leads. I'm telling you this because I think someone might be stalking me, and I have wondered if it's related to that long ago incident."

"What makes you think that?" asked Johnny, still reeling from the fact that she had kept that event secret. He bit the inside of his lip to keep from making any comment that would stop her from telling him more about her fears.

"There is a guy, probably around our age, whom I've seen in various places—when that bicyclist almost ran us over the other day, I thought it might have been him. Then there was the chapter I was writing that disappeared. If you hadn't made a hard copy, I'd have been in trouble. Maybe it's nothing, but still . . ." Kate again looked at Johnny. If his reaction to what she was saying was too heated, she wouldn't continue.

"Is there anything else you haven't mentioned?" he asked quietly, still in control of himself.

"Well . . . you know Eddie and I wrote letters to each other while he was away on digs. Some of his letters may have been taken from my mailbox. I only know this because he mentioned a few things he had written in them, and I didn't know what he was talking about." Kate blushed at what was, for her, a very personal revelation.

"This is serious, Kate. A stranger comes to your home, on your property, and steals your mail? That in itself is a federal offense. You have to tell Jablonsky. If you don't, I will."

CHAPTER 13

JABLONSKY CHOSE TO WALK FROM THE PRECINCT TO THE forensics lab. With his long strides he made the journey quickly, arriving at the forensics building feeling invigorated. Moving through the maze of workstations, he heard Lou Reed singing "Walk on the Wild Side." This wasn't the first time Jablonsky admired one of the technician's appreciation for early rock 'n' roll.

Bill Reeves, head of the lab, and the chief built their careers at the same time—they trusted each other implicitly. Coupe referred to them as "the old school justice league."

"Hey, Bill! Who is the tech that has the great playlist? Every time I'm here there is a Hall of Fame rock band playing."

"You must mean Hunter Lewis. Just for sport, we nicknamed him Huey. Very smart and hardworking, but on the strange side—extremely private, extensive tattoos, odd hairdos. He spends a lot of time at the gym with a group of guys who might go for the whole Iron Man competition." Bill shook his head, muttering, "Crazy," before changing the subject. "How's work on the miniatures at the train village going?"

"Pretty good. It's a nice group of retirees who help keep the display in shape—I'm not sure all of them know who I am, which is a bonus."

Jablonsky spent years building replicas of US battleships, then turned to helping the Pittsburgh Science Center keep its Christmas train display in shape. He enjoyed fixing the little houses and tiny people; he also liked the comradeship with the other men—they talked sports instead of crime.

Jablonsky noticed sheets of paper on Bill's desk. "What have you got there, Bill?"

"Here is the printout of Celine Arceneau's DNA. Next to it is the printout of the sample Detective Lemon took from Rose Delaney," Bill explained.

Jablonsky leaned over the desk, concentrating on the variously colored matching lengths.

"There is a familial match. Rose and Celine are half-sisters," stated Bill.

Unconsciously, Jablonsky offered Bill a stick of cinnamon gum, chewed one himself, then immediately started speculating.

"I guess Peter Smythe sampled more than croissants on his trips to Montreal," he smirked. "So did Peter know about this daughter? Did Ellen know that Celine Arceneau was Peter's child, and if so, how did she find out? Did Rose know that she had a half-sister? Is the simple fact of Arceneau's existence enough of a motive for murder?"

Bill chimed in. "The Smythes are a very, very wealthy family. Celine would be due a cut of that pie, but with so much money, would it really make a difference to any of them?"

"Bill, you and I come from the wage-slave perspective, but to the one percent, whoever has the most money at death, wins. I've just never been sure what they win, but they sure don't like to divvy it up," said a philosophical Jablonsky. "I guess this situation would be love betrayed—Peter's betrayal of Rose and Ellen. Strong motive."

Bill shook his head. "You and your team deal with the motives, I'm just the science guy. Now, let's talk about thallium, atomic number 81—a very potent poison.

"There's a famous killer in Britain, Graham Young, who murdered thirteen people—that they know of—with different forms of thallium. At fourteen, he murdered his stepmother with, I think, thallium acetate. Now, here's the thing, you can poison someone with sublethal doses over a period of time. Dr. Patel and I think this is what happened to Celine. We believe that she had been weakened by thallium, then the Bacillus cereus did her in."

"How would someone go about getting thallium? Would he or she have to have access to a laboratory where it is kept, like a nuclear medicine lab?" asked the chief.

"Thallium in the form of acetate is used as a medium in all kinds of experiments, so most likely it would come from a laboratory, of which there are many right here in this city." Bill shrugged, then continued.

"We've already asked the labs in the area that we know house radioactive isotopes to check if any thallium might be missing. So far, the lab directors we've been in contact with report that all their stock is intact—but that's not all the labs in the state, or even in all of Pittsburgh. Dr. Patel and I have also notified the Nuclear Regulatory Commission."

"She mentioned the NRC. So, the murderer might have procured it from a lab in another city." Jablonsky tapped his fingers on the desk. "Can you order it online?"

"It's possible. Start with the most probable and work outwards from there. If none of the labs in our city are missing thallium, then we have to cast a wider net—that's all I'm saying. Dr. Patel and I believe that the easiest form to get ahold of and use is thallium acetate, like that British man used." Bill Reeves stood and stretched, signaling the end to the conversation.

Jablonsky took a copy of the DNA reports and headed back to the precinct; thallium aside, he was excited about the first real piece of evidence that linked Ellen Smythe, Rose Delaney, and Celine Arceneau.

After letting his team know about Celine's paternity, Jablonsky wrote the same questions on the murder board that he had voiced to Bill Reeves, then turned to Lemon. "What do you have for me?"

"I reinterviewed the senior partner at the Cooper and Smythe law firm, this time pushing him to give me more detail about Peter's business travels to Europe and Canada. I politely asked him whether Peter was known to have 'liked the ladies.' After several disclaimers about gossip, he said that he and other older attorneys knew that Peter had been unfaithful to Ellen but did not know the particulars. He said it was, let me quote, 'An unfortunate aspect of being on the road so much.'" Detective Lemon frowned.

Both Jablonsky and Coupe voiced the same question at the same time. "Do we have any names?"

"I did ask him if there was someone in particular that he knew about. His answer was, 'Not that I can recall.'"

"How very lawyerly of him," remarked the chief. "Okay. We know that Adele Arceneau practiced law for the energy department of Canada, and with André Trembly's help, we probably can place her and Peter in the same city at the same time. Why would it take so many years for Celine to show up in Pittsburgh?"

"I suspect that Adele didn't tell Celine who her biological father was. The timing must have been really close—Adele is married but on a business trip, she does the dirty with Peter, gets pregnant, and decides not to tell her husband the baby isn't his. Then he dies in the skiing accident in Switzerland, and she's off the hook." Lemon finished with a sarcastic flourish.

"Why would she tell him? Surely she saw what Peter was? Baby or not, I doubt that he would have any intention of leaving Ellen. Was she trying to fleece some money out of him?" Jablonsky began his compulsive habit of tapping on someone's photo—this time it was Peter's.

Lemon quietly added another point of view. "Maybe she was in love with him. You're on a business trip, you meet in nice hotels, you have work in common, and you're out of normal life routines and constraints. It's a fantasy situation. And, Peter was the type of man who would have assumed that every woman in his orbit wanted him, so of course he would make a move."

"We have to find out if Ellen or Rose knew about Celine's existence. Let's look again at their social media and search records. Got that? Okay, moving on, our intrepid sleuth Kate Chambers has identified Ellen's companion as a Dr. Daniel Grusin."

Jablonsky wrote the physician's name under the empty outline on the board. Lemon immediately printed a photo of him from the internet—up it went over the mystery man outline.

"You two get me everything you can on Daniel Grusin. Ellen is a guarded person—would she have confided in him, or anyone, about Celine Arceneau?"

———

"Hi, Ellen. I'm heading to our committee meeting later today. Are you going? If not, I can stop by your office with our report—I need a signature. You're at home? Good. I'll cruise by." Kate hung up and gathered her things to head to Ellen's.

. . .

Kate sat in Ellen's kitchen as she signed the report. "I'm stepping back from the practice. I've been interviewing my replacement, a young physician I trained is interested. She would be a good fit for my staff and patients." Ellen announced this life-changing decision as if she were describing having found a good deal on a pound of ground meat—casually, with little fanfare.

"Is this because of the investigation into Celine Arceneau's death?" Kate was taken aback at how fast Ellen had moved on the idea of retiring.

"Yes, it is partly due to the fallout from the investigation. But I have been thinking about doing something other than private practice for some time. I just haven't settled on what will be next for me," Ellen said.

"Have you talked with anyone about this life-changing decision?" asked Kate.

"Actually, I have retained an attorney, Elise Rosen. I was worried that retiring would make me look guilty, but she said she didn't think it would make a difference. Well, there you have it." Ellen's gray eyes were warm and smiling, then suddenly, as if she remembered something, she snapped her fingers.

"Peter did the same thing. Right after his first round of chemotherapy for the leukemia, he went to see an attorney to discuss his retirement and his will."

"Kudos to him. Not many men seek advice about, well, anything. Did he consult a colleague?" Kate knew this could come across as nosy, but she didn't care; Ellen might pass over a detail not realizing its importance.

"He consulted an attorney he knew at a firm that specializes in estates. I'd met him, but I didn't attend the meeting," Ellen stated.

"Pardon me if this is too forward, but I don't understand

why you weren't at that meeting?" Kate was trying to grasp why a wife wouldn't be involved; Ellen looked at Kate's shocked face and gave out with a hoot.

"It's true that a husband and wife usually make their wills together, but from the beginning of my practice, I separated my earnings from the Smythe family trusts and their foundation. I know it sounds like a seventies manifesto, but I've always earned my own way. I didn't want to rely on his family money. Of course, Rose lives on a trust set up by Peter, and so does Patricia."

Kate put fresh bait on her hook and cast it into the water. "Do you know everything that is in the will?"

"He never hid the will from me—I have a copy around here somewhere. I cosigned it. I'm embarrassed to say that I didn't read the whole document—it's in the usual legalese. Rose took over administrating any annual bequests from the Smythe Foundation to nonprofits in Pittsburgh. She has the Smythe gene for generosity to the city—she's her father's daughter in that way."

"Did he seem relieved after getting the will settled?" Kate asked.

"No. You would think he would have been relieved, but instead he became quite introspective—I chalked it up to changes in his brain function, residual cognitive issues from the chemotherapy," Ellen explained.

Ever the scientist, thought Kate. *Overlooking the emotional aspect of relationships is a naive and dangerous thing to do in a family like the Smythes. Jealousy, envy, greed—that's the stuff that drives criminality.*

Kate left Ellen sitting in a patch of sunlight in her kitchen, sipping her coffee, a loafer dangling off one foot, one side of a heavily embroidered top slipping off her shoulder; her body language and dress evoked the picture of a young woman at the beginning of adulthood.

She's already made her decision as to what comes next. I wonder if it's related to Celine Arceneau or Daniel Grusin, or both.

. . .

After Kate's visit, Ellen found herself remembering her break up with Daniel.

They had been two students attracted to each other's commitment to medicine. At first, they were close friends who shared funny stories about dating—she talked about Peter and Daniel detailed his escapades with several girls in their class.

What began as a friendship, however, eventually escalated into an affair. Her memories of that pivotal day were still so vivid that as she sat in her kitchen in Schenley Farms she felt she had walked through a door into Daniel's old apartment. Annie Lennox was singing "Sweet Dreams" while she and Daniel were nestled on a floor mattress, surrounded by batik-printed pillows and an Indian block-print bedspread; the faint scent of pachouli oil was in the air.

"Let's go to the park and walk before we hit the books again." Daniel tied back his shoulder-length hair and put on a black T-shirt, grinning in appreciation as Ellen slipped into a peasant blouse and cutoffs.

With Peter, it was the little black dress, pearls, and country club dinners that included a crowd more than a generation older; with Daniel, she was fully part of her own generation. Ellen didn't come to realize the impact of that inequity until many years later when Peter had become an old man with whom she had nothing in common.

As they walked along the winding, tree-canopied paths in Schenley Park, Ellen felt nervous, but only understood half of the reason why.

"Daniel, you know that, over the last couple of years, Peter has been asking me to marry him. We've joked about it, but, well, a few days ago, I said yes." Daniel stopped dead in his tracks, his sharp features suddenly flushed with a sickly, aubergine color.

"What? What are you saying? I thought that was just a dalliance." Daniel grabbed her by the shoulders.

"You're telling me this after having just made love with me? What the hell, Ellen—I didn't think you saw him that much. I thought it was just an occasional thing." To Ellen's surprise, Daniel's lean body shook with anger as he unconsciously lifted his right hand; she realized that he could barely stop himself from hitting her.

"It hasn't been serious until recently. Really, Daniel, I don't understand why you are acting this way. You've seen other women on and off. . . ." Daniel angrily interrupted.

"I haven't seen anyone since you and I started sleeping together and you know it." He began to shout at her.

"I love you! You are the most important person in the world to me. I thought this May-December fling with Grandpa Smythe was just that. You can't do this to us—you are making a really big mistake and don't even know it! He had no right to ask you."

Daniel suddenly grew silent, then growled, "Is it for his money?"

"I can hear your knuckles scraping on the ground right now, Mr. Monkey Brain. I'll make my own money, thank you very much. Go cool off, and we'll talk later." Ellen stormed away, wanting to hide from his righteous anger. Yes, she loved Daniel, but—but what?

She hated to admit to herself that Daniel's intensity made her uneasy; with Peter, it was clear where she stood in his world—she was another of his accomplishments. Not very sexy, but a category that was full of empty space that she could fill with her patients and colleagues. Daniel however, wanted her heart and soul—subconsciously, she felt overwhelmed by his desire for her.

She left the park and went to Daniel's apartment, threw a few of her things into a bag, and went to stay at her parents. When they matched for their residencies, she stayed in Pittsburgh, and he went to California. They didn't speak for decades.

Daniel Grusin had never been in love, before or since, like he had been with Ellen—he was so devastated that no amount of time ever healed the wound. He stayed in California, married a nice woman for whom he genuinely cared, had a few children, then like many of his colleagues, divorced. From the outside, it looked like he was living a normal middle-aged life.

Over the years, he saw Ellen at conferences but never approached her. Then, Peter Smythe died.

CHAPTER 14

"CHIEF JABLONSKY? KATE HERE. I HAVE SOME INFORMATION that you might find interesting. Do you have a few minutes to talk?"

"Have you been interviewing people on your own again?" questioned the frustrated chief, who had warned her many times about the perils of behaving like she was an official detective.

"No, not really. Ellen Smythe and I were just talking together as friends—my tidbits come from our ordinary conversations." She layed out what Ellen had told her about Peter and his seeking out advice concerning his will.

"I thought it might be worthwhile to pay the estate attorney a visit. Follow the money, right? *Cui bono?* It sounds like parts of the will are in public records, but not everything. And, interestingly, it's Rose who handles distributions from the Smythe Foundation to the nonprofits they support."

On the heels of the DNA tests, and the speculation about Adele and Peter's relationship, this information is very salient, thought the chief.

"One more thing: Ellen said that after Peter put his affairs in order, he seemed more tense and introspective—not relieved at having all his ducks in a row. I wondered if there was more to his agitation than just being ill." Kate paused, anxious to hear the chief's response to her news.

After what seemed like an eternity, Jablonsky prompted her. "Anything else?"

"Well, it's a personal matter. Johnny said that if I didn't mention it to you, then he would." Kate managed an anxious laugh.

Having raised a daughter, Jablonsky knew that if a young woman confided in him, the content was important. "Go ahead, Kate. You can talk to me."

Kate described the recent bicycle attack on her and the missing chapters she had written for an academic book. "And there were a few other things."

"What other things?" Jablonsky's tone clearly indicated his concern.

She described the details of the attack at the all-state high school swim contest: Eddie and her grandfather were in the bleachers that day and spoke with the police—there was an official report.

"The Boston police never found the perp?" The chief had gotten out of his chair and was walking around his desk.

"I agree with Johnny. If it was just one incident, it could mean nothing, but you're describing a pattern of interference in your life that has taken place over years, and recently has accelerated, like accessing your office computer. Have there been more incidents?"

Kate told him about being viciously kicked while swimming at the university pool. She paused, then described the last of her concerns.

"When Eddie was away all those years, he and I wrote letters to each other. Through conversations with Eddie later on, I came to find out that some of them were missing—probably taken out of my mailbox. Now that he is gone, I keenly feel the loss of those missing letters. You understand?"

"You bet I do. Kate, let me and Coupe talk to the Boston

detectives who would be familiar with this cold case—let's see what we can find out about the situation. We have many new technologies for identifying people that we didn't have when the event happened—we might be able to get a hit on a likely suspect who was at the meet, and if that person is in any way related to the current stalker. Is it okay with you that we open an investigation on your behalf?"

"Yes! I'd be grateful. If my grandfather were still alive, he would help you, but . . . there's one more thing. I was born Kathleen Byrne. If you google Kate Chambers, you won't find any substantial material on me until my college years. After the attack at the pool, my grandfather legally adopted me, changing my name to his, Chambers. To protect me." The longing in Kate's voice for her grandfather touched Jablonsky.

"A smart man, your granddad. I think I would have liked him. I'll keep you posted, and thanks for the information about Peter Smythe and his will. We'll talk soon. Jablonsky hung up and continued to pace his office.

If the stalker had lost sight of Kate because of the name change, he's found her now, reasoned a worried chief.

"DeVille and Lemon. In here!" When everyone was settled in his office, he closed the door and told them about Kate's stalker. The detectives were assigned to start with the first swim incident and move forward.

"I'll cover the trial for the drunk driver who killed her parents," offered Coupe. "That would be in the public record. Kate hardly ever mentions it, but she was only five when it happened. I'll comb through the material."

"I'll look at the driver's family life and career," said Lemon, already out of her chair heading to the computers.

"Thanks for seeing me, Mr. Mallory." Jablonsky was seated in the office of Peter's estate attorney. He looked around at the luxurious red leather chairs, plush rugs, and numerous pieces of artwork. The area was replete with young women and men offering to satisfy his every drink need—would he like coffee, specialty teas, Pellegrino water, a mimosa, they asked. Reid Mallory was a local man: smart and successful but also approachable.

"So. You wanted to know about Peter Smythe's will? Much of it is public record because of the foundation. Was there something in particular that you wanted to ask about the personal side of the will?"

"It is a matter of some delicacy I have no need to remind you that our conversation is private. As you may know, we are investigating the murder of one of Ellen Smythe's patients. In this investigation, we have discovered that the victim was Peter Smythe's daughter." The chief paused to observe his reaction, but there was none.

"Go ahead," responded Mr. Mallory.

"We were able to match the DNA from Rose Delaney to that of Celine Arceneau, our victim. What I want to know is if Peter made any provision for this daughter in his will?"

"No. There was no personal provision made for anyone except Ellen and Rose. Perhaps this is indiscreet of me, but Peter did have a reputation for having affairs. Even so, I'm surprised there was a child. Does Ellen know?" Mallory seemed genuinely concerned about Ellen.

There is something about Ellen that elicits concern and loyalty even from people who are on the margins of her life, Jablonsky observed for the umpteenth time.

"If she did know, it would be an important fact in our investigation," replied the chief, avoiding a direct answer.

"Of course that would have to be true. It was a naive question on my part." Mr. Mallory seemed as if he were remembering something.

"Do you know Ellen?" Jablonsky inquired.

"Not really. We crossed paths over Peter's will, and I've sat with her at various social events. I like her. Not the typical rich man's wife—she has made a good career for herself—she struck me as serious and genuine. I'd hate to see her hurt."

Serious and genuine, and perhaps a murderer, mused the chief. "Did you know a Canadian attorney named Adele Arceneau or her daughter Celine Arceneau, our victim?"

"I didn't know either. I recognized Celine Arceneau's name only from reading about her death in an email from a colleague who knew Adele. There aren't that many law firms that were started in Pittsburgh that have gained an international clientele, like C&S has." In the chief's eyes, Reid Mallory began to become uncomfortable and, therefore, chatty.

"I didn't really know Peter all that well either. I would run into him at the downtown business club, and of course the time with him drawing up his will. Chief Inspector, is there anything else I can help you with?" Since it was the Chief of Detectives asking the questions, Mr. Mallory remained patient.

"Where there any offshore accounts that you know of? He was often in Switzerland. Any numbered accounts there?" asked Jablonsky.

The attorney shook his head. "If there were, I didn't know about them. That type of account would be hidden by tax attorneys, not me. It is illegal and unethical to sanction hiding money from the tax man. Others may look the other way, but I don't." Reid Mallory didn't appear to be offended by the question; perhaps it was one he was often asked.

"So Peter could have had an account that you didn't know about?"

"Absolutely. It wouldn't be in his name, but that of a shell company, which would have been overseen by businessmen that I wouldn't necessarily know about." Mr. Mallory shrugged, indicating the tangled web the rich weave in order to hide assets.

"One more thing. How would you describe Peter Smythe?"

"Describe him? Well, um . . . he was a family man. His daughter, Rose, was often with him around town and at society affairs." Once again, Mr. Mallory hesitated. Lawyers hated to express ideas before they knew where those ideas would lead them; *if you don't already know the answer, don't ask the question,* was the accepted wisdom.

"In terms of personality, Peter was direct and often forceful. He wanted what he wanted and stopped at nothing to get it. But having said that, I personally witnessed how sweet he was with Rose."

The two men rose at the same time and shook hands. "May I call on you again if I need to?" asked Jablonsky.

"Of course, Chief Detective. It is a novelty for someone like me to be even tangentially involved with a crime. I hope everything works out for Ellen."

Mr. Mallory couldn't have known that Jablonsky was headed back to the precinct to interview her as his primary suspect.

Ellen sat with Elise Rosen in the interview room. Coupe and the chief watched them through the one-way mirror for a few minutes, hoping to get a read on Ellen's mood. Unfortunately, the two women simply chatted and joked together, neither seemed worried about the interview.

"She's a cool customer," remarked DeVille. "Not a hair out of place."

Jablonsky entered the room, placed his small paper notebook beside a file on the table, then lined up everything in a neat row; Poirot would have approved.

Elise Rosen opened the conversation. "Why is my client here?"

"Dr. Smythe is here to answer further questions about Celine Arceneau. Let's begin. Here are the results of the DNA swab we took from your daughter, Rose, and the swab from Celine Arceneau." Jablonsky slowly placed the two sheets side by side in front Ellen.

After a few minutes of looking over the results, her comment was, "I see."

"What exactly do you see?" asked her attorney, who had looked at many DNA tests before but wanted Ellen to be specific and on the record in her interpretation.

"Rose and Celine are half-sisters." Ellen answered matter-of-factly. In the face of her nonchalance, Jablonsky decided to establish a quick pace with his questions.

"Did Peter tell you that Celine Arceneau was his daughter?"

"No he did not. I'm not sure he knew." Ellen's direct eye contact lent her an air of credibility.

"Now just a minute, Jablonsky," protested Ms. Rosen. "Whether Ellen did or did not know about Peter's half-daughter doesn't constitute a motive for murder. You are going to have to do better than this to drag a respected person like Dr. Smythe in here for this fishing expedition."

Ms. Rosen had peppered her words with a hefty dollop of indignation; Jablonsky was familiar with her theatrics, and to some degree, appreciated them—they kept things lively.

"We have been interviewing colleagues who knew Peter. All of them make some reference to his philandering. Did you know about the womanizing?" queried Jablonsky.

"Yes, I knew about it," Ellen replied.

"The fact that Ellen knew Peter routinely broke his wedding vows does not make her a murderer. Ellen focused on her career, taking care of her elderly parents, and on her daughter." This time Ms. Rosen harrumphed her disdain.

"Dr. Smythe, did Peter confess to having gotten one of his women pregnant?" Jablonsky pressed.

"Not to me." Ellen remained unphased.

Jablonsky leaned forward. "Once again, Dr. Smythe, did he tell you that Celine Arceneau was his daughter?"

"Asked and answered! Let's move on. That is, if you have any actual evidence tying my client to the murder," stated Ms. Rosen, using her best courtroom voice.

"Are you aware of any monetary provision that Peter made for Celine Arceneau?" asked the chief.

"I am unaware that Peter settled any inheritance on Ms. Arceneau. You can see his will or ask his estate attorney, Reid Mallory." Ellen folded her hands on the table, unshaken by the question.

"I've already done both. That's very careful wording, Ellen. 'I am unaware that Peter settled any inheritance. . . .' Did someone *else* give Celine Arceneau money? Did someone in Peter's extended family offer her a settlement?" Jablonsky and his team had been unable to find any moneys going to Celine. He hoped Ellen might slip and suggest if there had been a payoff.

"We are wasting time here. I don't care if you like Ellen's phrasing or not, she has answered your question. Evidence, Chief Jablonsky: there is no *evidence*. We are leaving." For emphasis, Ms. Rosen closed her laptop.

"I believe Dr. Smythe is lying to me. She's lying when she says Peter didn't tell her about Celine. Why would this partic- ular Canadian attorney take a sabbatical in Pittsburgh if not to get to know Peter's family and to demand her share of the Smythe family estate? Since Peter is dead, she would likely seek out his wife."

Ellen leaned forward. "Who knows how many children Peter fathered? I didn't know about Celine, or any others," she answered, voicing an uncharacteristic disdain for her dead husband.

"Was she blackmailing you for money? Did she threaten to tell Rose?" Jablonsky picked up the pace of his questions.

"No. I didn't know who Celine Arceneau was, but if she wanted money, I believe she deserved to have some. Peter fathered her, he should pay up."

The chief and Elise Rosen exchanged looks—this was a thoroughly ethical point of view, but hardly one that was ever expressed by a betrayed wife. Jablonsky returned to confronting what he saw as her constant perfidy.

"I believe you knew about Celine and that your motive for wanting her out of the way is the oldest in the world—you were protecting your own unstable child, like you have done in the past and continue to do in the present."

Jablonsky turned to Elise Rosen. "Dr. Smythe is a scientist. She could have easily acquired Bacillus cereus and hired someone to infect the guests at the farewell dinner. And she would know where and how to get thallium." Jablonsky sat back, enjoying the shock wave that eight letter word created.

"What?" Ellen was stunned. "Thallium? What are you talking about?"

"That's right. Celine Arceneau was being poisoned with sublethal doses of thallium. She wasn't suffering from IBS. It was thallium poisoning." The chief watched as Ellen wrestled with what appeared to be new information, but was her surprise an act or for real?

Almost to herself, Ellen said, "I'd never think to look for thallium poisoning, but it does match some of her gastrointestinal symptoms and the fatigue. I never asked about alopecia." She leaned forward over the table, curiosity wreathing her face.

"Did Dr. Patel say if Celine's hair was falling out? That would be the giveaway. Well, I'll be dammed. I missed the diagnosis entirely."

"That's correct, Dr. Smythe. You missed it entirely. Now why would that be?" Jablonsky baited Ellen with his sarcasm.

"She missed it because she isn't a double-o-seven, that's why. Dr. Smythe is a primary care physician, not a spy. Come on Jablonsky, my client didn't poison Celine with bacteria or —and I can't believe I'm saying this—radioactive material. You've got nothing." Elise Rosen's indignation bloomed to the size of a dinner-plate dahlia. She stood to leave.

"Dr. Smythe. Isn't it true that you know people in the hospital labs who could get you thallium acetate and who also would know how to handle it? Isn't it true you have the means to hire someone to poison Celine with the odorless, tasteless thallium? Isn't it true that a rich and powerful woman like you could hire someone to bribe a waitress to sprinkle Bacillus cereus on food served at the farewell dinner? Isn't it also true that poor, sick Celine would end up in your care at the hospital? You have the skill set and the deep pockets to have arranged all of this, isn't that correct, Doctor?" Everyone held their breath, waiting for Ellen's response.

"Prove it," said Ellen into the silence. She sat back in her chair and folded her arms across her chest.

Jablonsky was taken aback by her throwing out the two words most criminals use. He immediately thought, *This is about Rose. Ellen believes that Rose knew Celine and murdered her. It's the oldest story in the world—Ellen is willing to take the fall for her daughter.*

"Let's go, Ellen." Elise Rosen reached for Ellen's arm, helping her up.

"Not so fast, Elise. Ellen Smythe, you are a person of interest in the murder of Celine Arceneau. You will surrender your passport. For now, you are free to go, but know this for certain: I believe you were involved in Celine Arceneau's murder. I'm coming after you, and anyone else who helped you."

The chief remained sitting in the interview room twirling

his pen on the table like a child's whirly-bird toy. He knew that Elise Rosen was correct—he had no physical evidence that connected Ellen to the crime, nor did he have a witness to any aspect of her planning the murder.

Were Ellen and Rose in this together? Or, was it Rose alone?

CHAPTER 15

Back in the bullpen, Coupe recited the results of his search on Daniel Grusin. "Dr. Grusin does have an apartment a few blocks away from Ellen's. I questioned the housekeeper, Maria, who was quite forthcoming." He consulted his notebook and quoted her.

"'Dr. Daniel and Dr. Ellen are together, but no one knows about it.' When I questioned her as to why, she shrugged her shoulders and said, 'It's because of Miss Rose and her miseries.' I asked her to describe the miseries." Coupe clearly had enjoyed Maria's take on the dynamics.

"'Well, she has many miseries—she still has misery over her daddy's death, she has nervous misery, and sometimes can't eat or sleep, or think. She also says she has misery over Dr. Ellen not paying her enough attention.'

"At this juncture, Maria rolled her eyes like my grandmother does when she knows I'm shining her on. I asked her what she thought was wrong with Miss Rose and she said, 'She's a spoiled rich lady; her pee-sa-key-a-trist can't cure that!' We both had a good laugh over that gem of wisdom." Coupe grinned with the memory of the pee-sa-key-a-trist's limitations.

"Any irregularities in Grusin's bank accounts?" The chief took out a piece of cinnamon gum, always confident in its ability to help him reason clearly.

"No, not that I could find. He made a good living in California, but his wife really cleaned him out over the divorce—her demands looked more like a vendetta than a divorce settlement. When he came to Pittsburgh and resumed practicing, he replenished his coffers, but I would put it this way—Dr. Smythe has wealth, Grusin is just well-off," Coupe said.

"He's employed at the university hospital?" asked Jablonsky.

"Yes. He came several times for a series of interviews before he relocated; I have the dates. He's been working here for about a decade." Coupe moved to the murder board and jotted down the information.

"Okay. Lemon. What did you find out about Celine Arceneau's finances?" Jablonsky asked, turning to his number two.

"André Trembly put me in touch with Isabelle, Celine's close friend and the executrix of the will. She is, of course, anxious to help find the murderer. Isabelle is the sole beneficiary of Celine's estate, which includes the money Adele Arceneau left her daughter and what Celine had accrued in her retirement plan. All in it comes to around a million-five in American dollars. But there's more.

"The contents of the bank box included her mother's jewelry, birth and death certificates, passport, and, there was a sealed letter from Adele to Celine, to be opened upon Adele's death. Isabelle hadn't personally read the letter, but after her mother's death, Celine did. I asked her to please read it and scan a copy to me." Lemon clearly had something more to add, but waited until the chief prompted her.

"I just want to add that I've been to Montreal. It is a very expensive city. Celine's townhome is in an area called Westmount Circle, which some consider to be the swankiest part of the city. McGill University is there. Before she inherited money from her mother, how could she afford to buy there? I asked Isabelle about it, and she agreed, confirming that many of Celine's colleagues wondered the same thing. Where did the money come from?" Lemon tossed the question to the bullpen.

"Where *did* the money come from?" repeated Jablonsky. "So far there is no money trail leading from the Smythes to Celine—but that doesn't mean there isn't one. Get the cyber detectives on this; I want to know if any of these people had or have hidden accounts—Switzerland, Panama, the Cayman Islands—the usual suspects. Let's include Adele Arceneau in that search. And when is that sealed letter arriving?"

Coupe interrupted the chief. "Sir, Dr. Daniel Grusin just walked into the precinct and wants to talk to you."

"Oh really? Bring him to my office."

Jablonsky took the measure of the middle-aged physician as he sat down across from him. Dr. Grusin was a tall, fit man with salt and pepper dark hair, a beak-like nose, and piercing eyes; he shifted around in his chair, unable to make himself comfortable.

"I'm here because I'm worried about Ellen Smythe, who is a close, personal friend of mine. She told me that someone has been following her, so, well, I began to follow her."

"You did, eh? You seem like a smart man Dr. Grusin—but in this case, you're like a dog chasing a car—what's that dog going to do when he catches it?" taunted the chief.

"Okay, I take the point. But the person who has been following her is her daughter, Rose Delaney. I know it sounds strange, but you'd have to know the girl. She's like a child walking with a full glass of milk; no matter how careful she is, the milk always slops over. Have you met her?" Daniel looked at Jablonsky for confirmation of his assessment.

"Yes, I've met her, and I have a sense of what you are referring to. Why do you think Rose is following her mother? Aren't they close?" As was his habit, Jablonsky knitted together his horned owl eyebrows and built a finger steeple as he listened.

"Close doesn't even begin to describe it—it's more like a really neurotic relationship. Since Peter died, Rose is dependent on her mother. She wants to know where she is at all times," scoffed Daniel.

"You've known Ellen for quite a while, have you?" Jablonsky asked.

"Ellen and I were in medical school together. I went to California to work, then I married, then, you know how it goes—we divorced. After Peter died, Ellen and I reconnected, and it was around that time that I began to understand about Rose," answered Daniel, giving the bare-bones version of the relationship.

"You began to understand about Rose. That's an interesting way of putting it. Do you have a relationship with Rose?" The chief wasn't accusing, just walked along the edge of it.

"Ellen hasn't directly told Rose about us, but given the stalking, Rose might know already. Ellen feels it would 'destabilize' her daughter to know that she has a man in her life." Daniel sneered at the idea.

"Have you told Ellen that Rose is following her?" It was hard for Jablonsky to believe that Daniel had gone along with Ellen's rules for so long. *What does that say about him?*

"I haven't told her because then I'd have to admit to my own activities. Look, I know how all this sounds, but I love Ellen. Right now, I'm concerned about this murder investigation, so I'm trying not to create more stress for her. I also think you are looking in the wrong direction for Ms. Arceneau's murderer." Daniel was certainly forceful in putting forth that belief.

"Is this what you really came to tell me?" Now it was a direct accusation.

"Yes and no. I wanted you and your detectives to know

about Rose. And to tell you that it is not in Ellen's character to commit murder. She would never take a human life. Never. That said, can you do something about Rose's stalking?" Daniel angrily fired back.

"What exactly is it that you fear Rose would do to Ellen?" *Let's get down to it,* thought Jablonsky.

"I'm not exactly sure what it is I fear. Rose is intensely jealous of anyone who is close to her mother—for instance, Kathleen, Ellen's nurse, and even that physician assistant, Jake Albert. Rose bitterly resents their relationship with her mother. And there is another person, Dr. Kate Chambers, who works on committees with Ellen—Rose resents her as well. I ask myself the question . . . Would she hurt Ellen or a person close to her?" Daniel took a deep breath trying to tamp down his fears.

"You are afraid that Rose might hurt you, her mother, or others close to her, over jealousy. Okay. Good to know." Jablonsky stood and offered his hand without making any statement or commitment. "Thanks for taking the time to come in, Dr. Grusin. We will assess the situation."

As Coupe shepherded him out of the precinct, Dr. Grusin continued to sputter. "But wait . . . wait a minute. What are you going to . . . ?" Only the closing of the elevator doors silenced him.

"What do you think, Chief? Could he be right about Rose Delaney? Jealousy is a powerful motive: She's in the cooking class, so she had the opportunity and knowledge to place the bacteria. She has the money to grease some palms for assistance." Coupe stroked his face with his long fingers, then accepted a stick of cinnamon gum from Jablonsky.

Lemon weighed in. "I agree, Coupe. But what about the thallium? How would Rose have access to that? Dealing with radioactive material is high level science, and more importantly, the material is tightly monitored—Rose would have to hire someone to lace a food or drink with it, someone who didn't know what it was. That constitutes a lot of detailed and sophisticated planning for a person like her."

"Or else, Ellen and Rose were in it together. Aside from jealousy, the obvious motive is money—Celine Arceneau could claim part of the Smythe fortune. But, what about Dr. Grusin? He waited a long time to get back together with Ellen, would his own jealousy spark a murderous act? Was he tired of having Rose in the way?" Jablonsky wrote the questions on the murder board, then turned to face Lemon and DeVille, adding something they weren't aware of.

"Grusin mentioned that Rose is also jealous of Kate's relationship with Ellen. That's a worry, isn't it?

"Do we now have three prime suspects: Ellen Smythe, Rose Delaney, and Daniel Grusin? Is jealousy at the center of this fraught love triangle?" Jablonsky said to no one in particular.

Moonlight spilled into the bedroom, casting eerie shadows across the walls and the floor. Kate's condominium held that quality of silence that comes in the deep nighttime hours, when humans and objects alike exist in a heightened state of stillness.

Bourbon Ball, however, was awake, head and ears held on alert, his gaze focused toward the kitchen. He jumped off the bed, ran down the hallway, charged through the living room, finally throwing himself at the back kitchen door, growling and barking.

Johnny, who was sleeping in the guest room, made it to the kitchen first; Kate came running right on his heels. A man's face was framed in her kitchen window, and for a few seconds, she and the intruder locked eyes. Then he moved, and Kate screamed.

"Call the police!" shouted Johnny as he opened the door

to let Bourbon fly out after his prey. He grabbed the first weapon he could find—a kitchen knife—and wielding it like a saber, charged out onto the dark patio.

The snarling dog had attached his jaw to the intruder's pants and was being pulled along as the man tried to escape. The pants finally ripped, but BB managed to hold the torn fabric in his mouth even as he kept running side to side at the patio wall. The intruder athletically put one hand on the wall and swung his body over it, escaping into the shadows of the tree-lined driveway.

Johnny lowered the kitchen knife, trying to see through the darkness. Kate turned on her few patio lights and stepped out clutching her kayak paddle as a weapon.

"I called the police. They are on the way. Come here, baby," she cooed, calling her pup to her. Bourbon moved over and stood sentry in front of Kate, continuing to hold onto the piece of fabric.

Two police cars topped with flashing blues pulled down the driveway. Kate directed the officers to the side patio, then took a minute to talk with her robed, slippered, and very alarmed condo neighbors.

Johnny was already describing the event to the officers when Kate came back around to the patio. "I saw his face," she announced. "And you know, he looked somewhat familiar to me."

"Me too!" added Johnny. "His build and how he moved seemed familiar. I think I've seen him around here before . . . um, maybe even passed him on the sidewalk in front of this house."

"Do either of you think you could give a description to a sketch artist?" queried the female officer. Her partner continued to search the small patio and grassy area with a stunningly bright flashlight.

"I could." Kate began a preliminary description. "He was dressed in a black sweater—I could see his neck and face. He had multiple tattoos that ran on either side of his neck, and some that went up and around his ears. He wore a black ski cap."

Johnny jumped into the conversation when Kate paused, trying to get more air into her lungs; her body was still reacting to all the adrenaline coursing through her system.

"There were crosses on his forehead, and it almost looked like the scales of justice on either side of his neck."

"That's right," added Kate. "When I saw his face in the window, he stared at me intensely, almost like he wanted to communicate something. He had very dark eyes, and dark eyebrows. His nose was straight and thin. That's about all I can remember."

"When he was running toward the patio wall, I'd say he was a fit man, shorter than me, maybe five-foot-ten inches. Clearly no back or knee problems given how fast he got to the wall and catapulted himself over it—all that with Bourbon Ball chasing him," remarked Johnny, almost in admiration.

"Oh, and here's a piece of his pants." Kate held out the scrap of material, which the gloved officer examined and put in an evidence bag.

"It looks to me like there is some blood on the one end. That's good, right?" Kate asked.

"You bet it is. If it is blood, and this intruder is anywhere in the system, we can match his DNA." The young officer could hardly contain her enthusiasm over such a valuable piece of evidence.

She pressed Kate and Johnny about where they might have seen the perpetrator before, but neither could pin it down. Both agreed to stop at the precinct to meet with the sketch artist.

Johnny mentioned that they knew Jablonsky, and the name drop produced the desired result. The officers would get right on the situation by first letting the chief know what had happened.

Good, thought Johnny, who was shaken over what might have happened to his best friend had he not been there.

Kate took a few more minutes to talk with her neighbors. She cast the story as a local looking for something expensive to steal and hock. Everyone mumbled about new security cameras being on the agenda at the next condo meeting.

Bourbon Ball was crowned the king. He was petted, given treats and rubs, and in between, he drank copious amounts of water— being an attack dog was thirsty business. Labradors aren't bred to be watchdogs, but tonight, neither the Doberman nor the Akita had anything on him.

CHAPTER 16

KATE AND JOHNNY DIDN'T KNOW WHAT TO DO WITH themselves. It was now morning, and the sun was starting to rise. "I'm making some coffee," announced Kate, trying to avoid the inevitable talk about her not having adequate outdoor lighting; she dreaded the "I told you so" coming her way.

When Johnny started to speak, she interrupted with a preemptive declaration of guilt. "I know I should have gotten to the patio lights. I'll do it this week. I'm sorry."

"Lights or no lights, this was not your fault. Someone is stalking you, and now we have evidence, maybe DNA."

"I hope so! You know, the university pool opens at 5 a.m. for the swim team and the triathletes—your coach will be there. It would be relaxing to be in the water, and you'll get extra stroke analysis. I feel really spooked—I think it would help us both calm down."

Kate shuddered, rubbing her hands together as if to get rid of something noxious. Johnny had rarely seen her unnerved—anything that would help, he was going to do.

"I'm in. I have a swim suit here. I'll let my coach know we are coming. Jablonsky will get the report, then we can see the sketch artist later this morning."

Although it was just after dawn, the university pool was humming with lapping swimmers and a few platform divers and their coaches. This was the early morning world of aquatics. Johnny couldn't believe the activity; Kate reveled in it.

Her slow stretch fifteen hundred yards was just what she needed to blow out her anger. Since she finished before Johnny, she sat watching the divers twist and turn off the high platforms, mesmerized by their daring.

Kate knew that life was about the choices one makes in response to the unexpected. She had long resisted the choice to turn her anger inward, which surely would have resulted in depression. Instead, like the divers, she wanted to be brave.

"Damn the stalker!" she hissed under her breath, then thought of Marco and one of the haiku that he had sent her, focusing on the simple prose to calm her.

I am still myself, Kate declared to her herself, deciding not to cancel her early afternoon advising sessions or her meeting with Ellen. She wasn't going to stay home and hide; she was jumping off that platform.

Jablonsky rolled his chair over to the open office door and yelled into the bullpen. "DeVille and Lemon. Get in here."

"What's up, Chief?" Coupe asked as he strolled in and leaned against the wall. Lemon sat.

"Let's talk about Kate Chambers' situation—plural, that is —situations. We know about the stalker at her house last night. Whomever this is, his attempts to get at her are escalating." The chief's worry took its usual form of pen-spinning.

"I agree, Chief. Kate and Johnny just arrived and are with the sketch artist. I asked them to stop in to see you after they were finished," added Lemon.

"Fine. The ripped piece of pants was sent over to Bill

Reeves in forensics. He called a few minutes ago and said there is definitely enough blood for DNA—if this joker is in the system, we'll get a match. I've asked Reeves to put his best tech on it," stated the chief.

"Moving on: I contacted the Boston police, and they gave me one of the older detectives who had been involved in the assault on Kate at the swimming competition. With the technology available at the time, it looks like they did everything possible to find the perpetrator—it remains an open cold case.

"They believe it was a teenage male, someone who was either a participant that year or someone dressed as a swimmer. Kate was definitely targeted; no one else was hurt. That's all they have. What did you two find out?"

Coupe opened his laptop to view his notes on the driver who had killed Kate's parents.

"The driver's name was Henry O'Hara, and he had priors for drunk driving. This guy's blood-alcohol level would have stopped a moose, plus those priors, so there was no problem getting a conviction. O'Hara didn't, and couldn't, deny the results of the breathalyzer or the bloodwork taken at the hospital. He was sentenced to two consecutive twenty-year stints for vehicular manslaughter but died of cardiac disease after having served only one."

"Did he have any family?" asked Jablonsky.

"Yes. He was married with two children, a son and a daughter. At the time of his trial and conviction, the girl was a child, but the son was in middle school. Mr. O'Hara had worked as a biologist for a research lab in the Boston area; the missus worked part time in the cafeteria at the kids' school," said DeVille.

"After Henry was incarcerated, the wife struggled financially—she had to declare bankruptcy and unfortunately lost the house. In the midst of all that, she contacted legal aid and divorced the husband. Five or six years later, she remarried and is still married. After that, her life seemed to stabilize." Coupe closed his laptop, his report finished.

"What happened to the kids?" Jablonsky looked at Annie, who picked up the story line.

"My research found that the son, Liam O'Hara, acted out for a while. He was bright, but the school reports said that he had authority problems. There were some minor run-ins with the police, nothing serious. Eventually he buckled down, graduated, and went on to college. The sister, who was adopted by the second husband, also went to college and now lives and works in the Boston area. She's married and has one child."

"Where's the son?" asked Jablonsky in his just-the-facts tone.

"Liam O'Hara's college records show that he finished graduate school at SUNY. That's where the trail stops—we're still trying to track down his current job status and personal address." Lemon shook her head slightly, trials gone cold frustrated her.

"Search the change-of-name records. Also, see if he comes up in any of the national criminal databases. What was his major?" asked Jablonsky.

"Biology, like his father. Graduated cum laude," Lemon stated.

"Just like his father. Interesting. Good work, you two."

Betty Jane, the house sketch artist, politely interrupted their conversation. "Chief, I just uploaded my sketch. It should be in your inbox, and here are Kate and Johnny." Everyone crowded together around Jablonsky's desk to look at the computer image.

"These tattoos are really helpful. The crosses on the forehead are hard to hide, which makes identification easier for us. Coupe, send out an APB."

Kate and Johnny nodded their agreement with Jablonsky's tattoo comments—it felt good to do something concrete toward tracking down the stalker.

"Betty Jane, another outstanding sketch from you. Good work." Jablonsky was experienced enough to know that team-work always made the difference in catching a perp, so he handed out praise when it was due.

After Kate and Johnny left, the chief turned his attention back to the Arceneau murder, and they all moved into the bullpen and, like the Radio City Rockettes, lined up in front of the murder board.

Coupe went over the highlights of Rose Delaney's early life: "She attended private schools in Pittsburgh and then went on to university at Bryn Mawr in Philadelphia. Never worked, traveled with her father in the summers. Met her husband, Josh Delaney, in her early twenties, married, had one daugh-ter, Patricia, then within the next year, divorced."

"What does Josh Delaney do for a living?" asked the chief.

"He's a patent attorney. He left Pittsburgh to work in Silicon Valley," answered Lemon.

"What were the grounds for divorce? Did he get any of the Smythe money?" continued Jablonsky, taping on Josh's photo.

"It's just listed as 'irreconcilable differences,' and as far as I could see from the settlement papers, he refused to take any money. Patricia spent summers with him—it looks like they are tight—Rose never argued about custody. They were married for such a short time. I wonder what the real reason for his leaving was?" remarked Annie.

"Dig deeper," ordered Jablonsky. "For a guy to split after only twenty-four months into a marriage, not to mention leaving a little girl behind, something was really wrong."

Under Josh Delaney's photo, the chief wrote, "What did he find out about the Smythe family, or Rose, that made him move three thousand miles away?"

After the Lenten Fish Fry, the next best food festivals in Pittsburgh were the Greek Orthodox ones. Today, Jablonsky and Bill Reeves sat outside under one of the numerous tents that had been set up for the patrons of the Greek Orthodox festival in Oakland.

From their yearly attendance, the priests knew the chief and the head of the forensics lab—the serving ladies gave them special portions. They both had chosen the same dishes: lamb gyros, a wedge of pastitsio, and of course, a Greek side salad. As they ate, they discussed the Arceneau murder.

"We didn't find any residue of Bacillus cereus in Rose Delaney's purse, or in Ellen's purse or briefcase, or nurse Kathleen's, or in the briefcase that Jake Albert had with him at the hospital the day Celine Arceneau died," Bill Reeves casually remarked, focusing more on the food than the case details.

"Have any of the labs reported missing thallium yet?" asked Jablonsky, who was trying to eat his loaded gyro without the innards landing on his shirt.

"No. And I think almost all of them have reported in by now. Whoever did this must have gotten it from somewhere else," responded Bill, remaining unperturbed that that might be the case. "These days, the regulatory agencies can trace the origin of radioactive material like we trace genes. If it's from a reactor, they will soon be able to say which one."

"What did you find out about the intruder at Kate Chamber's house?" asked the chief, who was delighted with the creamy cucumber dressing on the gyros.

"The stalker's DNA wasn't a match with anyone in the convicted offender or arrestee index, nor in CODIS. The gyro meat seems better this year—so well spiced, don't you think?" remarked Bill.

"Maybe. I think the sandwiches taste better because we couldn't have them for two years during the COVID shutdown," posited Jablonsky.

"You're probably right. I could eat a third, but I'm going

to wait to see how these two digest. Any new substantial evidence on your side of things?" Bill slightly turned his chair so he wouldn't be swayed by seeing the people in line getting seconds.

"Yes. And quite damning too. The executrix of Celine's will forwarded a letter that Adele Arceneau had written to her daughter, to be opened upon her death—which Celine did. I brought a copy, take a look." Jablonsky handed the letter to Bill.

On the evening of 27 January 1984, I was raped by Peter Smythe.

I had been acquainted with Peter for a few years as an American attorney who specialized in international business; he was the attorney for several industries in Pittsburgh that produced parts used in nuclear reactors. In 1984, we were both attending the World Economic Forum in Davos, Switzerland, staying at the Steigenberger Grand Hotel.

Peter, myself, and our colleagues ate dinner in the hotel restaurant. He had been annoyed at what he saw as my opposition to certain of his contract demands. After dinner, he insisted on walking me to my room, saying it was for my safety, then he wanted to come in for a drink.

When I refused, he pushed into the room, aggressively threw me down on the bed, and raped me. His parting words to me were, "Don't ever stand in my way again."

When my obstetrician confirmed that I was pregnant, I described what had happened to me. I also told Peter that I was pregnant but wanted nothing to do with him. I told no one else. My physician said that I could privately pay for a test of paternity. The results are included with this letter, as well as the records from my obstetrician and the receipts from the hotel.

My darling Celine. I never told your father about the rape, mostly because he died so early in your life. In every way except biologically, he was your papa, he died loving his little baby girl as his own. If you wish to pursue legal action against Peter Smythe, you have everything you need.

Je t'embrasse,
    Mama

The awful content of the letter provoked silence. Both men, fathers of daughters, stared unseeingly into space; eventually, Bill spoke.

"Adele Arceneau went on with her career, raising and loving her daughter, all the while carrying that horrible secret. This explains why Celine waited so long to contact the Smythes—she didn't know who she really was until her mother died. The use of DNA for forensics wasn't common in the eighties, but it *was* used for paternity."

"Here's the thing, Bill: I don't know how long she waited to contact the Smythe's—they may have contacted her. According to our research, Celine lived in one of the most expensive neighborhoods in Montreal. How could she afford it?

"I think that someone in the Smythe family came to know about her and started paying hush money. Our financial guys are still looking for hidden accounts." Jablonsky arranged the salt and pepper shakers on the table into different configurations, as if the right design would help him figure out where the money came from.

"I'm highly suspicious of Rose Delaney. If she found out about the rape and Celine, I believe she was capable of hurting her—alone, or with her mother's help." Jablonsky looked at his watch.

"I really want to take another sandwich home for a late snack, along with some of that delicious baclava." The chief stood with his fingers grasping the back of the chair, as if that grasp would help him resist the third gyro.

In the end, both men ordered a to-go sandwich and dessert. The gyro and a cold beer would be for tonight; the sweet baclava would be breakfast. Later that evening, after Jablonsky had finished working on some miniatures for the Science Center's Christmas train display, he sat in his kitchen enjoying his sandwich and thinking.

His mind was focused on hush money, which he was positive Adele received. If he could track down the bank of origin, he would have a tangible link between the Smythes, Adele, and Celine.

Had Peter told Ellen about Celine and were they both involved in sending money to her? he wondered, wiping his beer mustache and enjoying a good burp. He had arranged for another interview with Ellen to present the new evidence from Adele Arceneau's letter.

Will she continue to lie to me? he wondered.

CHAPTER 17

Daniel Grusin accompanied Ellen to the precinct where they connected with her attorney Elise Rosen. Both women entered the interview room while he lurked in the hallway, hoping to catch Jablonsky.

"Why are you interviewing Ellen for a third time?" he asked, raising his voice, oblivious to the dangers of that behavior in a police station where everyone was armed.

"I have new information to present to her and her attorney. Dr. Grusin, I will interview her or anyone else connected to this case as often as I want," barked Jablonsky.

"I've told you already that Ellen could never be party to a murder!" Daniel shouted his complaints in a voice that indicated he was used to being in charge.

Jablonsky turned to Coupe. "Take Dr. Grusin to make a formal statement about his relationship with Dr. Smythe. And execute that search warrant for Ellen's and Rose's homes. Make sure we get all of the electronics."

As he was meant to, Dr. Grusin overheard the direction about the warrant; the ghost of a smile hovered around his lips.

He feels vindicated, thought the chief. *He thinks this is only about Rose.*

When Jablonsky entered the interview room, Elise looked at him quizzically. "Why are we here—again—Chief Detective?"

Jablonsky laid a copy of Adele's letter in front of Ellen. As she and Elise leaned in to read, the attorney protectively placed her arm on the back of Ellen's chair.

"What can you tell me about this, Dr. Smythe?" asked the chief.

Ellen breathed an exhausted sigh, then looked directly at Jablonsky.

"I can't tell you anything about this except that I'm revolted by Peter's actions. I've already told you that I knew he saw other women when he was traveling, but this—a rapist?" Ellen could barely catch her breath to speak.

Ms. Rosen looked through the additional evidence: the hotel receipts, the medical records from the obstetrician, and the DNA results.

"Adele Arceneau was a good attorney; this proof, plus her letter, would stand up in any American court. Plus, we now know that Peter had knowledge of the pregnancy. Interesting." She tilted her head and pulled down the corners of her mouth in disgust.

Jablonsky pulled another sheet from the folder in front of him and slid it to Elise and Ellen. "And here is the guest sign-in sheet from Peter's hospice that shows that Celine Arceneau visited him the morning of the day he died. Rose was there in the afternoon. I believe that Celine confronted Peter about the rape and announced that she was his daughter. She would have shown him this evidence.

"Did Rose ever imply, or outright tell you, that her father admitted that Celine Arceneau was his daughter?" asked Jablonsky.

"She did not," Ellen replied.

She's lying, but why? The chief shook his head.

"If she knew about Celine, she would have confided in you, correct?" Jablonsky kept after her.

"If she knew, and that's a big if, I'm inclined to say she would have told me, but the truth is, I'm just not sure." Ellen looked again at the sign-in sheet, subconsciously tracing Rose's signature with her fingernail.

"I had forgotten that she was actually with him the day he died. It was traumatic for her." Ellen's voice was wistful, and sad.

Jablonsky was inexplicably moved by Ellen's soulful show of emotion. Perhaps this is why people were so loyal to her. Is it possible that Peter told Rose about Celine, leaving out the rape, and that she had not confided in her mother, a mother upon whom she relied?

Was Rose even closer to and more protective of her father than we knew? Jablonsky shuddered as a feeling of revulsion shot through him.

Elise attempted to take control of the interview. "Why are we revisiting this issue? Dr. Smythe told you last time that she didn't know who Celine Arceneau was, and even if she had known, she had no motive to kill her. Whatever Peter did is on him."

Jablonsky ignored her and addressed Ellen. "Adele Arceneau told Peter about her pregnancy. Were you or Peter paying hush money to Adele for Celine?"

Ellen raised her voice. "I wouldn't know if Peter was paying her. As I've said over and over, he never told me about her."

Elise confronted the chief. "Have you found a money trail? Is there a bank account? Did Reid Mallory confirm that Peter was paying Celine? The answer is no to all of those questions." She threw up her chubby hands in frustration.

"Ms. Rosen. I'll say it again, Dr. Smythe is lying to me, and perhaps to you. On the day he died, I believe that Peter confessed to Rose, who then told Ellen." He locked eyes with Ellen.

"Did the two of you conspire to murder Celine Arceneau? Come on, Ellen, tell the truth for a change." Jablonsky rarely showed frustration in an interview, but he voiced it now, hoping to elicit the truth.

"I didn't conspire to do *anything* with Rose. Celine was nothing to me. You keep saying I have a motive when none exists!" Ellen slammed one hand on the table—shocking herself as much as everyone else.

In order to calm things down, Elise spoke very deliberately. "The letter from Adele Arceneau is inculpatory evidence of a rape, but that is about Peter, not Ellen or Rose. If you have something that directly ties the two of them to a conspiracy, show it."

"Celine was Rose's half-sister; that fact means Dr. Smythe had several motives, all variations on the theme of protecting her daughter. First and primarily, to protect Rose's mental stability; second, to protect the Smythe name, which she has carried for most of her life; finally, to protect Rose's inheritance. Hush money is one thing, a claim on the Smythe family trust is quite another."

It was Elise who stood up and interrupted Jablonsky's scenario, not Ellen, who had pushed herself away from the table but kept her fingers glued to the sides of her seat. Her face was a road map of cycling states of anger, tension, and frustration. Once again, Elise stated her position. "These allegations are conjecture. Let's go, Ellen."

Jablonsky stood and looked down at Ellen. "Dr. Smythe, we are searching your house and that of your daughter right now. I believe we will find evidence that implicates you both."

Jablonsky unwrapped a piece of cinnamon gum, manipulated it into a dumpling shape, and placed it in his mouth. He was satisfied that he had cracked Ellen Smythe's belief that she could control the situation in which she found herself; he hoped that through that fissure, the lava of truth would flow out.

Rose sat on her daughter's couch, wrapped in a soft robe, sipping a glass of merlot. Patricia was fussing around her, making sure she had everything she needed. She had lived through her mother's breakdown after her grandfather died and now was worried that the situation with her grandmother would produce the same result.

Patricia hoped some pampering would help soothe her mother's nerves. Between Rose and Patricia, the mother/child roles had always been reversed.

"On the news tonight, they showed a clip of your grandmother leaving the precinct—there was a man with her I didn't recognize. Who is he?" asked Rose.

Patricia looked at her mother, perpetually amazed at how obtuse she could be when it came to Grandma Ellen.

"Mom, that's Dr. Grusin. He and Grandma have been in a relationship ever since Pap died—they were old friends from medical school who got back together. How do you not know about him?"

"Well, I *don't* know about him!" Rose shouted. "How do *you* know about him, Miss Smarty-Pants? Why would my mother tell you about this man and not tell me?" The wine in her glass gyrated like it was in the spin cycle of a washer. Patricia reached over and steadied her mother's hand.

"Precisely because of how you are acting right now. You were so close to Pap that you never considered that Grandma would want another relationship—you know, for companionship."

In one of her sudden shifts in mood, Rose smiled at her daughter. "Okay. Come sit by me and tell me about this Dr.

Grusin: who he is, what he does, where he lives—all the details."

Rose sweetly patted the cushion next to her; one could say she was like a cat at the manicurist, wanting her claws to be filed just a little sharper.

Naively, Patricia prattled on about Daniel, so relieved to talk openly about him that she did not register the calculating look that came over her mother's face as she talked.

CHAPTER 18

ELLEN WAS HOME IN HER STUDY DELETING COMPUTER FILES when Maria tapped at the closed door. "I've straightened all the mess that the police made during their search. Everything is back in its place. And Dr. Chambers is here. Would you like me to make some coffee?"

No sooner was the question off Maria's lips than Kate walked into the room. Turning slightly in her desk chair, Ellen offered a warm, distracting smile to both while closing out of the file she was working on, but leaving the laptop open. *Who would look at it anyway,* she mused.

"Coffee in a little bit, after we've finished working, and since it is the end of the day, some cognac also. Thanks, Maria."

Before they attended to business, Kate confided in Ellen about the intruder at her condominium.

Ever the physician, Ellen asked a few questions, and when she was satisfied that Kate wasn't experiencing any transient post-traumatic stress symptoms, they turned to their committee assignments. The work took a little over an hour, after which they relaxed, waiting for Maria to bring coffee and spirits.

"Who would have thought two ordinary university women like us would be involved in such unsavory police investigations?" Ellen remarked. "The police searched my house today —now that's a sentence I never thought I'd utter!"

"The news had a little blurb on Celine Arceneau's murder. They showed a clip of you exiting the precinct. Was that Dr. Grusin with you? I don't really know him, but Joan Weisner introduced us at Mrs. Rossetti's funeral luncheon." Like a gardener spading around a delicate plant, Kate began a slow dig for the tender roots of their relationship.

"Yes. That was Daniel. We are friends and lovers, and have been since Peter died. I'm sure that fact hums along the hospital lines of gossip. Am I correct?" Ellen laughed so heartily that Kate was surprised. She enjoyed seeing the unrestrained reaction from the usually reserved Ellen.

Maria brought in steaming hot cups of strong coffee and a few dark chocolate truffles, placed a bottle of Martell XO on the sideboard, then excused herself. "I'm off to my apartment."

Ellen sighed, stretched her arms over her head, and slowly rotated her neck to relieve her tension. She looked directly at Kate.

"Nothing will ever be the same now. I've watched my patients go through this after they receive a lethal or debilitating diagnosis—they had one life and then, just like that, they have to start living another kind of life. Well, why not me? Bad things happen to everyone—now it's my turn."

"Bad things? Has something come to light in the Arceneau murder?" asked Kate, correctly reading the signals that Ellen wanted to confide something of import.

"Yes. I'm going to tell you a story that the police and Elise Rosen only know parts of." Ellen splashed a generous amount of cognac into her coffee cup and then told Kate about the letter from Adele Arceneau, and about the rape.

Kate was a professional listener; she nodded as Ellen

talked, showing no shock in response to the rape. Her female advisees routinely confided incidents of sexual harassment, and even rape, in the privacy of her office, so that aspect of a woman's life was nothing new to her. She hadn't grown immune to the reality; it still made her sad, and mad.

"So when Celine Arceneau came to your practice during her sabbatical year, it wasn't by chance." Kate stated the obvious.

"No. At first, I believed she wanted to see what kind of woman had stayed married to a serial philanderer. She asked a lot of personal questions about me." Ellen smiled at the memory of Celine, whom she had liked. "She introduced herself to me as Peter's daughter—I thought that took guts."

"I agree—that did take guts. Um, I hope this isn't impertinent to ask, but, were you surprised about Peter?" Kate leaned forward, completely enthralled with the whole story.

"I was," admitted Ellen. "Like I told Jablonsky, I knew Peter was aggressive in business, and I also knew about the other women, but rape. . . ." Her voice trailed off.

"So Celine knew." Kate stated the three words unemotionally. "She must have been so curious about Pittsburgh and Peter's family. Do you know if she contacted anyone else?"

"If she did, no one told me about it. She first came to Pittsburgh when Peter was dying. In fact, I just found out that she visited him the very day he died." Ellen shook her head.

"I remember the evening he told me about her existence, but not the rape. I wanted him to settle some money on her. It was only right, she was his blood and his responsibility; to me, it was no different than taking care of Rose. We argued about it. Finally, he agreed, but only for a limited period of time."

"Really? He agreed? Do you think Peter told Rose about Celine? Maybe he confided in her after he had seen Celine?" It was hard for Kate to imagine that Rose's father would not have told her; he might have wanted her to be prepared if Celine approached her.

Ellen sipped her cognac before continuing the story.

"I don't want Rose to have another breakdown. When her husband divorced her, she became debilitated. After Peter died, I worried that she had periods of being out of touch with reality. Patricia assures me that Rose has been taking her medications. That's something."

Kate drank her coffee, observing Ellen over the brim of her cup. She went back and forth in her mind, arguing as to the appropriateness of her next question. Emboldened by the atmosphere of women sharing, she decided to speak.

"If Rose knew about Celine, do you believe she could have murdered her?"

"Don't think I haven't asked myself that very question. I know people are tired of me saying it, but I simply don't know. She's smart enough to read about food toxins." Ellen left her chair and paced; she decided not to tell Kate about the thallium.

"I've never admitted this before to anyone, but there are aspects of Rose's nature that I just don't understand. I gave birth to her—I, well, I'm even having a hard time uttering these words. . . . Does she have it in her to murder another human being?" In a voice hoarse from emotion, she excused herself. "I'll be right back. I'm going to get some ice."

When she left the room, Kate also sought to relieve her tension by walking around. She landed at Ellen's desk and was gripped by an irresistible urge to find out what her friend had been looking at. Suddenly she acted; the laptop was miraculously unlocked. She immediately went to Documents and pressed "recent," and up came several files that were encrypted.

This dogged sleuthing was a side of Kate that her close friends and Jablonsky knew about; for the chief, it was a trait that had proven helpful for finding clues, but her friends sometimes felt her behavior trespassed customary borders of privacy. Kate valued justice over decorum.

In Kate's mind, Ellen was sabotaging her own innocence by not telling the whole story to the police, so she gave herself permission to look on the laptop for clues as to why that would be.

Ellen returned with an ice bucket, pausing in the doorway. "What are you doing, Kate?" There was no hint of accusation in her low, quiet voice.

Kate flushed at having been caught, but she didn't apologize.

"Well, I guess I'm snooping. I believe you are innocent, but I also worry that your need for privacy might be hurting you. For example, why encrypt some of your files and not others? That's a red flag for Jablonsky's team. Ellen, these types of files might make you look guilty of something."

Ellen moved into the room, set the crystal bucket aside, and poured both of them a generous amount of cognac. "Well, first of all, no one knows about this laptop, not even Daniel. I made sure the police didn't find it in their search. To answer your question, a few files are encrypted because I needed certain monetary transactions to be absolutely secure."

"What monetary transactions?" Kate tried to remain calm in the face of this juicy bit of information.

"I trust your intentions and instincts, Kate." Then, as if she were talking about the plot of a movie, Ellen calmly told the final part of her story.

"These encrypted files show bank transfers from one secret account to another secret account," Ellen said, calmly, as if secret accounts were an everyday fact of life.

"Secret accounts?" repeated Kate.

"The transfers in these accounts were the payments for Celine," stated Ellen.

Kate slugged down a mouthful of cognac, not even reacting to the burn of the liquor at the back of her throat.

"I have been monitoring the transfers ever since I successfully pushed Peter into doing the right thing by her." Surprisingly, Ellen smiled at Kate, clearly proud of that negotiation.

"Let me get this straight: You convinced Peter that since Celine was his daughter, he should financially treat her as such. Then you took on the responsibility of making sure he carried through on his promise, even after he died. That's really something, Ellen." Kate felt a surge of respect that Ellen's moral center had held, even in the face of Peter's despicable behavior and criminality.

"The money was paid out of rotating business accounts established in Panama—shell companies, difficult to trace. I'm not sure how Peter transferred the money into the accounts, but he set up Celine's when he was in Switzerland. I had nothing to do with the accounts except to monitor that the money was being transferred. The last payment was the week of her farewell party. There was nothing illegal in the whole deal, except perhaps the tax implications. That was on Celine." Ellen shrugged.

"Where did Celine think the money came from?"

"Apparently her mother told her it was an inheritance from some distant relative. When Celine was a youngster, Adele handled the account—she paid for Celine's private school education, her law degree, a down payment on a townhome—that kind of thing. When she died, the account transferred to Celine, who then read the letter and put two and two together." Like Kate, Ellen downed a mouthful of cognac to soothe her nervousness at telling the unvarnished truth.

"I think you need to talk to Jablonsky about this. You weren't doing anything illegal, nor was Adele or Celine. You can't lie to the chief of detectives without serious consequences. And if you don't turn over this computer, you could be charged with obstructing their investigation." Urgency filled Kate's voice. "Obstruction is a serious criminal charge, Ellen."

Ellen didn't respond to Kate's reasoning, so she took another tack.

"Years ago, Peter told you about Celine and you persuaded him to acknowledge her through money; then you agreed to follow the accounts to make sure he made good on his promises. You had no motive to murder her. All of this puts you in the clear."

"But what about Rose?" Ellen swirled the cognac in her snifter. Finally she added, "I'm just what the chief accused me of being—I'm a mother who has been lying to protect her child."

Kate didn't respond right away. Not having been raised by her own mother, the complexity of the mother-daughter relationship was always a mystery to her.

"Ellen. Rose is a grown woman. Through the picture Patricia paints of her in our advising sessions, I've come to realize that you are right to be worried about her mental state, but Rose's instability doesn't make her a child, or, for that matter, legally incompetent."

"Her anxiety can reach a level where I don't believe she is capable of making sane choices." Ellen threw up her hands in frustration at the whole situation. "What is the point of all that Smythe money if I can't use it to protect Rose?"

Kate didn't know what to say. *If all mothers had access to unlimited money, wouldn't they use it to protect their children?* she wondered.

"Please, Ellen. Please tell Jablonsky the whole story. He already knows about the rape—besides, you don't know if Rose is guilty of anything other than jealousy."

***

Kate was emotionally exhausted after her time with Ellen, but she left with a new appreciation of her mom dilemma. The situation only affirmed what she already had intuited: Celine

Arceneau had a connection to Ellen, and because of that connection, Ellen had become an accomplished liar. Kate didn't hold that against her; anyone close to Kate knew her motto—everyone is lying about something all the time.

Kate didn't believe for a minute that Ellen would contact the police, so she called Jablonsky and told him about the laptop his detectives missed and the payments from Panama to Switzerland. Jablonsky asked her to come to the precinct as soon as she could and to bring along Johnny.

CHAPTER 19

KATE COLLECTED JOHNNY FROM HIS UNIVERSITY OFFICE. SHE was nervous as to why the chief had asked them to come to the precinct—she zoomed down the steep, winding road through Polish Hill, and Johnny rocked from side to side, clutching his seatbelt as they took the hairpin turns.

Walking through the bullpen, Kate was surprised to see her picture on one of the murder boards. Coupe saw her reaction, so he quickly assured her that the board was just a visual reference for clues related to her stalker. "Don't worry, your picture being up here doesn't create any bad ju-ju for you."

Annie, Coupe, Johnny, and Kate crowded into Jablonsky's office. "Go ahead, Kate. Repeat what you told me on the telephone," prompted the chief.

Kate detailed what she had learned from Ellen concerning the monetary support of Celine through secret accounts.

"Ellen lied about knowing who Celine was, as well as having a separate laptop that she hid from your police search." Kate's strained expression evidenced the struggle between her friendship with Ellen and providing information that she knew Ellen hadn't.

"This clears Ellen, doesn't it?" she asked anxiously.

The chief built his finger steeple and stared at it before answering her.

"Not completely. She still could have acted as a co-conspirator with Rose. And right now, she is guilty of obstructing our investigation." He turned to Coupe. "Have someone pick up that computer."

Everyone was surprised when the typically unflappable Kate choked back tears. "I know Ellen's history of protecting Rose, I just don't think she would go so far as to commit a crime, particularly murder."

Johnny squeezed Kate's arm in support; he admired Kate's loyalty. He, like Jablonsky, knew that Kate was rarely wrong in her reading of people.

"We'll see how things go. For now, let's turn to your case. I want to show you and Johnny two pictures on our stalker board to see if you recognize either of them. Then we can talk through possible motives," said the chief.

The prison headshot of Henry O'Hara and a high school photo of his son, Liam, had been tacked under her own photo. The chief ran through the list of threats that Kate had suffered, starting with the long-ago shove at the swim meet.

"Do you recognize Mr. O'Hara and his son Liam?"

"I do recognize Henry O'Hara from photos that were in the newspapers at the time of the trial. My grandfather didn't allow me to attend the trial or speak to reporters. By the time O'Hara was convicted, I still was only seven." Kate stepped closer to the board, peering at Liam O'Hara.

"Whoever is stalking you started with physical intimidation at the swim meet, then disappeared for years, and has now resurfaced. Our primary suspect, past and present, is Liam. I want to review what we know about the son of the man who killed your parents."

Jablonsky turned to Annie Lemon. "Go ahead with your report."

"Liam O'Hara went every weekend to see his father in

prison. At first his mother drove him, but after the divorce, Liam went alone. I think it's possible that Henry filled his son with what I call 'a story of grave injustice,' which goes something like this: 'I didn't deserve the two sentences, the crash was an accident, my attorney wasn't any good, the jury was unsympathetic.' Some variation of those excuses."

From the corner of his eye, the chief watched Kate's response to these details. "Coupe, you weigh in on motive."

"Okay. Going further with Lemon's country western 'I've been wronged' song, Liam's father probably painted a picture that looked like this: 'Little Katie has a rich professor grandfather who sends her to private schools and summer camps. That grandfather locked me in prison for life while he and the privileged granddaughter are free. I'm the wounded one, I'm the one in jail without any hope of parole.'" Coupe paused, then articulated his main point. "A boy wants to believe in his dad, so Liam buys the story, lock, stock, and barrel."

All three detectives noticed that Kate was nodding in agreement.

"Liam wants to avenge his father, particularly after he dies in prison. And, he also wants revenge." Jablonsky was relieved to see that Kate wasn't showing any emotional distress from hearing a part of her life talked about like a criminal case. She endorsed Annie and Coupe's motives, then took it further.

"Aspects of our loyalty to and love for our parents exist below language—it's like an imprint on our very bones long before we can understand words and concepts like loyalty and love," remarked Kate, who then offered her own speculations.

"It could be that when Liam placed his love of his dad side by side with the choice his father had made to drive drunk, love and loyalty won. Perhaps all the injustices that his father claimed he had suffered, he projected onto my grandpa and me—that would have been an easier emotional position to take rather than deny his father's story. Somewhere along the

way, I became the receptacle for Liam's anger and blame."
Kate added, "It's one way of looking at the situation."

Johnny walked closer to the board and ran his finger back
and forth between young Liam's graduation picture to the
sketch artist's rendition of the stalker. He was possessed of an
art historian's eye; if anyone could spot even a hint of likeness,
it would be Johnny.

"Is this teen now this grown man?" he remarked in a
preoccupied voice.

Kate and all three detectives unconsciously took a step
backward, as if they were in a museum trying to sort out if a
John Singer Sargent portrait of Liam was the same as a
portrait of him painted by Picasso. No one, including Jablonsky, would confirm that the person in these two photographs
was the same.

"Plenty of men have elaborate tattoos these days. I know
I've seen someone lately with lots of tattoos, I just can't place
where," remarked Kate.

"My swim coach has tattoos. Maybe you are thinking of
him," prompted Johnny.

*Now that's an interesting detail, a swim coach—is there some kind
of symmetry here?* wondered the chief.

"Yes, but he doesn't have these particular markings." Kate
pointed to the sketch artist's rendering of the crosses on his
forehead.

"You are right about the type of tattoo—we have a viable
suspect with a strong motive in Liam O'Hara."

Before the chief could go any further, he was interrupted
by Bill Reeves and a posse of his technicians who swept into
the area as if they were bursting into a saloon—a palpable
energy buoyed the bullpen atmosphere.

Bill held up a photograph. "If you add a few years and
many tattoos to this picture, you've got Hunter Lewis—my
technician whose playlist you admire so much."

"What? You are kidding me—he's been right under our

nose the whole time? I never actually clapped eyes on him at your lab, I just heard the music coming from his station—and his playlist is from his father's generation," said Jablonsky.

Kate and Johnny grabbed ahold of each other in a mixture of excitement and anticipation while Lemon and Coupe pinned the photo on the board.

"Where is he right now?" demanded the chief.

"He's supposedly on vacation," added the technician who worked next to Lewis/O'Hara at the lab.

"Bill, give me everything you've got on him—oh, I see you already brought his employment file. I'll be damned. Liam O'Hara has been living as Hunter Lewis for all these years. Was he fingerprinted when he started the job?" asked the chief.

"Yes, we have his prints, but apparently he had never been fingerprinted as O'Hara. Like I said before, he was a smart guy who did good work but kept to himself. There was no answer at his apartment. He may have already skipped town," said Bill.

"Reeves, get your best people to tear his place apart. I want you to particularly search for a packet of letters that would be addressed to Kate Chambers from Eddie Fitzroy— he may have been stealing her mail. Between a match of his DNA to the blood on the pant leg the dog ripped off of him, and if we can find those letters, we can nail him. Coupe, you're with me," ordered Jablonsky.

The office buzzed with energy. Bill Reeves mobilized his technicians. Coupe organized a police sweep of the neighborhood around O'Hara/Lewis's apartment.

Lemon released the photo of Hunter Lewis with the caption "Armed and Dangerous." Even in the face of their begging to stay, Jablonsky ordered Kate and Johnny to leave; he would post guards at her condominium—Annie Lemon volunteered to be one of them.

Jablonsky began to carefully read through Liam's bogus

employment file. When the office quieted down, he added the new information to Kate's board. The picture of a driven, revengeful, and increasingly dangerous man took shape.

The chief pulled out a stick of cinnamon gum and folded it in half, then half again, and placed it on his tongue. His quiet chewing mirrored his worries. *Kate is in danger. This man has gone from wanting to scare her, to wanting to hurt her, to now wanting to kill her.*

A few hours later, DeVille returned from Liam/Hunter's apartment to report what his detectives did and did not find.

"The fingerprints at the apartment are a match to Hunter Lewis. No computer was located. It looks like he packed a bag—there are no toiletries in the bathroom, half of his closet is empty, same with his dresser drawers. We did find a photo of him and his father taped to the back of a poster. No letters yet—hopefully they will turn up somewhere."

Jablonsky added, "The city police are actively looking. His picture is out there and they have the make and model of his car—although I'm sure he has different plates on it by now. Hey, Reeves is back."

Bill Reeves had returned looking like a man who had just won a million dollars off a scratch lottery ticket. He slid into the chair next to Coupe, grinned at Jablonsky, then pushed a manila envelope across the desk.

Jablonsky opened it and let out a whoop. "Reeves! You're the man! Where were they?" Kate and Eddie's love letters fell out onto the desk, still tied with a Tiffany blue silk ribbon.

"They were in our lab. He made a false back to one of his workstation drawers and stashed the envelope in it. My technicians decided to examine Lewis's work area when we didn't find anything at the apartment. My people are the best!" Bill sat back in his chair, steeping in satisfaction over his team's excellent work.

Jablonsky felt electrified—he kept turning the packet of letters over and over in his hands.

"This was a mistake. Lewis made a very big miscalculation here. Up until now, he's been one slick criminal, but keeping these letters—it is uncharacteristically sentimental. He even kept the ribbon. I don't like what this may portend."

Jablonsky filled Bill in on how many guns had been purchased under the name of Hunter Lewis: there were two Glocks and two semiautomatic assault rifles, Colt AR-15s with large magazines of ammunition.

"There was no background check, nothing in place to stop him from arming up," mumbled Jablonsky. Like all smart policemen, he believed in getting military-grade weapons off the streets in order to protect his officers.

"Getting an AR-15 is really upping the ante. Don't you think, sir?" commented Coupe. "That type of weapon is typically used to kill the maximum number of people in the shortest amount of time. It seems out of character for this guy —up until now, his only target has been Kate."

"Yes, but I believe that this man thinks like a teenager. Like all the adolescent boys who commit mass shootings, he never learned to reason like a man. He's stuck in the adolescent idea that if he kills Kate, or anyone else whom she loves, he will avenge his father—which is pure diddle. Black-and-white reasoning is immature reasoning."

Coupe rarely heard Jablonsky spout psychology. *Kate's ideas have seeped into Jablonsky's point of view,* thought an amused DeVille.

"Let's turn up the heat on the search," Jablonsky ordered.

Bill returned to his lab. Jablonsky asked Coupe to arrange another interview with Rose Delaney.

"I know we are jumping back and forth between Kate's stalker and the Arceneau case, but I want to present Rose with

the new evidence that Kate gave us, along with the information we retrieved from her laptop. I'm hoping to shake a
confession out of her. Make the call," directed Jablonsky.

Like a juggler balancing on a unicycle, Jablonsky was
widely admired for his ability to keep multiple cases in mind at
the same time, without dropping any details.

When Jablonsky called Kate to inform her that they had
found the love letters, she naturally wanted to see them.

"You can see them, but I can't give them back to you right
now, they are evidence in this case. Kate, I'm putting more
guards on you—twenty-four-seven—I know it's inconvenient,
but there really is no other choice. You may continue to go to
your office. Annie Lemon will be the officer covering nights,
and I'll let you know about the other detectives. And always be
alert to your surroundings!"

"Will do. Chief, I don't think Liam O'Hara would not
want to end up like his father—that is, incarcerated for life. He
saw firsthand what prison is really like. Now that we have
identified him, he has nothing to lose. It makes him more
dangerous, doesn't it?" Kate didn't shrink from the truth—
Jablonsky admired her grit.

"Yes. It makes him more dangerous. I will get him, Kate.
He is almost in my grasp."

CHAPTER 20

Jablonsky grabbed his small paper notebook, a file, a fresh cup of coffee, and a small gold-toned Apple laptop—he was feeling invigorated from the breakthrough in Kate's stalker case. He and Coupe headed toward one of the interview rooms. "Has she been Mirandized?"

Coupe nodded.

Attorney Jeffrey Edwards, a junior partner in Elise Rosen's firm, felt protective of Rose Delaney, naively viewing her as half-child, half-adult. He was oblivious to the fact that she used her porcelain doll appearance to manipulate people to get what she wanted.

Today she sat next to him wearing a somber navy suit with a lapel pin in the form of the letters C and S, which were encrusted with diamonds and sapphires. Jeffrey had commented on it, and she confided that her father had had it designed just for her; she felt it would bring her good luck. He also noticed the faint scent of a man's cologne.

Mr. Edwards assured Rose that in the unlikely event she was bound over for trial, she would never go to prison. Lawyers call that a misleading statement—she may never go to prison, but she might be committed to a psychiatric facility. Would a jury see her as mad, or bad?

Jablonsky came into the room and studiously placed copies of Adele Arceneau's statement on the table in front of them. Rose read it, and with a quick whoosh, pushed it back to the chief.

"These are lies. That woman just wanted my father's money." Rose looked directly at the chief. "This proves nothing to me."

Speaking slowly, the chief tried to educate her. "This document has a seal on it, a notary seal, proving it was a statement signed in front of an official. It's real, all right."

The chief laid Rose's laptop on the table between them. "Your attorney was made aware that our examination of your laptop showed that you had been tracking Celine Arceneau from the time your father died, until her death. You lied to me when you said that you didn't know who she was, and you continue to lie now, right to my face." Jablonsky stopped, watching for any reaction; when there wasn't one, he changed his approach.

"Rose, why not tell me your side of the story? Just start at the beginning—start when your father told you the truth about your half-sister."

"I don't have any half-sister!" Her nervous habit of picking imaginary lint off of her clothes asserted itself; red-painted fingernails carefully picked at the sleeve of her jacket, flicking invisible nothings to the floor.

"Here is the result of the DNA sample that we took at your home. Here is Celine Arceneau's sample." Jablonsky traced the long matching threads with the tip of his pen. "These colored horizontal rectangles show how much you and Celine shared in your father's DNA."

Rose grabbed the reports, crumbled them into small balls, and threw them on the floor. She pushed back her chair and shouted at the chief.

"I said, I do not have a half-sister! All of this so-called evidence is a lie. Give me my laptop!" Just as quickly as she reached for her computer, the Great Horned Owl shot out his talon and placed it on the laptop.

Rose stood, trying to yell at Jablonsky through her rapidly increasing breathlessness.

The chief turned to Mr. Edwards. "Get your client under control." Jeffrey Edwards left his chair and gently pulled Rose to the corner of the room.

"Rose, your computer is evidence, you cannot take it. Later, when all this is over, it will be returned to you."

"But," she gasped, "my pictures of Daddy are on it. All my pictures of our . . . (gasping) . . . of our trips. I need those. . . . I need . . . (choking) . . . those pictures! Don't you understand?" Rose suddenly looked lost and unable to focus. She turned the grayish-white color of a sand dollar, and, fearing she might faint, Jeffrey Edwards guided her back to her seat.

Jablonsky shook his head, marveling at this woman's ability to turn on a dime—was it real emotion?

"How did you get the bacteria onto the greens at George's bistro?" His question caught Rose so completely off-guard that her shallow, rapid breathing stopped. She narrowed her eyes, then looked down at her painted fingernails, assuming a coy posture.

"I didn't place any bacteria on any greens served at that dinner. I wasn't there," Rose said coolly.

"Yet," responded the chief softly, "we found a search on your computer of common pathogenic microorganisms that can cause food poisoning." Dr. Patel had been educating Jablonsky in the vocabulary of things that live on food that can kill you.

"Woo-Hoo! Pathogenic microorganisms! You've been doing your homework, Chief." Rose's flirtatiousness now had a hard edge to it as she continued her defense.

"I had an assignment from the cooking class I'm taking at

the bistro. Ask Henry, the sous-chef, he'll tell you." It was clear that Rose was confident she had covered her tracks.

"We did ask Henry. And we asked the other students. There was no such assignment. I'll put the question to you again: how did you acquire the bacteria and how did you get it onto the greens?" Jablonsky moved Rose's laptop closer to him, unsure of the extent of Rose's desire to protect the pictures of her father.

"Well, Henry gave me different assignments because I was more advanced than the other students. Besides, Henry has a thing for me. I'm a special person." Rose began to stroke her lapel pin, avoiding looking at the chief.

"Yes, I can see that you are a special person," remarked the chief. He became confrontational. "Did you ask your mother to procure the food toxin from one of the university labs?"

"No! I would never ask my mother to do anything illegal."

"Did you ask your daughter Patricia to procure the bacteria?"

"I would never, never, ask my daughter to 'procure' anything," Rose answered adamantly.

"Were you in the hospital the day Celine Arceneau died?" Jablonsky relentlessly continued.

"No, I was not. I was getting my hair done. My stylist will confirm that." In the infuriating way a thirteen-year-old taunts her parents, Rose smirked at Jablonsky.

"By the way Rose, the bacteria didn't kill Celine Arceneau. It was thallium poisoning. But you already knew that, didn't you?" asked the chief.

Rose's attorney interrupted. "Wait a minute, Chief Jablonsky. What do you mean thallium poisoning? You mean the stuff the Russians use to kill political enemies?" Elise Rosen hadn't clued the junior partner into the real cause of death.

"Yes. The same. Someone had been giving Celine sublethal doses of thallium. That, in combination with her reaction to the food poisoning, was what killed her." Jablonsky leaned back in his chair and just stared at the attorney.

"I don't know anything about some radioactive thing-a-ma-jig. How could anyone get ahold of that stuff anyway? It would poison them." Rose looked as innocent as her namesake.

"That's right, Rose, it would kill them, unless they knew something about handling radioactive elements. Like your father would have. All those years representing businesses that fabricated tools and parts for nuclear reactors . . . he would have known all about radiation. Did he explain things to you? Did he tell you how to handle a radioactive element like thallium? Come on, Rose, tell me the truth." Jablonsky leaned in.

"My father never talked business with me. Never," snapped Rose.

"Yet he put you in charge of the Smythe Foundation. You clearly know a great deal about business, don't you Rose?"

"Come on, Jablonsky! There's no correlation between the work a foundation does and the nuclear business. This line of questioning is absurd." Jeffrey's attempt to interrupt Jablonsky's momentum fizzled.

"Why did your husband leave you suddenly after just a few years of marriage and a new baby?" asked Jablonsky.

"You would have to ask him." Rose returned to petting her lapel pin. Jablonsky noticed a pained expression briefly skip across her face.

"We did ask Mr. Delaney why he left. He said that it had to do with your father's behavior. . . ." The chief waited for her to finish the sentence.

"I never knew what behavior he was talking about—I didn't know then, and I don't know now. We only speak when it has to do with Patricia." Rose crossed her legs.

"He was talking about your father's philandering—the numerous affairs with other women. And, he said that he felt your father would veer too close to breaking the law when it came to getting what he wanted for his clients. Your father's behavior must have been pretty bad for your husband to leave you and Patricia and move three thousand miles away," Jablonsky stated.

Mr. Edwards shouted at the chief. "That's enough! What do the details of Mrs. Delaney's divorce have to do with the murder of Celine Arceneau? Your emotional manipulation of her is unconscionable."

Jablonsky ignored him and moved forward in his attempt to illicit a misstep from Rose. "Did you conspire with your mother to murder Celine Arceneau in order to protect your father's reputation?"

"That's it! I'm leaving. I never asked my mother to do anything criminal! And I don't know anything about radiation poisoning." Rose almost ripped off the buttons to her suit jacket as she tried to close them. She grabbed her purse, pushed Jeffrey Edwards' hand off of her arm, and wobbled on her stilettos toward the door.

"Sit down, Mrs. Delaney," barked the chief. Rose was so startled that she slowly dropped one cheek of her derriere onto the chair farthest from him.

"Mrs. Delaney. Your mother has been monitoring payments to Celine Arceneau—payments that your father set up when Adele Arceneau told him she was pregnant. Your father knew Celine was his daughter, and your mother felt she deserved part of her rightful inheritance. Just like you." Jablonsky placed his elbows on the table and steepled his fingers in front of him.

"So what? My father and mother can do what they like with their money." For the first time, Jablonsky saw that Rose had been caught off guard. She slowly inched back up to a standing position.

"Did you see Celine Arceneau at the hospice the day your father died?" Jablonsky's tone told her that he already knew she had been at the care facility.

"No." Rose wasn't giving in to anything, yet.

"Did your father tell you that day that Celine was his daughter?" he pressed.

"No," answered Rose.

"Rose, you are lying to me again. We have evidence from your computer that you started tracking her the day your father died. We have evidence that you were researching bacteria on foods. It is not a stretch that, as Peter's daughter, you would know about radiation and the uses of radioactive isotopes. Did you kill Celine Arceneau? Tell me the truth right now," demanded the chief.

At this point, along with Jeffrey and Rose, Jablonsky was standing. He did not lean over the table toward Rose, but he did decide to give her one last emotional shove.

"You know, Rose, I feel sorry for you because it will be Daniel Grusin who will be with your mother when she retires. Maybe they will move to California, where *his* children are. She will have a whole new family. Unfortunately, you will be in prison. In prison, alone, without her."

Rose began to scream, "Shut up! Shut up! Shut up! She is MY mother—MINE! Screw Daniel Grusin!" She kicked her chair against the wall, and, like a six-year-old child, blocked his words by putting her hands over her ears. Two officers ran into the room and restrained her while she continued to scream.

"Jablonsky, I'm taking her out of here." Mr. Edwards grabbed his briefcase and started to leave.

Coldly, the chief gave his proclamation. "I am arresting Mrs. Rose Delaney for the first-degree murder of Celine Arceneau. Her shrink may visit her in holding. Now, Mr. Edwards, now you may go."

Because of the Smythe influence in the city, Jeffrey Edwards knew that with the right judge—even with a first-degree murder charge—he could get Rose released on bail.

She would, however, have to sit in a cell for a while as he called in favors.

Before Mr. Edwards left the interview room, he made a demand. "Jablonsky, I want her placed under a suicide watch while I procure bail."

"Of course, Mr. Edwards. You can have as many people as you want watch her."

Jablonsky walked back to his office and stood staring out of his window. A loud clap of thunder announced the arrival of the storms that had been traveling down into Pittsburgh from the Great Lakes. The thunder, lightning strikes, and sheets of rain suited his mood.

Coupe attempted to tamp down his jittery storm nerves by poking his head into the chief's office and giving his rendition of the song "Agent Double-O-Soul." The corner of Jablonsky's mouth twitched in recognition of Coupe's allusion to espionage.

"Go make yourself useful, DeVille." After he left, Jablonsky returned to thinking about Rose.

I'm sure Rose is guilty, I'm just not sure she was alone in planning and carrying out the murder, he thought. *How did she get ahold of thallium, and who did she hire to dose Celine?*

Early the next morning, the door to Jablonsky's office was flung open, banging it against the wall. A flushed DeVille stepped in and breathlessly made his announcement.

"There's been an accident on the river involving Kate and Johnny. It's bad."

CHAPTER 21

KATE NEEDED TO DISCHARGE HER ANXIOUS ENERGY AFTER HER meeting with the chief and having to bear the twenty-four-hour detail of protection. She recruited Johnny to meet her at the launching area for kayaking. They paid their money, donned life jackets, and pushed off. Right behind them was Annie Lemon, glad to be outside after her night shift—she kayaked alone at a discreet distance—her life jacket hiding one of her weapons.

Today, Johnny insisted that they get a two-person kayak. Kate knew him well enough to understand that his desire to keep her close provided him a sense of control over whatever new situation may crop up. It was an irrational position toward the unexpected, but one most people took. There had been no sighting of Liam O'Hara; he was still out there hunting her.

The temperature hadn't yet risen above seventy degrees as they started, their perfectly synchronized paddles dipping into the water. At first they were silent, breathing deeply and soaking up the diffuse sunlight. A small group of puddle ducks were effortlessly gliding along the side of the riverbank, looking for a morning meal of the seeds of underwater plants or some juicy insects. On the riverbank, a lone fisherman had cast his line, retreating to his portable lawn chair to enjoy a cup of thermos coffee, most surely spiked with a generous amount of whiskey.

In the distance, Kate saw a beautiful cabin cruiser making its way up the river.

"Hey Johnny, look at that 29 OBX Regal. Don't you think the upward curve from the stern to the bow is stunning? And what a great wraparound swim platform—it sits so low to the water you could easily get in and out."

"The only thing I see is that beautiful color on the sides. I think they call it burnt orange. I had the big box of crayons when I was a child," he remarked, chuckling over the box with three tiers of different colored crayons that still resided on his desk at home.

"The Regal's signature FasTrac hull design gives it plenty of giddy-up. That boat can fly."

Johnny burst out laughing. "Really Kate, you know about hull designs? Who are you? Just when I think I know you, you reveal how much of a polymath you are; Joan has nothing on you!"

"I'm the girl who grew up around water, raised by a grandfather who loved boats. I know guy things." They paddled onward, alternating slow strokes with fast ones, sometimes just gliding along in silence.

The cabin cruiser kept a polite distance as it passed them. Without anyone realizing what was happening, it made a sharp turn and came barreling back toward them, creating an arrowhead of wake close to their kayak.

Johnny planted his feet and grabbed the side of the madly rocking vessel, trying to stabilize it. Then, the cruiser executed another U-turn and again came flying toward them. This time Kate was knocked into the river with Johnny tumbling in right after her.

As calm as the surface of the river appeared, the

Allegheny was known to have dangerous undertows, and it was this undertow that had Johnny in its grasp. After only a few swimming lessons, he didn't know how to stay afloat. Kate could see him repeatedly sinking below the water, then resurfacing with arms flailing—his life jacket wasn't holding him up.

My God, Kate thought. *He's going to drown.* Her decades of training kicked in and she plowed through the still-choppy water toward Johnny, finally close enough to grab his jacket. Treading water, she was able to turn him on his back and secure her hand under his chin, keeping his nose and mouth up out of the water.

"Relax, Johnny! I've got you! Don't fight me—I won't let you go under." Johnny did as he was told; Kate's strong legs and absolute determination kept them both upright.

Annie Lemon and several other kayakers were paddling madly toward them. When they finally came close, Kate and Johnny grabbed ahold of the side of the savior outriggers. The small group was relieved to see a motorboat coming their way, its captain throwing life preservers into the water as he moved near.

The captain glided one side of his boat close enough to the kayaks so that Johnny, Kate, and Annie could climb up the ladder onto its deck. When they were safe, the other kayakers involved released their adrenaline by clapping and cheering.

Catastrophe had been averted, for today. The skipper of the small craft wrapped the soaked and shivering victims in blankets and headed straight back to the shore. Annie showed him her badge, then notified the river police; she also called Coupe.

Kate and Johnny changed into spare clothes given to them by the launching center crew, but even though they were physically dry, they couldn't stop shaking. They greedily consumed cups of hot chocolate that magically appeared while they tried to give their report to the river police. Kate's knowledge of pleasure cruisers provided them with good details, and the skipper of the motorboat and the rescue kayakers talked over each other, each describing the incident from their perspective.

At a certain point, Kate put her face in her hands and gave in to her tears of relief: she was alive, and so was her best friend. Johnny knelt in front of her, covering her bowed head with his hands.

"You saved my life. I was drowning, and you caught me," he whispered in a hoarse voice. The group unconsciously closed around them, shielding them from the gathering spectators.

They were all still at the launch giving their statements when Jablonsky showed up.

"Everyone okay here? Stay put until the paramedics check you out. I'm going to talk to Lemon and the river police, then I'll be back. Kate, you and I need to talk." Jablonsky conferenced with his fellow officers from the river force—they had good news.

"We've already found the cruiser that tried to run them down. It was abandoned at Leroy's Dock, just about a mile from here. Keys were left in it; no trace of the perpetrator and no witnesses. It's a weekday, so there were no boaters there, and the dock crew were inside. We'll have forensics go over the boat for prints."

"Does Leroy's crew know the boat owner?" Jablonsky was so irritated he could hardly stand still; needing to chomp on something, he reached in his pocket for a piece of cinnamon gum.

"Yeah. It's registered to some doctor—they all know him —nice guy, never any trouble. He was at his office at the time of the incident and is still there," assured the river officer in charge.

"I'll send a man to talk with him. Any unknown car

parked at the marina this morning?" Jablonsky asked, his eyes scanning up and down the river.

"No. This guy just completely disappeared, poof, like he was Houdini," replied the officer.

"Do we know for certain it's a man?" asked Jablonsky.

"Yes," affirmed Lemon. "When he made the U-turn, I saw him, and so did the other kayakers."

"Detective Lemon, make sure you show Liam O'Hara's photo to the other kayakers." Jablonsky turned to the officer in charge. "This man is dangerous, probably heavily armed—be careful, don't approach him."

The river police were an integral part of Pittsburgh's force, smart and experienced with criminals of all kinds. Jablonsky respected them; he knew they would do anything to help capture the man who violated their turf.

By the time Jablonsky walked back to Kate and Johnny, they were being examined inside an ambulance. He stood outside the door, and like a priest in a confessional, he averted his gaze while he reported that they had found the cruiser, but not the perpetrator.

"The APB and the photo will eventually give us a hit. After you two get settled, call me. I've asked Lemon to stay with you until more detectives are dispatched to Kate's condo."

Jablonsky talked with the witnesses and was able to put together a picture of what he considered to be an attempted murder. The good news was that a few of the witnesses saw that the boat driver had tattoos. He then called Bill Reeves, discovering that the river police had already notified him—forensics would meet them at the marina. He sent Coupe to interview the owner of the boat.

Jablonsky was enraged. Houdini was an apt reference the slippery Liam O'Hara. The chief jammed another piece of gum into his mouth and left for the precinct.

There's another attempt coming. Kate may not be so lucky next time, he worried.

———

Johnny went home with Kate, not wanting to leave her alone and not wishing to be alone himself. Lemon talked to the two detectives who had arrived to cover the premises.

Kate decided to shower. Once the water was on full blast, she crouched down under the pelting spray, keening her shock at the attempt on her life. If there was one thing that separated Kate from her peers, it was that she had suffered such devastating losses; she didn't want to walk through the maelstrom of losing someone else.

One thought spun round and round in her head. *What if I hadn't gotten to Johnny in time?*

She stayed in the shower trying to emotionally gather herself. Bourbon Ball lay outside of the shower stall, knowing something was amiss—his nose detected that those weren't Kate's clothes, and that that was not chlorinated pool water on her skin. As she toweled off, he leaned against her legs, licking them while looking at her with full-on Labrador love blazing from his dark brown eyes. She leaned over and kissed his head, then sat on the toilet lid petting him, finally feeling her blood pressure drop.

Now in their own comfy clothes, Kate and Johnny stood in front of the open refrigerator door, blankly staring in.

"We should eat. Are you hungry for anything in particular?" Johnny asked.

"I can't eat anything, Johnny. I'll make coffee."

"No, I'll make the coffee, you go sit down." Johnny opened the kitchen door to the patio and moved Kate through it.

Kate did as she was told, too exhausted to offer resistance. Johnny carried their cups and saucers outside to the patio table and sat, warming in the sun, waiting for the water to percolate through the grounds. When Kate got up to get the coffee carafe, she also grabbed some brandy. Placing everything on the table, she said, "We need this."

She sensed that Johnny wanted to say something but instead shyly occupied himself with Bourbon Ball.

As if it were tequila, he threw back his brandy, then poured himself another. Kate grinned at him, commenting, "Good man," and then she threw back a shot as well. Johnny grabbed her hand, only able to choke out one sentence.

"What kind of small talk does one make after your best friend saves your life?" In that moment, no declaration could have been more full of the mystery of love than his.

"Liam tried to kill me today. Before the river, I think he just wanted to ruin any achievements or any happiness I've made for myself. Now I know he wants to kill me. I say the words, Johnny, but I can't fully comprehend that someone wants me dead." Kate shivered.

"I can't either." Johnny paused, then quietly added, "You fear that to hurt you he might also try to hurt me." Kate shrugged her acknowledgement.

Have you talked to Joan and Marco about Liam O'Hara?" Johnny asked.

"I really haven't had the chance; everything has happened so fast. First there were these seemingly random events, then he shows up at my house, then we find out he's actually working forensics, and now we know who he is—now he's real." Kate looked and sounded exhausted. "I'm going to sit here in the sun for a while," she added.

Johnny went inside to putter with the dishes, giving Kate her privacy, then he quietly telephoned Joan and Marco.

A bright red cardinal dropped down from one of the shade trees and stood on the rim of Kate's birdbath. Sporting his black mask, he looked around, then waded into the water, took a drink, then began to flap his wings and dunk his head, creating a small shower of droplets in the air.

Kate was mesmerized. She felt one of the lacerations in her heart began to knit together; it was a little red bird magic. The cardinal flew up into one of the trees, continuing to preen and dry itself. Finally, it gave out with its song—complex whistling sounds that ended in a slow trill—it was beautiful to hear.

In an odd psychological twist, Kate found herself thinking that even though she hadn't been able to save her parents, she had saved Johnny. She knew it was a totally irrational thought, since she had only been five years old when they were killed, but right now, it somehow made perfect sense. She had squared the circle.

A picture of herself as a little girl flashed before her— Kate spoke to her child-self. "I saved Johnny, I kept him from drowning."

As she continued to listen to the cardinal's song, a profound fatigue overtook her. She went into the kitchen, gave Johnny a cheek-kiss, then went to her bedroom. She finally registered that her shoulders and legs were aching and rubbery from her extraordinary treading effort in the river.

Kate climbed under the bedcovers while Bourbon Ball jumped up and settled next to her, placing his big block head on her belly. When Johnny came in the room to check on her, he found the two of them deeply asleep.

In the privacy of the guest room, he had his own cry. He wept into his pillow, partly out of relief that he was alive, and partly in fear of what might befall them next.

A few hours passed before Kate woke up. Groggily, she and Bourbon Ball wandered out to the living room. She sat on the couch, feeling like she had been beaten with a baseball bat. Suddenly, she wondered where Johnny was. Mirroring his earlier behavior, she peeped into the guest room and found him asleep, so she quietly removed his cell phone and closed the door. Back sitting on the couch, her phone rang.

Twice in her life, the ringing of the telephone or a knocking at the door forebode existential changes—once when her parents died, and recently, when Johnny arrived to tell her about Eddie's deadly accident. When she was feeling vulnerable, like today, the telephone ring felt like a lightning strike in her body. She took a few deep breaths to calm down. She noticed that it was Jablonsky calling.

"How are you two?" he asked with such kindness in his voice that she responded with the honest truth, not trying to put up a brave front.

"We are both wiped out. I just got up—Johnny is still sleeping. What's going on?"

"Kate. I wanted to warn you that I spoke with some reporters who showed up at the marina. They interviewed the kayakers who helped you—have you seen the news?" asked Jablonsky.

"No, but thanks for the heads up—I should call my friends and my boss." She hesitated, then asked, "Any word on O'Hara?"

"No, not yet. Kate, is there any place you can stay until we arrest this guy?"

"Um, Johnny knows some people in Key West. I guess I could go there." Kate was stunned at the suggestion that she leave her home, but then, her life was at stake.

"I can't protect you in Key West. Some place closer," Jablonsky insisted.

"Let me think about it. Would this mean you don't want me to go into the office?" Kate felt frustrated; since the COVID lockdown ended, she was really enjoying seeing her students face to face.

"Yes. I don't want you out and about at all," Jablonsky answered firmly.

Kate's heart sank. It would take a lot of maneuvering to

extricate herself from her university duties right now. She knew she must do what he said, but she didn't have to like it.

Bourbon Ball was fed and ready for his walk. For the first time since moving to Pittsburgh, Kate hesitated to take him around her typically safe neighborhood. *What if someone tried to grab BB?* she fussed.

Kate stood in the kitchen paralyzed by the thought that something might happen to her beloved pup when Joan suddenly appeared at the side door carrying a bag of deli-made sandwiches, a six pack of beer, bottles of wine, and brownies. She put her arms around Kate, declaring, "Johnny called me. I just had to come and see you in person."

Kate confessed her anxiety about going out, so Joan, ever the physician, diagnosed her feelings as perfectly normal and took charge of BB's walk.

On her way down the drive, Joan and BB ran into a hurrying Dr. Rossetti. "Is she all right?" Marco didn't wait for the answer—he blew by Joan to get to the kitchen door.

"Kate. Kate?" he called out as he let himself in. Before she could answer, he wrapped her in a boxer's full-body clinch. She inhaled deeply—there was that delicious soap scent.

When he finally released her, he started squeezing and moving her limbs. "Are you in one piece? Any damage?"

Kate wasn't used to being manhandled—for a second, she was irritated, then she stepped back from him, laughing. "Yes Mr. Surgeon, I'm in one piece, still."

By that time, Johnny had woken up, luxuriated in a second hot shower, walked into the kitchen, and found them hanging on each other in the hysterical laughter that bubbles up after having dodged a bad situation.

"Hey man, good to see you here." He and Marco exchanged an elaborate handshake and a manly shoulder tap. Johnny didn't admit he had called Joan and Marco to let them know what had happened; since Kate always hid her pain, he knew she wouldn't.

"I guess you know that my best friend saved my life today," was all he said.

Kate turned up the volume on the news; she didn't want any sentimental scenes. They watched the segment about the incident, experiencing a kind of body doubling: the situation had happened to them, but now their experience belonged to the news audience.

"I guess that's how Dr. Smythe must feel," remarked Kate. "A part of her life belongs to the public. And now, so does mine. I hate that!"

Annie Lemon tapped at the kitchen door.

Kate looked around her crowded kitchen. "If there was a VW Bug here, you'd all be trying to jam into it!" Her joke lightened the mood.

Lemon enjoyed this group of friends—she accepted a coffee, comfortably listening to the news with them. "I have to remind you that the chief wants you out of this condo."

"You could stay at my place," offered Marco, itching to be helpful, and to spend more time with Kate.

"My official address is my mother's, but I own a place on Mount Washington. It's in the Crown Building—you know, very tall and sleek, expansive views of the city, plenty of security cameras, underground parking. I've made sure no one knows about this place. And, Kate could bring Bourbon Ball."

Lemon responded before Kate could. "I know that building, it looks like a Miami condo tower. There aren't many ways to get to it—definitely would be easier to guard Kate there. Perhaps Johnny could stay also?"

"Kate is not going without me. The semester is over, and I'm free. Marco, I'm your house guest." Johnny flashed Marco a wry smile.

Lemon pulled up a Google map of the Mount Washington neighborhood: It was a small community, 367 feet high above downtown. Access to the Crown Building was limited to the main road, Grandview Avenue, a secondary back road, and the Duquesne Incline, a funicular that connected the riverbank of the Ohio River to the top of the bluff.

"You would have a broad range of vision," remarked a preoccupied Marco, who was leaning over the map. It dawned on Kate that Marco had just spent time in a war zone, where understanding how the enemy would make its approach was a matter of life and death.

I guess that's true for me as well, she ruefully thought.

Joan returned with BB, then helped Kate decide what she needed to take along—she promised to grab more clothes for her if the manhunt went on for an extended time. Kate's boss gave her permission to return to Zoom meetings with her advisees, which was a relief—she hated not following her students.

Marco and Johnny gathered Bourbon Ball's toys, bed, food, and treats, and stowed them in the car. They then left to go to Johnny's place to pack his gear. They would all rendezvous at the condo where Lemon would begin to set up Kate's security detail.

CHAPTER 22

COUPE STOOD AT THE MURDER BOARD POSTING THE THREE pictures of people who routinely saw Celine Arceneau in and around the law school: James prepared her morning French roast takeout at the law school café. Lou made her afternoon cup of espresso from his food truck. Missy was the line cook who made Celine's lunch salad from the restaurant that sat between the law school, the university's main library, and the venerable Carnegie Library.

"Anyone that you like as an accomplice?" asked the chief, who walked into the bullpen, pausing beside his number one.

"Yeah. It's this guy," he answered, pointing to Lou's photo. "He made Celine's daily espresso. His food truck wasn't as crowded as the café in the lobby, and, well, he has a certain hustle about him. He flirts with the women, tells jokes, always has a witty sports comment for the men. He remembered Celine right away—he sometimes carried certain pastries in order to tempt her to stay around and chat."

"Do you think he's involved?" Jablonsky offered Coupe a stick of gum.

"I'm not sure. He's got the kind of energy that gives me the impression that, for the right price, he'd be open to low-level bribery. Considering the Smythes' wealth, there is plenty of available cash to spread around." Coupe sniffed the cinnamon, which he liked, and following the chief's habits, rolled it into a Tootsie Roll shape and popped it in his mouth.

"You're thinking that it would be easy to sprinkle thallium powder into espresso, but, do you think Lou is sophisticated enough to handle the powder without getting sick himself?" Jablonsky banked his gum wrapper off the murder board into the waste basket.

"No. In fact, I doubt he knew what the powder was. I think someone could have convinced him the powder was something else," said Coupe.

"You mean, something a Canadian might enjoy in their espresso? Because he liked this law professor, he would want to please her. Very devious. Good thinking, Coupe." Jablonsky tapped on Lou's picture.

"Is he sick? I mean, does he show any symptoms of thallium poisoning himself?" Jablonsky was concerned about DeVille being around someone who had been exposed.

"Before I talked with any of these three people, I asked Dr. Patel what the risks were to everyone, me included. She wanted information about the truck—was Lou in a closed environment for such-and-such period of time that he would inhale the powder. She also talked about skin absorption. He wears gloves when touching all of the food, and he would have sprinkled the powder on right before sending the coffee out through the window—there was little chance of prolonged exposure. Dr. Patel wasn't concerned for me, but she advised that Lou see his physician. There is no risk to you or me for an interview." Coupe paused.

"What did you say to this Lou fellow?" Jablonsky asked.

"I told him that Celine Arceneau had been poisoned and that we wanted to rule out his food truck, the restaurant, and the café as possible sites. I emphasized that there was a slim chance he might be in danger from the poison, which I did not name, and that he should see his doctor." Coupe looked to the chief for confirmation on how he handled the issue.

"Get him in here. You did a good job of protecting him without giving away too much."

Several hours later, Lou Christie arrived at the precinct for his interview. He looked around the room, then stood in front of the one-way mirror and combed his hair, apparently unaware of the detectives observing him inches away from his face. Mr. Christie was of medium height and build, with sculptured features, and no beard, no sideburns, no weird goatee chin hair. Jablonsky found his clean-shaven face a relief from the current beard fad for men; he found facial hair to be disgusting.

DeVille walked into the interview room with the chief. "Hey, man," was Lou's greeting to Coupe, as he stood and offered his hand. "This must be the boss," he remarked, turning to offer his hand to the chief.

"I am Chief Detective Jablonsky. Take a seat, Mr. Christie." The chief grinned at Lou, who ducked his head.

"I know, Lou Christie, like the singer. My mother's family is Italian, from the Moon Township area where Christie went to high school. Since our last name was also Christie—well, anglicized—my grandmother insisted that my first name be Lou.

"He toured with Dick Clark's Caravan of Stars, did you know that? Who can forget 'The Gypsy Cried'—not my grandmother and her sisters, that's for sure. They played his music constantly." Lou settled into his chair.

DeVille was right about both the man's innate charm and his hustle; he was hard not to like.

"Mr. Christie," Jablonsky said, starting the interview.

"Just Lou, Chief,"

"Okay, Lou. We are investigating the circumstances of the

death of Celine Arceneau. Detective DeVille tells me you saw her almost every day that she was here on her sabbatical. Is that correct?"

"Absolutely correct. Nice Canadian lady. Always ordered a double shot of espresso around three in the afternoon. Paid with cash. A little old for me, but still good looking," said Lou.

Since Celine was only in her early forties, the chief let the age comment pass, particularly since this young man was in his late thirties. *Lou must look at himself through male delusion goggles,* he thought.

"Did anyone approach you about Ms. Arceneau? For instance, asking if you knew her, if she was dating anyone, was she really from Canada—that kind of thing," suggested Jablonsky.

Lou's dark eyes darted from Coupe to the chief and back. He hesitated before answering, crossing his arms.

"Well, my uncle wanted to know about her. Since he put up the money for my food truck, he comes around a fair amount. Big Moe, that's his name, said he wanted to get to know the law professor, although he is old enough to be her father, and looks it, if you know what I mean. A real beefy burger."

"Did he ever ask you to give her anything special?" asked Jablonsky.

"Give her anything special? Now that you mention it, he did occasionally bring some beaver tails from a bakery that carries a few pastries based on Montreal treats—he just gave them to me in case she would want one. He said to keep the money from the sale of them. Did I do something wrong?" Lou shifted, his trim body seemed to become longer and thinner; a wariness settled in his eyes.

"No, you didn't do anything wrong in terms of accepting the pastry. Was there anything else he asked you to give Professor Arceneau as a special treat? Something specifically

French-Canadian?" Neither Coupe nor the chief changed their posture or tone, they wanted to keep Lou comfortable.

"Yeah. He gave me a tiny jar of sugar—he said it was a special vanilla sugar that the Canadians like with their espresso. He said, 'Just swirl a pinch into her cup with a tiny spoon, she'll love it.' What's going on here, Chief? Was the vanilla sugar bad? Did it make her sick? Is the sugar the reason DeVille told me to go see my doc?" asked Lou.

"Slow down, Lou. Let's take this one question at a time. Did your uncle pay you to put the vanilla sugar into her coffee?" asked Jablonsky calmly.

Lou cleared his throat several times before answering. "Yes. He did shoot some bills my way, which he sometimes does, nothing unusual in that. Big Moe thought the sugar would be a special treat for the professor—something from home."

"Do you still have the jar it came in?" asked the chief.

"I think so. It's on the food truck somewhere. I'll look for it." Lou was an accommodating kind of guy.

"Detective DeVille will accompany you to the truck. It might be evidence in Ms. Arceneau's case. We are just covering all the bases. Detective DeVille asked you to see your physician for a checkup just to be on the safe side—just in case the vanilla sugar contained a poison."

"Jeez. A poison, eh?" Nothing seemed to upset this man.

"When was the last time you saw the professor?" asked Jablonsky.

"I saw her a couple days before she was to go home. Her pals at the law school were throwing her a shindig at some bistro over in East Liberty." Lou remained his calm self.

"Did your uncle tell you where he bought the beaver tail pastry and the special sugar?" asked Jablonsky.

"No. He just said he knew a pastry guy. I'm not in any trouble, am I? I mean, I saw on television that she had died in the hospital from food poisoning from that last supper—well, not *the* last supper, but at her party. Other people got sick too, right?" Lou was finally feeling some anxiety, it pushed him to inch forward on his chair.

"That's correct, Lou. A bacteria was found on the greens used in the salads. But, back to your uncle. Will you give us your uncle's name and address so we can contact him?" requested Jablonsky.

"Absolutely, yes!"

I guess in Lou's life there are a lot of absolutes, thought the chief. He couldn't help but like the man.

"Detective DeVille will meet you at your food truck to get the sugar jar. You've been a good citizen, Lou, but you aren't out of the woods just yet—stay in town. We will speak to your uncle and follow up with you soon."

Bulls eye! Jablonsky was stoked. *Finally, the weapon that killed Celine Arceneau—that is, if Lou still has the jar. Could Big Moe be the key that unlocks this mystery box?*

CHAPTER 23

KATE, JOAN, AND JOHNNY WALKED INTO MARCO'S TOP FLOOR condominium on Mount Washington, trying not to gasp. Every room had a panoramic view of the city skyline: Point State Park, the three rivers, and Northside, where both the baseball and football stadiums were. They were so stunned at the pristine beauty of the rooms that they carefully set down their luggage, remaining transfixed.

"Not too shabby, Marco," joked Joan, breaking the ice. Without another word, she walked done one of the long corridors to the bedroom area. Joan never needed an invitation when she was curious about something.

"I'll say," added Johnny, who, as if he were in a museum, strolled around looking at the art on the walls and the several blown glass pieces secured in the back-lit modern breakfront.

"You've got the eye, Marco, very nice collection," remarked Johnny.

Kate and Marco remained in the entry.

"Do you like the place?" he asked, nervously.

Kate just looked at him as if he were crazy. "What's not to like? It's, it's . . . so perfect."

"Well, these public spaces are in order, but not my study

and bedroom," Marco replied, hoping to have time to straighten up his bedroom before anyone saw it.

Kate moved slowly into the living room, letting her hand drag across the back of the Italian leather sofa, then feeling the texture of the wooly throws; her fingers gently touched the glass art and circled around the top of the crystal martini glasses. In the kitchen, she turned the red Wolf stove knobs on and off and slid open the filled spice rack drawer next to it. The Sub-Zero refrigerator was ginormous, but mostly empty.

"Did you design everything yourself?" she asked, not facing him.

"Well, I've been collecting art, particularly glass, for a while now. A designer did the kitchen. . . . I don't cook much. I do still try to bake a little." Marco moved next to her.

"Do you think you will feel safe here?" he asked nervously.

"Oh yes. I know I'll be safe here." Quick as a butterfly skipping along a flower bed, Kate kissed his cheek. "Where is my room?"

Before he could answer, Joan called out to her. "Come see your room! You'll never want to leave here."

Kate and Marco giggled like children caught with their fingers in the cookie jar; he grabbed her suitcases, and they walked down the hall to one of the guest rooms.

The room was painted a pale azure blue, with matching bedspread and shams. The room color extended out through the tall French doors to the blue of the sky—a startling *trompe l'oeil*.

There was a small, white desk where she could place her laptop and two creamy-white swivel chairs for reading. The bathroom was also white with blue bath towels hung on their rods and a white, fluffy robe resting on the hook on the back of the door.

Kate reached over to the L'Occitane products placed in the shower and on the sink—she sniffed their fragrance—this was the scent she loved on Marco: Almond. Almond body cream, almond shower scrub, almond hand lotion, almond soap.

On the desk, she found a volume of haiku poetry. "He's thought of everything, hasn't he?" remarked Joan, pinching Kate's arm. "This is a man you could get used to spending time with real fast."

"Joan, don't even start down that road—help me unpack." Instead of helping Kate, Joan sat on the bed and filled her in on the actual cause of Celine Arceneau's death—thallium poisoning.

"Ellen didn't tell me that. She talked about food poisoning, not radiation poisoning. That's an interesting omission. What do you know about thallium?" Kate sat down in one of the chairs, confident that Joan would have the information; Joan knew everything.

"It used to be in over-the-counter rat poison. Many people were probably poisoned with it. I think it was banned commercially in 1975. Here's the thing: Dr. Patel would have had to report that Celine Arceneau was poisoned with thallium to several regulatory agencies—the Nuclear Regulatory Commission, the Environmental Protection Agency, Federal Drug Administration, and the state government."

"Wait, why would the FDA be involved?" asked Kate.

"Because thallium is regulated like a drug. Whomever got this stuff knew where to get it and how to handle it—you can't just walk into a lab and steal a little powder. It is all carefully accounted for. Celine would have felt increasingly sick from the poison over a period of several weeks," Joan answered.

"So, someone really wanted Celine to suffer before she died. The killer must have ice in their veins—that doesn't describe the Ellen Smythe I know," remarked Kate.

"Agreed. The other thing is that Ellen is in primary care, not a specialty. This murderer would have needed access to a nuclear medicine laboratory or even to an actual reactor that makes radiopharmaceutical material. According to my research, there are many of those in Canada. Interesting isn't it, since Celine Arceneau was Canadian," said Joan.

The two women continued hanging and sorting and putting away things while Johnny and Marco stood out on the deck talking about what was happening to Kate.

"Thanks for doing this. I wouldn't know how to get along without her. She's beyond a blood sister to me; we understand each other," explained Johnny.

Marco turned to face Johnny. "She's becoming important to me as well. I think I'm falling in love with her. Well, honestly . . . I *am* in love with her. I've even started writing bad poetry." The two chortled over the things a man will do when he's falling in love.

"Johnny, I have to ask. Do you think that Kate will ever truly get over Eddie Fitzroy?"

Johnny responded without hesitation. "I do. I've noticed that she has switched from wearing his emerald ring on her left hand to wearing it on her right, and recently, she sometimes wears the ring on a chain around her neck. I believe this change reflects her effort to find the right spot in her emotional life for her memories of him. How Kate wears the ring symbolizes the status of her grief, wouldn't you agree?"

"I'm a surgeon, Johnny. Symbolism in the grief process is something that I might have written about in a college paper —after stealing the idea from someone like you!" Marco blushed at this confession, particularly since he was a bona fide genius. That said, his IQ didn't guarantee human insight.

"Don't underestimate yourself Marco. You are the one sending Kate haiku poetry. She didn't mention it to me, but I saw some of the post cards. You clearly aren't dense when it comes to emotional subtleties. Cut yourself a break." Johnny tapped Marco on the arm in brotherly support.

"Sending her a few haiku is different than expressing my feelings in person. I'm a cautious man, Johnny." Marco looked down at the city below.

"You know, Marco. I think you and Kate are like a Venn diagram: you've had overlapping experiences. You are both serious individuals who had significant people just disappear from your early lives—no wonder both of you are wary of intimacy—you're always waiting for the person you love to disappear or for something bad to happen to them. You are capable of understanding her far better than Eddie ever did. My advice is to keep writing that bad poetry—maybe even send her some," Johnny offered.

Marco was a bit shocked at the accuracy of Johnny's analysis, but before he could respond, Kate and Joan wandered onto the balcony. Everyone was drawn to the railing —the wide vistas engulfed their senses in the same way that the expanse of the ocean does. In this moment, the fact that a killer was hunting Kate seemed utterly improbable. It was Johnny who broke the spell.

"I'm going to unpack and set up my computer."

"And I have to head to the hospital. Marco, you keep our girl safe." Joan briskly walked to the private elevator, then shouted back over her shoulder. "I'll pick up Bourbon Ball and bring him over later. He'll be walked and fed." Like good dog-aunts and uncles, Kate's friends loved and cared for BB like he was their own.

"I also have to get going, I have a few patients to check on. You and Johnny settle in and—" before Marco could finish, the ping of the elevator announced the arrival of Annie Lemon and another police officer. Marco gave them a quick tour of the condominium, then rode down with them to the lobby.

Lemon introduced herself to the building's security people, who showed her through the workout room, the lap pool area, and the underground garage, pointing out all the inside cameras. Aside from Marco's, there was only one other suite that had a private elevator. Four elevators went to the six other floors from the lobby.

They trooped outside and walked around the building, which wasn't built on the bluff of Mount Washington but rather sat back on firmer ground. There was a manned guardhouse where visitors had to stop and show identification before being allowed onto the premises. The whole Crown Building and its surround were tightly monitored, every nook and cranny was videoed day and night.

Lemon called Jablonsky. "I'm happy with the security situation here, Chief. Someone would have a hard time getting to Kate while she's in the building."

"Good, that's one thing settled. Right now we're setting up an interview with Lou Christie's uncle. Let Kate know I'll drop by later," stated Jablonsky.

While Lemon and the guards were getting to know each other, Kate decided to walk to the small local grocery to lay in supplies. She was summarily stopped at the lobby door.

"Where do you think you are going?" Lemon demanded.

"I'm just walking up the block to the grocery. Not okay?" responded Kate.

"I'll go with you." Lemon's handgun was tucked in her shoulder holster, concealed under her sweater. A backup was strapped to the inside of her left leg.

The local grocery was unexpectedly delightful. It stocked everything needed for a simple egg, butter, and milk run to items deemed necessary to the gourmet palate. Kate purchased so many groceries that she was glad Annie was along to share the load.

"I see there's an indoor lap pool—only twenty yards long, but it'll serve the purpose. Would it be okay if I used it?" Kate didn't like asking permission but also didn't want to court danger.

"No problem. One of us will be with you—just let me know when you want to work out. And Kate. Don't make routines. Don't swim, use the weights, or the elliptical machine at the same time each day. Criminals look for routines. Be random. Got it?" ordered Detective Lemon.

"Got it. I can be random. Thanks, Annie. Come up to the condo when you want a good cup of coffee. Actually, Marco's espresso machine is even more elaborate than Johnny's—it could launch a cup down to you. By the way, I was hoping to see my letters? The ones they found at O'Hara's workstation."

"I understand. Jablonsky would have to bring them to you. Chain of custody and all. He mentioned that he would stop around soon." Lemon left it at that.

Kate unpacked the groceries, talked to Johnny, then went to her room and contacted her office. This was going to be her life until Liam O'Hara was caught. She was anxious for Bourbon Ball to arrive. Nothing soothed her overwrought nerves like petting her sweet pup.

CHAPTER 24

ONE OF THE COMPUTERS IN THE BULLPEN WAS RUNNING A photo of Lou's uncle through criminal data bases—periodically Coupe would check it, but so far there were no hits.

After the interview, he had taken Lou to his food truck where the tiny bottle of poison powder had been unceremoniously left behind a large box of sugar on one of the shelves. Using gloves, DeVille placed it in a glass container, dropped it at forensics, then returned to the precinct.

Jablonsky stood in front of the murder board, staring at Lou Christie's photo. He had already marked down the salient details of the interview, and just in case he was lying about everything, the detectives had given Lou's apartment a good toss—nothing turned up. His bank account showed a recent cash deposit of five hundred dollars. If he was their guy, he certainly didn't do anything to hide the fact.

Imagine depositing cash? thought an amused chief. *Cash is walking around money.*

"What did forensics say about the bottle?" he asked Coupe.

"They just called—it's our culprit. They found residual

amounts of thallium acetate powder; no muss, no fuss," stated Coupe.

The chief was frustrated that the scientific and medical laboratories in the area continued to report that they were not missing thallium in any form. Where did the perpetrator acquire it?

"We got a match!" called Coupe. The computer had stopped its scroll, flashing two photos side by side. Jablonsky and DeVille looked closely at the picture, then the chief remarked, "Lou's uncle is head of security for the Copper and Smythe law firm."

"Do all the security firms list their employees like this? I'm not sure I actually knew that fact." Coupe turned to the chief for confirmation.

"After 9/11, security guards at certain types of facilities were required to be fingerprinted, provide proof of citizenship, and have a photo placed in a police database like this one. This is the generous uncle—Mr. James Zwicki, nicknamed Big Moe. Well Big Moe, let's get you in here to tell your big story." Jablonsky rubbed his hands together in anticipation of the interview.

It was clear why "Big Moe" Zwicki was given his nickname. He was a tall, thickset man, with several strands of hair combed across the top of his scalp. Zwicki's bulk pressured his chest, making his breathing labored, both as he walked, and also when he sat. His face was as round as a cherub's and his rosy checks and easy smile distracted from his beefy, intimidating, towering presence. His pale blue eyes were clear and held an expression of curiosity. Big Moe was clean and nicely dressed in a maxi-sized cotton shirt and pressed khakis.

"He wears Old Spice, Chief. It's so dated that I kind of like it," announced Coupe. "It's fresh."

"Hey, careful there Detective," cautioned Jablonsky. "I

wear Bay Rum, but my dad and every one of his brothers wore Old Spice. It's a classic, and certainly better than the usual stink that pervades the interview room." Jablonsky smiled to himself as he opened the door to the interview room.

"Thank you for coming in today, Mr. Zwicki. We are hoping you might be able to offer some insight in an ongoing murder investigation." As was his habit, the chief placed his small paper notebook alongside the printout of Zwicki's work history.

"Call me Big Moe, Chief Jablonsky. Everyone does. My nephew Lou said you folks were interviewing anyone who had contact with the professor who died. What's cookin'?" His face glowed with the shine of helpfulness.

"You have had a long tenure at Cooper and Smythe. Did you personally know Peter Smythe?" Jablonsky wanted Big Moe relaxed, so he started conversationally, setting the tone for a kind of Mr. Rogers story time.

"Peter Smythe hired me. Years ago I worked at WABCO —Westinghouse Air Brake. When that closed, I transferred to the Steiner Company, which fabricated parts for nuclear reactors—that's when I met Mr. Smythe—his firm handled their international business. We kind of hit it off, so he hired me away from Steiner's to oversee security at his law firm.

"They had just bought their downtown building. He gave me free rein in hiring the men and women who would protect the practice. They still list me as the head of security, but I'm really retired—you caught me on one of the days I fill in for an employee who is on vacation." Big Moe's presentation was direct and unassuming. Jablonsky wondered how many secrets this man knew about the firm and its members.

"You must know where all the bodies are buried, eh?" stated Jablonsky.

"Well, since it's a law firm, there aren't too many bodies around, just a lot of attorneys working late nights. Burning the midnight oil is the norm because of their overseas business." Big Moe relaxed into his chair, beginning to feel comfortable.

What a political answer, observed the chief. *No wonder Peter Smythe liked him.*

"Did you ever do small side jobs for Mr. Smythe?" asked Jablonsky.

"I take it you're asking if I did anything on the down low. The answer is no, just some private security work. When Peter was away in Europe, he would ask me to swing by his house on my way home to make sure the wife and daughter were okay. Or, if a really big client came into town, he would request that I be the one to pick him up at the airport. That kind of thing," answered Big Moe.

"Did you spy on his wife, Dr. Ellen Smythe? Did you ever have cameras installed in her home or put taps on the phone?" The chief went right for it.

"No! Never, not ever. If there were cameras hidden in the house or phone taps, I had nothing to do with it." Big Moe seemed more annoyed than offended by the implication.

"I will say that after his daughter Rose was divorced, he asked me to assign someone to watch her house and to follow her around—just for the first few months. I didn't like the idea and told him that I wasn't in the private eye business. Obviously, I don't look like the original Magnum PI or the Magnum redux. Once Rose moved in with her mother, the surveillance stopped."

Jablonsky laid a picture of Celine Arceneau and Lou Christie on the table. "What can you tell me about these two people?"

Big Moe reached over and, with his fat fingers, moved the two photos in front of him. "You already know Lou is my nephew. He needed something steady so I invested in a food truck—he runs the show. I've seen this woman at his truck, but I didn't actually know her. Her name was Celine something."

"You saw her at his food truck? Go on," encouraged Jablonsky.

"I sometimes stop at Lou's truck in the afternoons, which is when this woman would come by. Lou liked her, and well, so did I. I'm a widower now. I like to look. She was some kind of law professor."

Very charmingly put. He just likes to look *at younger women,* thought the chief.

"You don't live in the university area. Why would you stop at this truck? Checking on your nephew?" asked Jablonsky.

"I sometimes take the university classes offered for seniors. Recently I've been auditing the one on the Homestead strike," offered Big Moe.

"I take it you're registered for this class?" Jablonsky scribbled in his notebook.

Big Moe nodded.

"I'm sure we will find all the correct paperwork at the registrars. At the truck, did you introduce yourself to this Canadian professor?" continued the chief.

"No. I would say hello or something about the nice weather. Mostly I drank a soda and listened to Lou chat her up." Big Moe continued to look unbothered.

"This Canadian professor's full name was Celine Arceneau, and she was poisoned," Jablonsky stated.

"Food poisoning, right?" He paused. "You can't think Lou had anything to do with her death. He's a good kid."

"It is an avenue we are investigating, just like we are investigating you," said Jablonsky.

"Me? Come on. Hey, do I need an attorney here?" Like a flight of sandpipers, Big Moe's fat fingers were suddenly active —fluttering in agitation around his comb over.

"Mr. Zwicki, you have a right to an attorney. Do you want to suspend this interview and call one? You know enough of them," stated Jablonsky bluntly.

Big Moe's adipose shook with the effort of thinking

through his dilemma. "Well, I guess not right now. Get where you are going, Chief."

"Tell me about the tiny bottle of sugar powder you gave Lou. You told him it was vanilla sugar to be put on the Canadian professor's espresso," stated Jablonsky.

Zwicki lowered his head in deliberation; the strands of hair fell forward onto the bridge of his nose.

"There was a youngish man, obviously a runner, who used to stop for iced coffee. Since I'm a security guy, I could tell that he listened in as Lou and I talked about the professor. One day he sat next to me at the picnic table. He pulled out this tiny bottle and said that it contained a special sugar that the French Canadians sprinkle on their coffee. He wanted to help out us 'mokes' . . . that's how he said it, 'mokes.' The bottle was in a plastic container. I was suspicious of him, so I asked, 'What's in it for me?'"

"Did he then offer you money?" asked Jablonsky.

"A few hundred, that's all. He gave me the bottle, shook my hand, and said, 'Give it to Lou, you'll both look good in the professor's eyes—like you're culturally sensitive.' He said that last part sarcastically." Big Moe frowned.

"He left, I showed it to Lou, and we both thought, How can it hurt?" Big Moe's pale eyes became wary. The chief couldn't believe Zwicki's statement.

"How can it hurt? Let me count the ways. You didn't know this guy, he offers you a bottle of white powder to sprinkle on a foreign professor's coffee, then he gives you some cash, and you take it. Is there a special school where naive security guys go? Even a civilian knows not to take a powdered substance from one stranger to give to another stranger!" The chief couldn't believe this guy's ignorance.

Jablonsky sighed deeply, wrote a few notes in his notebook, then continued. "When was the last time you saw Professor Arceneau?"

"A couple weeks ago. She hadn't been around lately. Now I know why," responded the clueless Zwicki.

"When was the last time you saw Ellen Smythe and Rose Delaney?" queried Jablonsky.

"The Smythes? Um, let me think." Big Moe rubbed his eyes, then snorted like a whale rolling in Pacific waters. "I saw them both at Peter's funeral. That's got to be almost a decade ago."

"What was the content of your conversation with them?" asked Jablonsky.

"I didn't have any conversation with them. I went to the funeral luncheon, waited in the line to offer my condolences, sat and ate with the other security people, then left. That's it." As if confiding a secret, he leaned in and lowered his voice.

"You know, Peter Smythe could be sort of strange. I mean, he loved his clients in the nuclear business, and especially loved all the gizmos that went into the reactors. He kept some of them in his office."

"He kept parts that were designed to go into a reactor? That is an odd thing to collect. Where were they taken after he died?" Jablonsky made a note for himself and DeVille.

"I guess they went to the family, or else a museum— maybe the Heinz History Center—maybe there?" offered Big Moe.

"Why are you telling me about this aspect of Peter Smythe's personality?" asked the chief, almost as much to himself as to Zwicki.

"I'm not really sure. It's just that, I liked Peter Smythe, and he was good to me, but . . . there was always something about him that didn't seem completely upstanding. I have never said this to anyone before, but being around him was like being in Miami—where the water is blue, the hotels are gorgeous, the people are happy on their vacations, but there is an atmosphere of criminality that lingers in the air."

"Did you ever personally see Peter Smythe commit a

crime? Or hear of one second hand?" Jablonsky knew many people who lived in "an atmosphere of criminality"; he rolled the phrase around in his mind, deciding he liked it.

"I never knew or heard that Peter committed any crimes. He was, however, a ladies' man. There were always rumors floating around about his activities. Are we finished yet?" Big Moe was becoming antsy.

Jablonsky chortled. "Finished? We are a long way from finished. Here's the salient fact—it was that pretend sugar powder that killed Professor Arceneau, not food poisoning. You are in deep trouble, Big Moe. What did you think this interview was about?"

Zwicki's voice cracked, and his pale blue eyes grew as large as a bunny's. "You gotta be joking. I'm just a guy who was helping my nephew get in good with a lady. What could you charge me with?" Big Moe was stunned.

"What can I charge you with? The small fish is aiding and abetting, but the big kahuna would be conspiracy to murder." Jablonsky raised his eyebrows but revealed nothing in his tone.

"Conspiracy to murder? What would be my motive to kill a professor I didn't know? What the heck, Chief? I'm a security guy, not a criminal. Please, Chief. You've gotta help me out here!" pleaded Big Moe.

"No Zwicki, you've got to help *me*. Did you ever hear of Peter obtaining thallium from his friends in the nuclear business?" asked Jablonsky.

"Thallium? Like the poison? I would have no idea if Peter acquired some—that doesn't mean he didn't have it. It's just the kind of weird thing he would have liked to own." Big Moe returned to his low, confiding tone of voice.

"People like Peter Smythe can purchase anything—if he had asked, someone he knew in the industry might have obliged him by pinching some from a laboratory. Oh, like that tiny bottle of special sugar. . . . Oh man, I get it now." Big Moe took out a real handkerchief and mopped his brow.

"Was Peter Smythe a spy?" asked Jablonsky.

"A spy? Like a secret agent? Nah. He was just a rich guy who wanted what he wanted. I never saw politics enter into his life, unless it had to do with getting the best deal for his clients. Peter didn't care about politics; he cared about power."

"Some people would say that's the same thing," the chief commented. "Were you ever in the family home in Montreal?"

"Yeah. Early on in my employment, I was there many times. Very beautiful—designed for outdoor sports. More of an estate really. He and Rose spent a lot of time there, but not the missus," added Big Moe.

"Did he keep any of his reactor gadgets there?" prompted Jablonsky.

"Now that you mention it, I think he did," said Big Moe.

"Could he have kept thallium there?"

"Absolutely. The house is outside Montreal in the foothills of the mountains, rather isolated. If he had any, that's where I suspect he would store it."

"Mr. Zwicki, get yourself a good criminal attorney from your friends at Cooper and Smythe because you are a person of interest in the murder of Celine Arceneau. We are considering charging you and Lou with, at least, aiding and abetting. Take this seriously," warned Jablonsky.

When Jablonsky walked back into the bullpen, he quietly remarked, "Big Moe might be telling the truth. The most important thing he offered was that Peter Smythe collected parts that go into a nuclear reactor. Did he also collect radioactive elements? Before we go to Montreal, let's have a look-see in the outbuildings at Rose's and Ellen's homes."

DeVille responded the way Jablonsky liked him to. "I'm on it."

CHAPTER 25

DEVILLE AND A FEW OFFICERS ARRIVED AT ROSE DELANEY'S house with a second warrant, this time one that permitted a search of the grounds and the garage. She was beside herself with anxiety and anger—she called her mother, who told her that the police had searched her garage and Maria's apartment as well. Ellen drove over to Rose's house to see if she could lower the temperature of the situation.

"Is there anything I can help you with, Detective DeVille?" asked a very civil Ellen, who had surrendered her secret computer to the detectives, hoping it would keep her from being charged. Elise Rosen said that she could be charged with obstructing the investigation, along with lying to the police, but there had been no charges yet.

"It came to our attention that Peter collected items related to nuclear reactors. He kept some in his office—where did they go after he died?" Coupe was equally civil, but not friendly.

He watched Ellen look through him into the past, trying to remember Peter's odd collection; she didn't deny that he had them but apparently couldn't quite place where they went.

"I remember his collection but I'm not sure who has it. I

know it's not at my house. He may have stored it here at Rose's. Look at anything you want; I'll go into the house and call one of Peter's retired colleagues to see if he knows what happened to it."

Coupe and his officers located the key to the apartment over the garage, trudged up the steps and unlocked the door. There was no puff of dust nor any of the usual spider webs that adorn unused spaces.

The apartment was clean and tidy, with a living room, kitchenette, bathroom, and two bedrooms. Coupe and his guys walked through all of the rooms, opening and closing bureaus and closets, looking in the kitchen cabinets, the stove, refrigerator, and freezer. There was nothing.

Returning from making her call, Ellen walked right into Coupe's frustration; she ignored it.

"Peter's colleague said that he might have kept some things at the family estate outside of Montreal—Summit Park, Westmount area."

"Do you give us permission to search that home?" asked Coupe.

"Of course. Let me find keys for you, and I'll write something in case the Mounties don't like your intrusion into their territory. I will also contact the consul, André Trembly—whom you must already know—he'll smooth the way," said Ellen.

"Yes, we know Mr. Trembly. Dr. Smythe, please hurry with the arrangements—we will want to get a flight to Montreal as soon as possible," stated DeVille.

Rose had posted two million dollars for her bail. After Jablonsky arrested her, she turned in her passport, sat through booking with her attorney, then finally was released. She was so spooked that she called a private security group that she typically used for social events and booked two men for twenty-four-hour, on-site protection from the media. When Ellen came back into the house, she found a disgusted Rose pacing in the entry hall.

"Are those people still here? What are they looking for? Let's go to the library," requested Rose.

Rose had changed into a cashmere lounging outfit, and her hair was pulled up and secured with a large sparkly clip.

She looks like she's eighteen, Ellen observed, fondly remembering her daughter at that age.

Ellen asked the ubiquitous mom-question. "Have you eaten anything?"

"There is some leftover Chinese in the fridge, Mum. I'm not hungry. My glass of wine is doing the trick for me."

Ellen poured herself a cognac from one of the crystal carafes sitting on the bookcase shelves. She smiled; Rose always kept a bottle of Martell XO for her.

"Rose, when was the last time you were at the Summit House in Canada?" asked Ellen.

"I'm not sure, Mummy. Why do you ask?"

"The police are looking for your dad's collection of parts and tools used in nuclear reactors—one of your dad's colleagues thinks they might be at that house. Do you remember seeing anything like that?" Ellen kept her tone even as she asked her questions.

"No, Mummy, I don't. His suite of rooms was on the other side of the house—I rarely went there," explained Rose.

Ellen knew the house was really a sprawling mansion—Rose was probably telling the truth that she wouldn't have bothered traipsing to Peter's quarters.

"Tell me about Jeffrey Edwards. I've met him in passing at Elise Rosen's office, but I don't have any substantial impression of him," prompted Ellen, changing the subject.

"Well, he's very direct. He says that unless the detectives find another prime suspect, I'm it, and could be tried for first-

degree murder. He thinks that the police have a strong circum-
stantial case against me," said Rose.

"The process goes like this: There is a preliminary hearing
where the evidence will be presented to the judge. If the judge
thinks that the case is good, then there will be a trial. The fact
that this Arceneau woman was related to me seems a big deal
in the eyes of the court. Did you know about her, Mummy?"
There was no accusation in Rose's tone.

Ellen was astonished at Rose's composed recitation of the
legal facts. It was almost as if she were talking about someone
else—but then again, her father and husband used to talk law.

"Did I know about her? Yes. Your father told me. Did he
tell you?"

Rose poured herself more wine, avoiding the question.
"The police said he was paying that Celine person hush
money."

"It wasn't hush money, Rose. She was his daughter, she
deserved some of his estate, the same way you deserve it. You
must face that fact," lectured Ellen.

"Do you think he raped that woman's mother?" Rose
asked, picking invisible lint from her sleeve.

Ellen didn't like to lie to Rose, so she took the long way
around the question. "He never directly told me that he raped
Adele Arceneau, but, I believe it was possible that he might
have. Adele Arceneau signed a notarized statement to that fact
—you read the letter."

Rose shrugged off the last sentence. "Daddy would never
rape anyone. He was too sweet and loving a person. I can't
believe you would even consider rape as a possibility. Whoever
that Adele Arceneau and her daughter were, they are out of
the picture now."

Rose picked up her glass and drained it. Ellen's maternal
antenna was spinning—she moved close to her. "Do you want
to ask me about anything else related to this? Like Daniel?"

"No, Mummy. I'm too tired. I took my medication right

after I came home, and between that and the wine, I'm sleepy. We can talk about him some other time."

Relief and worry collided in Ellen's mind—all she could think to say was, "Okay, just close your eyes and rest. I'm going to eat some of that takeout and then clear the dishes." She knew that the sound of someone bustling around the house would be a soothing, homey noise for Rose.

Ellen felt calmed as she went about the normal, everyday activity of reheating food. She ate a small serving of shrimp over vegetables as she watched the news—she was startled and saddened to see the report on Kate's near miss on the river.

I should insist that she come into the office so I can examine her. She called Kathleen and asked her to make an appointment for Kate.

Ellen loaded the dishwasher, looked out the window at the security detail, then returned to the library.

She sat down next to Rose, who immediately leaned over and rested her head in her mother's lap. They remained together like that for a long time—Ellen stroked her daughter's hair as if she were still a little girl.

"I want you to know that your father's last words to me were about you. He said, 'Always protect our Rose.'"

Through a deep sigh, Rose whispered, "I loved him, and he loved me. I was his little bonbon."

Ellen continued stroking Rose's hair as her daughter's breathing deepened; she felt compelled to ask her the burning question.

"Rose, darling. Now tell Mummy the truth. Did you poison Celine Arceneau? No matter what the answer, you are still my daughter and I will stand by you," said Ellen.

It was almost a minute before Rose responded.

"No, Mummy. I didn't put any poison in anybody's food or drink."

An hour later, Ellen slipped out from under her daughter's sleeping body, depositing a kiss on the top of her head.

Why would she say drink, and not just food? And, just because she didn't personally place the toxins, she could have paid someone to do it. Ellen's mind was spinning, but she didn't question Rose further. Did she really want to hear the answer? Instead, she called Daniel, then drove to his apartment.

"I have something to tell you, Daniel." Ellen drew in a deep breath.

"She murdered Celine, didn't she. Did she confess?" Daniel couldn't hide his excitement at being right about Rose.

"No. Well, not exactly. She said that she didn't put poison into anyone's food or drink."

"That could mean anything. She could have hired someone else to do it." Daniel paced back and forth while Ellen threw up her hands in frustration. She didn't confide her worries as to how much Rose knew about thallium, or with whom she might have collaborated to poison Celine. Nor did she mention the Summit House; it would only inflame Daniel's distain for the Smythe wealth.

Daniel walked to his kitchen window and stared out into the night. Was Rose out there right now, stalking them?

CHAPTER 26

THE HOUSE IN SUMMIT PARK HAD BEEN BUILT IN THE STYLE OF an eighteenth-century stone mansion with turrets, a porte cochere, large bedroom wings, and central gathering rooms with wood burning fireplaces. It could, and often did, accommodate ten guests; the stables housed a string of well-tended trail horses for riding on the vast property. There was a large indoor swimming pool, workout equipment, and two classic pool tables.

André Trembly had telephoned the house manager, letting her know that several American detectives and forensic technicians, plus the chief of the local constabulary, would be arriving to search the house; that tidbit would be fodder for gossip in the town for months to follow.

"When was the last time someone from the family stayed here?" Coupe's men had immediately swarmed all over the house and grounds, while he remained in the living room questioning the affable house manager, Beatrice.

"Well, Miss Rose was here recently with some friends from Pittsburgh. Let me check my diary." Beatrice retrieved a computer tablet from her wide sweater pocket and scrolled through the calendar.

"Yes. She was here in early spring; there were five guests. I remember that one of them had been raised in Montreal—he was a chef, named, um . . . Hank, no, named Henri, you would say Henry. Nice young man. He had quite a shopping list for me, I can tell you that. He cooked for the group."

"How long did they stay?" Coupe couldn't believe his luck. *So Henry from the bistro stayed here with Rose. They both have been lying to us—that's obstruction plain and simple.*

"Looks like it was around four days. They were active—jogging the trails, riding, swimming."

"Do you have a list of their names?" asked Coupe.

Beatrice gave him a shocked look. "No. And unless she had a special reason to give the names to me, Rose would never have mentioned it. It would be discourteous and inappropriate for me to ask."

"Yet you knew about Henry."

"He introduced himself," Beatrice replied, showing a bit of temper.

"Have you ever seen this man?" DeVille opened a photo of Big Moe Zwicki on his phone.

"No. I don't remember this man. Before Mr. Smythe died, I only worked here for special occasions. In years past, many family members and friends came and went and I didn't see them," Beatrice stated.

"Is this the young man who was the chef?" Coupe showed Beatrice a phone picture of Henry.

"Yes. That's the chef who was from Montreal," confirmed Beatrice.

"Detective DeVille, sorry to interrupt, but we are not able to access one of the rooms." The young forensic tech led the way to the area.

Without being asked, Beatrice followed Coupe and the local chief on the long walk to the other side of the house. *I feel like I'm at Manderley,* Coupe thought, hoping there was no smell of smoke.

They finally arrived outside of a large, closed wooden door, which no one was able to open.

"Beatrice, can you unlock this door for us?" requested DeVille.

"Yes." She flipped up the lid to a small wall box by the side of the door. Inside was a retinal scanner.

"You have to put your eyeball close to this gadget, it scans it, and then opens the door. Miss Rose and I are the only two people whose eyes it is programmed to recognize, since Mr. Smythe died that is." Beatrice demonstrated, and the door opened.

The room inside was clearly a collector's lair: There were many shelves of tools and parts for nuclear reactors, as well as pictures of the smaller Canadian reactors which produced radiopharmaceutical material for use in nuclear medicine. There were also photos of heavy water reactors, alongside pictures of Peter shaking hands with men in suits wearing hard hats and lapel dosimeters.

"Thanks, Beatrice. We will call you if we need anything else." The techs took samples and photos of everything. Surprisingly, they couldn't find a personal safe. DeVille left the room for the stables, where the staff had pointed out a locked cabinet in the office.

"What's in this cabinet? he asked the groomsman.

"The veterinarian keeps a few animal drugs in there for the horses. I'll open it for you."

The groomsman sorted through the stash. "Ketamine, Adequan, alcohol rubbing lotions, ace bandages, not anything unusual."

As Coupe slowly scanned the rustic office, he noticed a fresh scar on the wooden floor.

"Someone has recently moved this desk. Push it out of the way, and let's take a look at what's under here."

They found several of the old wooden floor slats had been lifted, so they did the same.

"Now we're cookin' with a spoon," exclaimed DeVille.

The techs pulled out a small, thick metal box with even smaller glass bottles in them. One was missing.

"This is it, this is our powder of thallium acetate. I'd stake my life on it." Fist bumps occurred all around: Coupe thanked the local commander, Beatrice, the groomsmen, and his men, then left.

He called Jablonsky on his way to the airport. "Sous-chef Henry was there with Rose and some other friends eight weeks ago. Perhaps he was the one to help Rose on both counts—the Bacillus cereus and the thallium acetate."

"Good work, DeVille. See you back at the precinct."

***

Several days had passed since the team returned with the goods from Summit House. Bill Reeves confirmed that the found bottles held thallium acetate and that the bottle taken from Lou's food truck was of the same kind. They were closing in on the perpetrator—the chief was leaning toward the idea of co-conspirators, perhaps Rose and Henry.

Under a good grilling at the precinct, Henry admitted to having been at the Montreal house, but didn't admit to anything else. He vehemently claimed he knew nothing about any small bottles loaded with radioactive poison.

Before he lawyered-up, he did give the names of the other guests, one of which immediately drew the chief's and Coupe's interest, but not surprise.

Henry pleaded, saying he was deeply sorry for having lied: lied about being in Montreal at Rose's house, lied about his friendship with her, and lied about knowing the other people who were there. The chief charged him with obstruction.

The day after Henry let her know that he had been charged, Rose awoke early. Opening the drapes at the bedroom window, she nodded her approval at seeing the two private security guards walking around her property, keeping the media at bay.

Her longtime masseur, Mr. Chen, was stopping by; she had already laid out her clothes for the day. She had picked a white pair of shorts with a gold belt and a matching white blouse. Alongside her clothes lay a small, gift-wrapped box and card. She felt the pockets in the shorts, nodding in approval at their depth and width. She would shower and dress after the massage.

Rose slid into her silk robe and meandered into her closet, busying herself with tossing clothes into the hamper, hanging some blouses, and putting shoes in their individual, clear plastic boxes. She pulled out a small suitcase from the wall safe, opened it, took out the contents, then placed the suitcase back in the safe. The doorbell rang and the security guard called to her—Mr. Chen had arrived.

During the massage, she mentally picked through a conversation she had had with Patricia.

"Did your grandmother tell you that she is definitely retiring?" Rose had asked.

"Well, yes. She mentioned it when the three of us had dinner together, don't you remember?" Patricia had responded cautiously.

"Does that Daniel person know?" Rose asked without emotion.

"Yes, I think so. With everything going on around the Arceneau case, Grandma didn't want to burden you with other considerations—like her retirement." Patricia strove to shelter Rose, just like Ellen always had. Generational habits of secrecy and over-protection remained firmly in place between these women.

The masseur interrupted her musing. "Rose, you are tensing. Relax. Let me work out these knots in your shoulders and back."

Rose took a deep breath and did as she was told, putting aside all thoughts of whether her mother might leave Pittsburgh with Daniel. Besides, she had decided last night what she was going to do about her situation, there was no use dwelling on it now.

Jablonsky was reviewing the case in his office when Coupe barged in.

"There's some kind of standoff outside of Dr. Smythe's home. One person is armed—one that we know of. Officers are on the scene; the area has been secured."

Jablonsky unlocked the desk drawer and took out his shoulder gun, then secured his backup to the inside of his left calf.

"Let's roll," he growled. They flew down Penn Avenue and up over Polish Hill, and in ten short minutes, entered the Schenley Farms neighborhood. They parked at the bottom of Dr. Smythe's street, keeping their badges visible as they moved up the slope to her house.

Jablonsky took in the particulars of the situation as he jogged: The police had cleared several streets around this one, cautioning homeowners to stay in their homes. Officers were crouched strategically behind their vehicles, guns loaded and pointed at the four people on the sidewalk. A paramedic bus had arrived. He heard Ellen Smythe trying to reason with Rose, who stood across the street holding what looked like a .38 Saturday Night Special.

The gun was pointed at Daniel Grusin. Jablonsky noted that Daniel kept trying to maneuver Ellen behind him. Maria was also with Ellen in front of the house.

"Move aside, Mummy. I know that you are thinking of

leaving the city with that man. I am the one who should be with you. Me! Not him!" Fragile, anxious Rose had disappeared, and an armed and dangerous Rose had taken her place, or, had she been there all along?

"Rose, it's Detective Jablonsky. I'm going to move a little closer. Just drop the gun, and you can go to your mother. You can be with her right now; all you have to do is drop the gun."

Jablonsky laid his gun down on the pavement, then moved very slowly toward Rose. He had already communicated a plan to Coupe, who at this moment, was coming around the side of one of the houses behind her, his weapon held down at his side. Annie Lemon was right behind him. Their plan was to tackle and disarm Rose when Jablonsky distracted her.

"Please, Rose, drop the gun. You are scaring your mother. See how she is crying? You can go and comfort her if you just drop the gun."

"Stop right there, Detective!" Rose yelled. "Don't come any closer, or I'll shoot you."

When Jablonsky stood still, out of the corner of his eye he saw Daniel Grusin unobtrusively reach behind his back and take hold of a pistol he had tucked into the waistband under his shirt. Jablonsky also noticed that Ellen saw his movement; she turned slightly toward him and the chief heard her say, "Daniel, don't do anything. This is my daughter, for goodness' sake!"

Daniel clenched his jaw. "Am I the only one who gets how crazy she is? She is pointing a gun at us! Just stay behind me!" Ellen turned her attention back to Rose.

"I would never leave you, Rose. I love you with all my heart, you know that. Please drop the gun. Think of Patricia." Desperation burned in Ellen's eyes.

While Ellen pleaded with Rose, Coupe was inching closer, now almost within tackling range. Rose suddenly became aware of the movement behind her, spun around, saw

DeVille, and then, with hummingbird quickness, spun back around and fired at Daniel.

When Rose fired, Coupe took his shot; his intent was just to wound her, but Rose had been pushed backward into his bullet by the recoil of her weapon. As if in slow motion, Rose collapsed onto the pavement, the gun still grasped in her hand. For a few seconds, there was complete silence on the street.

Jablonsky moved rapidly toward the body: Coupe and Annie Lemon stood over Rose, their guns trained on her. The chief felt for a pulse.

"Everyone stand down," he commanded; the officers came out from behind their cars, holstering their firearms while murmuring relief.

Daniel was holding his left side as blood soaked through his shirt. The paramedics ran forward and helped lower him onto his back. Maria stood behind Ellen with her hand on her shoulder, their heads turning in unison as they looked across the street toward Rose's body—Jablonsky locked eyes with Ellen, and shaking his head, confirmed that she was dead.

With dilated pupils and ashen skin, Coupe forced himself to look directly at Ellen. When he lowered his head, she let out a sound as old as the human species—the loud, sustained wailing of a mother who had witnessed the death of her child —everyone cringed to hear her agony.

The work of securing the scene began. The paramedics did their job; one ambulance took Daniel and Ellen to the emergency center at the university hospital, and a second had arrived to take Rose's body to the morgue. Daniel was alert, and the medics had stopped his bleeding. Even though they believed his wound to be a through and through, there still might be bullet fragments in his body. Pictures would be needed.

Ellen, wrapped in a warming blanket to help stave off shock, sat beside him, slightly rocking back and forth. She didn't speak—her mind was whirling with the image of Rose's body lying in the street.

Bill Reeves came in person to oversee his forensics team. High-definition cameras clicked, blood particles were sealed in tubes, bits of debris were placed in baggies, all the while neighbors buzzed in anxious conversation from the safety of their porches.

Jablonksy stood with Reeves and DeVille, who, knowing the inquest that was to come, had already handed his gun to his chief. Jablonsky reassured him, "It was a righteous shoot. Almost twenty officers witnessed it. Don't worry about anything."

Coupe said, "There was no registration on Rose's .38. No one knew she had it."

Lemon searched the area across the street for Daniel's bullet. She then examined the area in front of Ellen's House. The chief walked over to her.

"You heard it too? Yeah, there was a fourth gun shot." The two continued to search; finally, Lemon called to him.

"Got it," she said, dropping a fragmented bullet into one evidence bag and two fully intact bullets into another—she handed them to a tech.

"This bullet went through Daniel and landed on the cobblestones; it's got some tissue on it. That's one. Here is the casing for the shot Daniel took at Rose. That's two. Coupe's bullet of course, remains in Rose's body. That's three. Here is where I found a fourth casing." Lemon continued her work, glad to be in on the action, rather than watching the Crown Building where Kate was.

Coupe, trying to steady his nerves after his first-ever kill, remarked, "Daniel Grusin was armed. I can't believe he fired at Rose."

Jablonsky reminded Coupe about their look at Dr. Grusin's gun registration.

"Judging from the records at the gun range, if he hadn't been hit, he could easily have taken her out. He had become a crack shot. He didn't believe Rose's mental health story, but rather felt that she was a manipulative, entitled woman who stood in the way of him marrying Ellen."

The chief grew quiet, then added, "I'm not sure Rose expected to live past trying to shoot Daniel."

"Suicide by cop?" asked Reeves.

"She must have known she would be shot by someone. We have a strong case against her. Unfortunately, we still don't know who gave the thallium poison to Lou and Big Moe—I do think that Rose hired someone to give it to the food truck guys, I'm just not convinced it was Henry," said Jablonsky. He turned to Reeves.

"Bill, someone else was here on the street and fired a gun—I need the info on all the bullets and casings ASAP."

Kate was making dinner in Marco's now fully stocked kitchen when she saw the news coverage of the shooting at Dr. Smythe's house.

"Johnny! Come look at this."

Johnny hurried in from the terrace where he had been arranging potholders and tongs on the shelf of Marco's never-been-used gas grill.

"Rose Delaney has been shot and killed while she was trying to shoot Dr. Grusin. A neighbor caught everything on their phone." Kate gaped at the TV.

The two friends watched in horror as Jablonsky, DeVille, Lemon, Ellen, Maria, and Daniel were all in harm's way, trying to control the armed confrontation. Luckily, the news producer had the sensitivity to refrain from showing Rose fall from DeVille's bullet.

"I hope that won't be me," Kate quietly remarked.

"As my mother would have said, 'Oh go on with ya.' Nothing is going to happen to you. You are secure here." Johnny stared at Kate in earnest, as if he could will it to be true.

Kate apologized when she saw how upset Johnny was by her spontaneous comment.

But it could be true. I might well be shot and some stranger will photograph it and post it to social media. What an ignominious end that would be.

Trying to be positive, she quoted The Beatles, "With a Little Help From My Friends" to Johnny. She shook off her fears and returned to cooking.

Staying at Marco's was ambiguously a respite and a confinement. Kate saw her advisees through Zoom, emailed her reports to the office, and worked out in the condo's facilities, trying not to create observable routines. The last part was almost impossible since all exercise is constructed around routines; lapping in the pool helped her bind her frustration at being cooped-up. At least she could walk to the local grocery, which she did daily, but always accompanied by one of her assigned security officers.

Johnny, on the other hand, loved staying at Marco's. He busied himself with getting some publishable articles going, and he used Marco's high-tech television to take virtual tours of the world's greatest museums. To honor the recently deceased Pittsburgh artist Ahmad Jamal, jazz became the musical backdrop to this time of captivity.

He was free to come and go, but Johnny chose not to, afraid he would be followed. Kate marveled at how he created such a rich, artistic world for himself, speculating that he had learned that skill as a young gay teen living with his abusive father in their working-class neighborhood—survival necessitated creating his own sanctuary.

As she shaped the hamburger patties, her mind drifted away from her own troubles to Ellen. Kate knew better than to try and telephone her; the police would be busy with interviewing everyone—and she would have to formally identify Rose's body.

Tears unexpectedly filled her eyes. Kate's recent loss of Eddie made her uncomfortably empathetic to grief. She wiped her hands, then reached up to touch the emerald engagement ring he had given her, now hanging on a chain around her neck.

Suddenly she was overcome with the urge to take it off— she uncoupled the clasp and held the chain and ring in her hand, not sure what to do next. Finally, she placed them in a small jewelry box in her bedroom.

Recently, the feel and sight of the engagement ring had begun to amplify her emotional response to all the events happening around and to her: the unknown rushing toward her, her grief, now Ellen's dramatic loss of her daughter, the murder of Celine Arceneau, and Liam O'Hara still being on the loose—everything was weighty and stark. Sometimes she felt like she wanted to jump right out of her skin.

"What's going on, Kate?" Johnny had quietly walked in from the balcony. "Everything okay with you?"

"No. But I don't want to go on about it. Help me finish dinner."

The house smelled of summer when Marco arrived from the hospital. The sliding doors were open and the breeze from the rivers pulled through the rooms, carrying the tantalizing odor of grilling food. Kate surmised that bustling activity in his condo was new to him; his face held the wondrous look of a small child who had captured a firefly in a bottle.

Marco sat at the kitchen island watching closely as Kate constructed her summer salad: quartered pieces of English cucumber and cherry tomatoes, strawberries and watermelon, pieces of ripe avocado, and a few chopped pecans, all placed over red leaf butter lettuce and drizzled with a balsamic vinegar reduction. Perhaps it was Kate's knife skills that held the surgeon's rapt attention, or just the pleasure of watching the woman with whom he was falling in love.

Johnny had streamed the old video of Michael Jackson's "Thriller," and enticed Kate out from the kitchen to learn the moves. From the corner of her eye, she noticed Marco enjoying their sibling-like antics; he joined in with hoots of laughter and a few "OMGs," but no active participation. Marco had never cavorted in his life.

When the video was over and Kate had returned to finishing dinner, he remarked, "Rosalie would have loved that." His simple declaration made Kate realize how much he still missed his older sister and brother. Kate and Johnny were each other's chosen siblings, but for better or worse, that relationship was different than that of a blood sibling.

She understood that Marco's brilliance had relegated him to the sidelines interpersonally. In middle school, he was taking high school classes, so his same age classmates weren't really his mates—nor were the teens who were in those high school classes.

As an adult, Marco was liked and respected, but as a youngster and teen, he was viewed as alien, weird. When his two older siblings went missing, he became an "only"; having been an "only" herself, she empathized. She hoped her and Johnny's animated relationship might act as wall spackle in the cracks of his missing experiences.

Kate had also noted that Marco closely observed how she and Johnny lived; for example, they always set the table for everyday meals—placemats, napkins, the correct flatware, water glasses, wine glasses, condiments in tiny bowls instead of the bottles on the table, fresh flowers in a vase. It was a style of living that Marco appreciated, but never had created for himself.

The dinner menu was simple: hamburgers with the fixins, her summer salad, and homemade pineapple upside down cake. It was cold beer in frosted mugs for Kate and Johnny, but not for Marco. Like Joan, he refrained from drinking on work nights.

The topic of conversation over dinner was the death of Rose Delaney, Daniel Grusin's recovery, and Ellen.

"I didn't know her daughter, but I do know it's a life-changing loss for Ellen. I saw that change with my own parents when my siblings were missing. The news report implied that there is more to this story than an unstable daughter gone over the edge," remarked Marco. Kate and Johnny exchanged glances but didn't offer any information.

After Marco and Johnny cleared the table and loaded the dish washer, they all proceeded with their coffee and cake to the deck, drinking in the glorious view of the city and the shimmering waters of the three rivers. Kate watched Marco sink into his chaise lounge with a sigh, the deep facial lines carved by his daily life-and-death responsibilities softened in relaxation.

When Johnny excused himself to work at the computer, the two remained on the balcony, talking about the vicissitudes of growing up: his medical school, her doctoral program, his mother, her grandfather, his work in Ukraine, her worries for Ellen.

Marco hadn't, and wouldn't, approach her; Kate knew that since her time at the condo wasn't volitional, he would consider physical advances bad form. He was an old-fashioned gentleman who lived by certain standards, and his restraint felt mature to her.

Smack dab in the midst of murders and manhunts, a romance bloomed between them. The constraints of her confinement dictated that none of the usual rituals of courtship occurred: a first dress-up date, an athletic date, a movie date, a necking date, a sex date.

Instead, it was like being friends in an apartment building where after work, everyone was in sweatpants and tees, hanging together on tiny side porches sipping wine and listening to a playlist. As friendship moved toward love, Kate felt her frozen heart begin to thaw.

When getting ready for bed, she found a romantic haiku on her pillow. In a teenage girl moment, Kate kissed the paper, then put it in her jewelry box for safe keeping.

CHAPTER 27

Daniel Grusin was settled in one of the hospital's private rooms. Ellen sat close to the bed, silent; she looked frail, her large gray eyes made even more luminous by periodic tears.

Several physicians had stopped by to support the two well-known colleagues. Beyond "how are you feeling?" no one knew what else to say in the face of the bizarre and devastating circumstances.

Elise Rosen had arrived and was shocked to see two officers accompanying Jablonsky into the hospital room. "These men will guard the room," was all he offered Ms. Rosen, who departed in puzzlement.

"How's the wound, Daniel?" Jablonsky asked, sitting down and pulling out his notebook. "Are you up to giving me a statement?"

Daniel made light of the wound, even though his hands shook as he settled the bedsheets. "They did a CT of the area and didn't see any bullet fragments—I think I'm okay."

"Tell me about the events leading up to the shooting," requested Jablonsky.

"Ellen and I were at her house having breakfast with

Maria. It seems like that was eons ago, not just hours. Well, Rose showed up, stood outside, and shouted for me to come out. I didn't know she had a gun, so we all went out onto the porch. You know the rest."

At hearing Rose's name, Ellen excused herself and went out into the hall. She had called Patricia when she and Daniel were in the ambulance. Right now, it was all she could do to keep herself from screaming. Although Coupe's deadly shot had temporarily deconstructed Ellen's sense of self, she knew that seeing her granddaughter would stop her from losing her mind altogether.

"As you know," Daniel continued, lowering his voice, "I felt all along that Rose was dangerous. I've had a registered gun for several years, and at the time I bought it, I took some lessons on how to use it. I had the idea that Rose would never let Ellen remain with me—that she might kill her, and perhaps me, rather than allow us to marry. I'm glad I had the gun with me." Considering he had just been shot, Daniel's responses were remarkably calm.

You think you are home free, thought Jablonsky.

"We were aware that you had registered a gun, as well as how often you went to the practice range; you've become quite a good shot. Was it your intention to kill Rose today?" asked the chief.

There was a slight smugness that momentarily pulled down the corners of Daniel's lips, quickly replaced by the look of feigned shock.

"What are you talking about, Chief Detective? If you hadn't noticed, I'm the one who was shot. All your people saw her try to kill me."

"That's correct, everyone saw that you had been shot. That scene was a fortunate turn of events for you, wasn't it, Dr. Grusin? While you have been steadily casting Rose as an unstable lunatic, we have been checking into your own background. I'm here to arrest you for the murder of Peter Smythe." Jablonsky motioned to the two officers.

"Peter Smythe? What are you talking about!" shouted Daniel. For a few seconds, the chief glimpsed the angry, resentful young doctor who had lost Ellen to the older, wealthy Peter.

Daniel looked up and saw Ellen standing in the doorway. "Daniel, what is he talking about?"

"Before your so-called serendipitous reconnection with Ellen at the conference in Florida, you had been actively interviewing with various practices here in Pittsburgh; we have all those dates. During those interviews, you found out two things —that Peter was dying and the hospice where he was a patient. We have witnesses that place you at his hospice late in the day of his death. Come on, Daniel, you hated him for years, and you were tired of waiting for Ellen to be free." Jablonsky paused.

"Dr. Grusin, why don't you tell the rest of the story?"

Daniel stared down at the sheets. He reached over to the patient table and pulled out an antiseptic wipe from its container, using it to clean his hands. Slowly he raised his head and locked eyes with Ellen.

"I've loved you since I was twenty years old." Daniel's throat closed up, and he started to choke.

"Get ahold of yourself, man," chided Jablonsky. "Out with it."

"Yes, I murdered that old, corrupt, worthless shell of a dying man." Daniel found his voice again, and like a pack of wolves jostling at a fresh kill, his words tumbled over each other as he told his story.

"I went to the hospice in my white coat, and the people at the desk checked my hospital badge and let me in. I went into Peter's room and closed the door; he opened his eyes and stared at me. I said my name, then jabbed a needle loaded with a lethal dose of morphine into his boney ass. He was already on comfort measures—I just made him, well, more comfortable." His sarcasm ricocheted around the room like an ice-bullet, chilling everyone.

Daniel suddenly tried to get out of the bed, attempting to rip out his IV line. He began to beg.

"Ellen, I did it for you. I did it for us! You were free to have a life again. It wasn't really murder. He was almost dead anyway."

Daniel's theatrics reminded Jablonsky of his last interview with Rose. *Maybe they weren't so different,* pondered the chief.

Ellen hadn't moved from the doorway. She repeated Daniel's words, drawing them out to emphasize the level of his depravity.

"He was . . . almost . . . dead . . . anyway?" Her whole body contracted inward with revulsion. She slowly straightened, and with no histrionics or recriminations, turned, walked out of the room, and out of Daniel Grusin's life.

Jablonsky closed his notebook and stood.

"Daniel Grusin, you have confessed to the first-degree murder of Peter Smythe. Guards will remain posted outside your room until you are physically able to be processed for your crime."

Ellen leaned against the wall in the hallway, looking like she might collapse—who could blame her? Within a matter of weeks, her life had fallen apart. Jablonsky softened his posture and his words as he approached her.

"I'm so sorry to remind you that you will have to identify Rose's body. Dr. Patel will arrange the identification for any time that suits you."

"Thank you, Chief. Right now, I'm waiting for Patricia. She will want to see her mother." At the word "mother," she covered her face with her hands, moaning softly.

Patricia was hurrying down the hall in her Dansko clogs as

Jablonsky was leaving. Not yet aware that Daniel Grusin had murdered her grandfather, and had tried to murder her mother, she stopped and quickly gave a report.

"I just checked with Daniel's physician, who said that he will be fine—the bullet moved through his side missing any of the vital organs. How is my grandma?" Patricia asked.

Jablonsky looked at her intently, surprised by her collected demeanor.

"Your grandmother is waiting for you; your presence will be the medicine she needs right now. I want to say how very sorry I am about the loss of your mother. The situation gave us no choice."

The genuine fatherly kindness in his tone cracked her public facade. She momentarily lost her balance—Jablonsky reached out to steady her, and without any awkwardness, Patricia rested her head against his broad chest and wept. The hospital staff let them alone for a few minutes, then they helped the chief guide her further down the hallway into her grandmother's waiting arms.

On his way to the morgue, Jablonsky thought about Patricia, who was around the same age as his Carly and had carried the heavy emotional burden of her mother. It was her maturity that had pushed aside the irony that she had been comforted by the very detective who had ordered her mother shot.

Jablonsky knew from experience that many would say Patricia's wealth and privilege balanced the scales of her burdens, but he also knew that money alone never corrected the emotional cost to a child raised by an unbalanced parent —which Rose surely was. The triptych of therapy, time, and love was necessary to heal those wounds.

Walking along the dimly lit hallway, Jablonsky's mood, typically upbeat when he was about to see Dr. Patel, was

subdued, even melancholy. He entered the morgue quietly—
Dr. Patel was at one of the microscopes.

"Stefan!" Aashi immediately read his mood and in a
lowered voice said, "What a sad day this is. Come, the body is
over here."

She lifted the sheet to reveal Rose's barely dead corpse.
"She looks at peace, doesn't she?" remarked Aashi.

Carefully raising Rose's head, she pointed to the entry and
exit wound."

"Detective DeVille was hoping to just wound her, but the
kickback from her pistol pushed her backward into this
bullet." Jablonsky sadly stated the details of the shot.

"She died instantly. There was no suffering. Is Ellen
coming for the formal identification?" asked Dr. Patel.

"Yes. She will come with her granddaughter, Patricia.
And, just so you know, we arrested Dr. Daniel Grusin for the
murder of Peter Smythe," said the chief.

At Aashi's startled look, Jablonsky said he would tell her
the whole story later.

The chief was glad when she placed the sheet back over
Rose's face. He had viewed countless bodies in his long tenure,
but seeing Rose's still pale-pink, lifeless body on the slab, when
she had been so madly alive just a few hours ago, stung him.
His team had shot her, and he would, and could, live with that
fact, but he didn't want to continue looking at her young, fresh
corpse.

Dr. Patel moved back to her microscope and searched
around beside it. "Ah, here it is. This is the bullet that Detective DeVille fired. Do you want it, or should I send it directly
to Bill Reeves?"

"I'll take it. I need to see Reeves anyhow. There was a
fourth gun fired at the scene; we are hoping to identify it by
the bullet." Jablonsky stood there staring at the evidence bag
in his hand.

In an uncharacteristically personal response to his mood,

Aashi remarked, "I understand there was quite a wrangle outside Ellen's house. I'd like to hear about it if you care to tell me. Drinks and dinner?"

Jablonsky was taken aback by this generous offer. He attributed it to her kindness and decency, but whatever had moved her to make the offer, he was accepting it. This was a happy step beyond their breakfast meetings.

"Text me where and when, and I'll be there." Walking back through that dimly lit hall, he unwrapped a piece of cinnamon gum, and with profound need, chewed it.

Ellen and Patricia arrived at the morgue along with Maria, who had wanted to accompany them for the formal identification. Maria drove so that Patricia and Ellen didn't have to focus on anything other than this first step into the reality of Rose's death.

Dr. Patel met them. "Do you want to see her through the viewing window or in the morgue?" she asked. "I know you and Patricia are physicians and used to death, but this is different."

"We want to come in." Dr. Patel had warned her staff that Dr. Smythe might want to touch and spend time with her daughter; everyone busied themselves, giving the grieving mother and granddaughter their private space.

Dr. Patel led them to the table, then slowly drew back the sheet, gently tucking it around Rose's shoulders.

"Dios mio! She looks like she is sleeping," uttered a shocked Maria, who flushed, then stepped back behind Ellen and Patricia, wiping her face with a lacy, starched handkerchief.

Ellen leaned over and moved a few strands of hair away from her daughter's face. "My beautiful little rosebud," she whispered.

As if she were in front of a firing squad, Patricia stood frozen, her eyes wide and filled with fear.

"It's okay, Patricia. Say your goodbyes, honey." With that urging, Patricia leaned over Rose, laid her forehead on the sheet, and cried out her heartbreak. Even seasoned Dr. Patel sighed deeply, lowering her head in deep human empathy.

Their farewells were long, but Dr. Patel didn't hurry anyone; she was the kind of medical examiner who respected and advocated for the dead and their families. When they turned to go, Maria stayed behind to cut a small bit of Rose's hair.

"A memento for Miss Ellen," she whispered to Dr. Patel, whose own culture sometimes did the same.

CHAPTER 28

DEVILLE AND HIS OFFICERS HAD SURROUNDED THE APARTMENT building in the Strip that they had been casing for some time. They entered, showing their badges to the manager at the desk. DeVille sent a few officers to the back of the building, two remained in the lobby, and two went to the underground garage. Coupe rode the elevator to the third floor, then pulled his gun and cautiously walked down the corridor.

"Jake Albert! This is the police, open the door! We just want to question you, come out now!" They waited a few seconds, then kicked in the door. They searched each room, calling "clear!" as they went.

Coupe spoke rapidly into the walkie-talkie. "He's not here. Looks like he took some of his belongings—he's going to run. He might be on the way to the garage. Heads up everyone!"

Coupe and his guys ran to the elevator, the outside officers sprinted to the driveway that led to the garage. They heard squealing tires and saw a black Dodge Challenger SXT come barreling up the grade, crashing through the boom barrier; everyone jumped to the side to avoid being hit.

DeVille immediately reported the car and within minutes, black-and-whites blew past the building in pursuit of Albert.

Penn Avenue, the main road in the Strip, was packed with traffic and pedestrian shoppers. The Charger wove in and out, staying on Penn.

"He's heading to the Sixteenth Street Bridge to cross over to Route 28. That will get him on open highway," yelled Detective DeVille, communicating with the lead car.

"Don't worry, Coupe. We'll cut him off before he gets there," was the confident reply. As if by magic, two police vehicles had gotten to the bridge before Jake Albert, who spun into a one-eighty when he saw the blockade; he remained seated in the still-running car.

DeVille had arrived on the scene and, with all the other officers, waited to see what Jake was going to do. Coupe finally stepped forward, shouting, "Get out of the car, Jake! You are surrounded. No one wants to shoot you. Open the door, put your hands out first, then your legs, and remain standing."

Jake Albert did as he was told: he scooted himself out of the car, raised his hands, eyed the officers who were about ten feet away from him on either side, then like a jack rabbit, he suddenly leaped up and rolled over the hood of his car, sprinted to the bridge, and jumped.

"Holy crap. We've got a leaper!" screamed Coupe. "He's a triathlete, he's a strong swimmer. . . . Call the river police, he might survive this fall and make it to the other side."

Jablonsky will never let me live this down, he thought as he hotfooted it to the bridge, leaning over the railing, scouring the waters of the Allegheny for any sign of Jake Albert.

The river police came flying toward the bridge at full speed, slowed, then dumped two divers into the water while the boat decelerated to a full stop. The regular police had crawled down the steep slope to the river's edge, watching the water with military grade binoculars.

Coupe believed that Jake survived the jump and swam under the bridge to hide behind the giant cement pillars, where he could catch his breath. He called to his men to center their search on those pillars, also asking the divers to do the same.

"There he is!" shouted one of the divers. Before they could get to him, Jake dove under and didn't surface until he was on the other bank of the river.

He scrambled to dry land, made it to the railroad tracks that ran alongside the river, and even after all that physical effort, he still had enough in the tank to begin a measured run. Several officers jumped back into their cars and drove over the bridge, hoping to cut off Jake's escape.

"Don't shoot him! I want him alive," commanded DeVille.

Officers from other precincts began to arrive and swarmed down to the tracks. Jake suddenly disappeared into a large drainage tunnel that went under the road—he emerged on the other side of Route 28. The police stopped all the traffic on the four-lane highway; curious drivers got out of their car to watch the action.

"He's heading up the hillside. Shoot above his head and warn him!" shouted an almost hoarse DeVille.

Jake's magnificent escape ended when he lost his footing on the hillside, unceremoniously sliding on his butt down to the road.

"We got him!" The police cuffed him and put him in the back of one of the city police cars. The river police tooted their loud foghorns and the men cheered; Jake Albert took the prize as the most slippery and amazingly fit perpetrator the police had ever seen. There would be many embroidered stories told about this "almost" great escape.

"Take him to the hospital. Jablonsky and I will see him there." DeVille was pumped.

Coupe stared at his cell phone, took a deep breath, and called the chief; he started with the good news, then gave a brief description of the chase.

"He what? He jumped off the Sixteenth Street Bridge? And how did it happen that he was able to get to the bridge?

Jeez o'man, Coupe. How many city resources did it take to catch him after you all let him slip through your fingers? I'll meet you at the hospital."

For all his bluster, the chief was happy they nabbed him, but he wasn't going to tell Coupe that—not just yet.

A very badly bruised Jake sat upright in his hospital bed. The emergency physicians decided to keep him to rule out any concussion from the jump. Large purple contusions were beginning to form on his arms and legs. He had a long cut on the side of his face, already cleaned and sutured.

In a configuration reminiscent of the recent interview with Daniel Grusin, Jablonsky pulled a chair close to the bed, and DeVille slouched like a cowboy against the wall. Two officers sat outside the room; there would be no more escape attempts.

"Mr. Albert. I understand you have been Mirandized, but refused counsel? Yes? That is your right. Now, when did your affair with Rose Delaney begin?" the chief asked, cutting right to the heart of the matter.

"It started several years ago," was Jake's clipped answer.

"Tell me the story," ordered Jablonsky.

Jake took a drink of water, wincing at having to move. "I met Rose at Dr. Smythe's office. She frequently stopped in to see her mother."

"And?"

"And, at first she treated me like the help. Over time she saw how much I respected her mother, and she would kibitz with me. Finally, I asked her out." Jake winced.

"And?" The chief wanted details.

"And, we fell in love." At that declaration, Jake looked defiantly at Jablonsky. "We fell in love and remained in love."

"Was your apartment in the Strip District the secret meeting place?" asked Jablonsky.

"Yes. We spent time there together. We did the things every couple does: cook, watch television, see movies, make love." Once again, Jake's look was defiant.

Jablonsky understood that Jake was trying to normalize the relationship—was it for himself or for the chief?

"A normal, loving relationship. You did things together that other couples do. Except for the part about planning the murder of Celine Arceneau. That's not really so normal, now is it, Jake?" The chief pulled out the gift box that Rose had left in her bedroom, placing it on the hospital bed, but not addressing it.

"Why all the secrecy?" continued Jablonsky.

"That was Rose's call. And, well, Dr. Smythe is also a very private person. I didn't want to bring my outside life into the office."

The women in this family—privacy was always code for secrecy, thought the chief. *As Kate would say, everyone is lying about something all the time. Here it's the Smythe women, and even their lovers.*

"When did Rose begin to talk to you about Celine?" asked Jablonsky.

"It was after the first time Celine came to the practice. I never spoke about patients with Rose, but somehow, she already knew about her. I didn't know where she got the information. Sometime after that, she told me the story of her father and Celine's mother. Her dad had told her about the half-sister when he was dying." Jake ran his hands over his neatly clipped hair; his breathing was labored and heavy with fatigue.

It struck Jablonsky that the young man could barely sit upright. *This is more than the effects from the jump. This guy feels guilt. He knew what he was agreeing to was murder.* It was rare that Jablonsky had someone on the other side of the metaphorical table who was troubled by a conscience.

"At what point did you agree to help Rose kill Celine?" asked Jablonsky.

"There was no one moment, it just . . . evolved. Look, Rose was a special person, she needed a lot of love and attention. She didn't like me at first simply because Ellen did— everyone in her life became competition for either her dad's affection or her mom's," said Jake.

"Is that what broke up her marriage? Was her husband 'competition'?" asked Jablonsky sardonically.

Jake looked directly at Jablonsky with his bloodshot eyes.

"Yes. Rose told me that Ellen really liked and admired her husband. Rose resented that. Plus, her husband didn't like Peter." From various kinds of pain, Jake's jaw clenched and unclenched.

"Celine was heading back to Canada. In what way would she be a threat to Rose?" queried Jablonsky.

"In my mind, Celine wasn't a threat, but Rose felt she was. I tried to help her see another side of the situation, but she wanted her gone—not just gone to Montreal, but really gone."

Jablonsky could hear the struggle between Jake's conscience and his fear that he would lose Rose if he said no to her.

"Was it you or Rose who decided to sicken everyone by coating the greens with bacteria in order to hide the intended murder?" asked Jablonsky.

"You have to understand that at first, it was just a conversation between us. She would say things about how easy it would be to hide a murder in the middle of a group of people getting sick. Rose called it an Agatha plot—like in an Agatha Christie novel. She made a joke about it." Jake was visibly shaking now.

"Some joke. Go on," said the chief.

"Rose had started taking cooking lessons at the bistro because she had ferreted out that it was the place where Celine's farewell dinner would be held. She talked to Henry about the menu, how many people would be there . . . things like that."

Jake shifted in the bed, flexing his arms and hands, trying to relieve the pain of the trauma to his tendons and muscles. The chief saw that Jake was aware of how his statement sounded—his life was like toilet water, ready to be flushed away.

"Continue," prompted the chief.

"On my morning runs, I started passing the bistro. The produce delivery trucks arrived like clockwork in the alley, then the guys would go in and have coffee with George. Henry was already there, cooking. I knew the routine," Jake stated.

"Tell me about the bacteria, the Bacillus cereus."

"So, the box of arugula was still on the truck. I coated the greens with it—I was done in a minute." Bizarrely, Jake downplayed his quick, cool nerve in the situation.

"Where did you get the stuff?" asked Jablonsky.

"I'm not going to tell you that. I'm not implicating anyone else. I got it, I put it on the greens, I helped sicken those diners," Jake said.

"If you had stood up to Rose the same way you just stood up to me, your life wouldn't be over," remarked a frustrated Jablonsky; he hated waste.

"We know why Celine became sicker than the others. When did you and Rose decide to start poisoning her with thallium?"

All the blood seemed to drain from Jake's face; the slash stood out in its angry redness. He quietly repeated the name of the poison. "Yes, the thallium acetate."

"As a physician assistant, you understand that poisoning someone with thallium produces suffering—at sublethal doses, it makes a person suffer, Jake. They suffer *before* they die," said Jablonsky.

"You don't understand how persuasive Rose could be.

And, she greased palms freely. People around town knew about her and her, um, generosity." Jake grimaced.

"You're talking about the men at the food truck, Lou Christie and Big Moe?" prompted Jablonsky.

"Rose knew Celine's daily routine. She told me about how Celine stopped at the truck for an espresso," admitted Jake.

"Was the thallium stored at the Smythe house in Summit Park?" asked the chief.

"Yes. We went there often—sometimes alone, sometimes with friends. Henry and a few of my training buddies went in the spring—that's when she showed me her father's stash hidden in the stables. She figured if she offered Big Moe or Lou enough money, they would sprinkle it in Celine's coffee." Jake stopped.

"Rose told me—and I'm not sure I believe this—that Peter's last words to her were, 'Get rid of that Canadian bitch.'"

Coupe and Jablonsky exchanged a look filled with revulsion. Jablonsky had seen and heard of many perverse relationships between fathers and daughters, but this was on a new level.

Jablonsky leaned forward. "There is something you aren't telling me. Something important. The more cooperative you are, well, it might be to your benefit at sentencing."

Shockingly, tears began to slowly course down Jake's cheeks.

The tears repulsed the chief. "Come off it, Jake. Take responsibility for the decisions that you made. What are you holding back?"

"Rose wanted to be the one to approach the men at the food truck. I—I—I talked her out of it. I didn't want her to be connected to the poison, so I insisted that I would set it up."

Jablonsky couldn't resist a moral lecture.

"Mr. Albert. You are a young man who has the second half of his life yet to live. You have a profession with a code of ethics, you have respect from colleagues, you are a triathlete—why would you agree to help Rose murder a woman who was, in reality, no threat to her? Not just murder her, but *make her suffer?*" asked Jablonsky.

"Man, don't you think I've asked myself that question over and over?" Jake rubbed his eyes, as if trying to wipe away the mysterious film that had blinded him to the truth of his choices.

"I'd never met anyone like Rose. I loved her, I loved her beyond reason."

Jablonsky drank deeply from his water bottle, trying to wash away the foul taste of Jake's weakness and the betrayal of his professional code of ethics—something that the chief despised in his own profession.

"Let's turn to the morning that Rose was shot. How did you know that Daniel Grusin had a gun?" asked Jablonsky.

"I have friends who spend time at the shooting range. They told me about Daniel, what a marksman he had become. Rose never actually told me that she planned to kill him, but once she found out about his relationship with her mother, I knew she wasn't going to let him live." Jake hung his head, perhaps in guilt.

"You knew Daniel had a gun, you knew Rose was planning to kill him, so why not call the police?" Jablonsky couldn't believe this guy's cascading stream of bad-to-worse decisions.

"Okay! I get your point. I made stupid choices—and I'm going to pay for them!" shouted Jake, showing the first anger of the interview.

"After Celine was dead, I realized that my love would never have been enough for Rose, just like her first husband's wasn't enough—Rose only wanted her mother," Jake said bitterly.

"That's a lot of psychology, Jake. Here's what I'm hearing:

you were crazy about a crazy woman and became a criminal because of it," stated the chief.

Jake slowly exhaled while his fingers gripped the railings around his bed. "I loved her so much. When I was with her, the rest of the world disappeared. It was like endlessly coursing down a water slide, exhilarating and scary."

"You could have gone to a water park for that," said Jablonsky sarcastically. "Now, you stated that you knew Rose intended to shoot Daniel Grusin."

"Yes."

"When you showed up with a gun at Dr. Smythe's house, who did you intend to shoot?" asked Jablonsky.

Jake's face twisted into a tortured roadmap of pain; he broke down completely, covering his face and sobbing.

It took all the chief's strength not to roll his eyes. "I'm asking again. Who did you intend on killing?"

"Rose!" screamed Jake. "I was going to kill Rose because loving her was killing me! Rose, Rose, Rose! I meant to shoot Rose."

"I see. Rose would shoot Daniel Grusin, and you would shoot her. Jake, my detectives were under orders to fire if she tried to kill her mother or Daniel. You didn't kill her," Jablonsky stated.

Jake stared at the chief, as if his words had no meaning. "What are you saying?"

"You didn't kill her. Rose shot Daniel Grusin. Detective DeVille shot Rose—your bullet didn't hit anyone." Jablonsky took no pleasure in his statement.

Nothing moved in the hospital room: not a muscle, not an eye blink, not an intake of breath. Then, Jake suddenly started to shake, his limbs and torso jerked as if he was convulsing from a high fever.

Jablonsky put his hands on the young man's legs. "You're okay. You are just having a reaction to the news. Take some deep breaths."

Minutes passed. When Jake's autonomic reaction settled down, Jablonsky slid the gift box over to him. "Rose left this for you. Open it."

Jake wiped his face and, with still shaking hands, unwrapped and opened the box. He lifted out a wristwatch. It was a Påtek Philippe; the engraved sentiment read, *To mark our sweet hours.* There was also a tiny engraved rose at the end of the sentence.

Jake touched the engraving with his finger, then slid it back to the chief.

"This is evidence. You will get it back—at some point." Jablonsky stood up, and Coupe moved forward to stand beside him.

"Jake Albert. I am arresting you as a co-conspirator in the murder of Celine Arceneau. I'm also arresting you for the attempted murder of Rose Delaney."

Jablonsky zipped the watch into an evidence bag, pulled out a stick of cinnamon gum, and walked out of the room and down the hall with Coupe, who couldn't resist a quip.

"I kept hearing Percy Sledge's song, 'When a Man Loves a Woman.'"

"How does a youngster like you know Percy Sledge? But you're right on target with its sentiment—he couldn't see just how bad she was. To him, she could do no wrong." Jablonsky shook his head.

"That water slide dropped him right into a shark tank, didn't it, Chief? Were you ever in love like that?" Coupe asked.

"Are you asking me about my personal business, Detective?" Coupe buttoned his lip, and the two men headed back to the precinct, each silently reminiscing about their own first crazy-in-love infatuations.

CHAPTER 29

Jablonsky gave a brief statement to the press, naming Jake Albert and Rose Delaney as co-conspirators in the death of Celine Arceneau. Rose Delaney, now deceased, had also attempted to murder Dr. Daniel Grusin.

Additionally, Dr. Daniel Grusin was charged with the first-degree murder of Peter Smythe.

The missing thallium was finally traced to one of Canada's small nuclear plants that produced radiopharmaceutical material; the regulatory agencies had done their job.

The person responsible for stealing the thallium was never identified, but it was noted that Peter Smythe's firm represented the Pittsburgh manufacturer who built parts and tools for that plant. The Canadian press had a field day with suppositions and speculations, none of which could be proved.

The news reports on social media used a blackboard diagram so that readers could follow the interlocking relationships of all the attorneys, physicians, lovers, and adult children involved in the case.

Out of Jablonsky's earshot, Johnny irreverently remarked to Coupe, "It's like Carrie Fisher's diagram of her famous parents and Hollywood celebrities from her HBO special 'Wishful Drinking.'"

The chief brought Ellen into his office for a debriefing of sorts, where he presented the details of Jake Albert's involvement in the poisoning of the bistro diners and of Celine Arceneau. He also told her that Jake had gone to the scene planning to kill Rose, whom he had "loved beyond reason."

"I had no idea that Jake and Rose were a couple. They kept it completely hidden from me. I guess I was doing the same with Daniel."

Ellen grew quiet, then added, "Maybe Daniel loved me 'beyond reason.' I've made some lousy choices of men, haven't I?"

The chief completely agreed about her lousy choices of men. He had decided not to bring charges of obstruction or lying to the police against Ellen; the loss of her daughter and Daniel's betrayal seemed enough. The chief was wise as to which battles with the law and the community he would pick.

Privately, his assessment was that Ellen and Patricia would be fine eventually. They'd have each other to lean on while they sorted through the trauma of their shared loss.

After Ellen left, he walked out to the bullpen where everyone was celebrating the closure of the Arceneau case. Jablonsky gave them their due, then invited Coupe and Lemon into his office for the ritual toast with some Jameson Black.

Lemon couldn't stay long as she was needed back at the Crown Building for security watch over Kate. The three talked about Liam O'Hara, who was still on the run.

"This man disappeared once before for years, and now everyone fears he has done it again," remarked Coupe. "There were no leaks to the press as to what exactly he was wanted for, just that he was armed and dangerous."

Jablonsky decided it was time for him to take Kate's found love letters to her at Marco's condo.

Jablonsky rode the private elevator to Marco's four-thousand-square-foot apartment in the sky. He was greeted with a head-butt from Bourbon Ball, who then sniffed his crotch for identification, then his pockets, searching for treats. With dogs around, there simply was no dignity.

Kate was busy in the guest bedroom working at her computer. Johnny had his laptop open on the dining room table with a stack of art books beside it; he was busy filling a legal-size paper tablet with notes Johnny had switched from listening to Ahmed Jamal to the band Pink Martini.

"John, doesn't look like you are having much of a vacation here, but I do like your choice of music. My daughter listens to that group," said Jablonsky.

"It is so easy to get articles written when there are no distractions! I'm taking advantage of being in this beautiful place. Kate, on the other hand, does nothing but see her clients on Zoom, work out, and play with Bourbon Ball. She does, however, do the cooking." Kate walked in from the back bedroom and chided Johnny.

"Thanks for that, buddy boy. Speaking of cooking, we've made some lunch for everyone—eat-in for us, and takeout for the detectives. I'll finish getting that together while Johnny shows you the rest of the condo."

Jablonsky laid the manila envelope with her letters on the dining room table, then followed Johnny for the tour. In Marco's study, the chief's detective eye spied a note pad on which poems in various states of completion were scribbled. One read:

> *deep, far reaching roots*
> *entangle 'neath the surface*
> *lovers truly tied.*

He exchanged a knowing look with Johnny, who remarked that Marco was writing poetry for Kate. "He has it bad for our girl." The two men ended the tour on the deck in companionable silence.

Kate watched the chief with Johnny, knowing how much it meant to this gay professor of art history that Jablonsky trusted him to help secure her safety. She knew that he had never had a strong paternal figure who liked and trusted him; Jablonsky meant a great deal to him.

Back inside, they found the dining room table ready to be set for lunch. Johnny took the cue, removed his computer and books, and finished readying the table. He put on another album from Pink Martini.

Kate had steamed Silver Queen corn on the cob, grilled locally-made kielbasa with sweet onions, in honor of the chief, and tossed a fresh green salad with tomato vinaigrette. There was home-brewed iced tea with mint, but today, no dessert.

In between bites of delicious kielbasa, Jablonsky reported on the hundreds of tips the police were receiving and the ongoing canvassing of the city neighborhoods for Liam O'Hara.

Watching her as they ate, Jablonsky noticed that although she had lost weight, Kate's face showed less strain than the last time he saw her at the precinct. Dressed in black yoga pants and a Pittsburgh Pirates T-shirt, with her glossy, black hair pulled up into a simple ponytail, she could have been a college girl. After Johnny cleared the table, the chief slid the envelope with the letters across the table to her.

"Here are your letters. Take a look at them now, and then I'll take them back with me." Jablonsky left the condo to talk with his detectives, followed by Johnny, who was delivering lunch to Lemon and the other officers.

The room was flooded with afternoon sunlight. Bourbon Ball dozed under the table. It was an atmosphere conducive for remembering. Kate sat holding the manila envelope, but she didn't open it. Instead, she propped her chin with cupped hands and thought about Eddie.

Kate didn't keep a journal; she was so private about her inner life that she feared someone would find it. Since his death, she didn't know what to do with the memories of Eddie, so she had taken to writing down some of her most vivid images on small pieces of paper, and then burning them. Today she wrote:

My life so far has been cut into segments—life with my parents,

life without them. Life with my grandfather, life without him. Life with

Eddie, life without him. What will be next?

She lit the slip of paper on fire and watched it burn as the breeze from the balcony scattered the ashes. Strangely, she felt so light and energized that she decided to change into a swimsuit and work off her lunch in the water. She alerted Detective Lemon that she was heading to the pool.

Kate, Detective Lemon, and Bourbon Ball rode the elevator down to the lower level of the building. BB was now quite familiar with the lap pool—he jumped up onto one of the lounge chairs and pretended to close his dark chocolate eyes—Bourbon, however, knew where his mistress was at all times. Lemon went about her routine of checking the perimeter of the room before posting herself at the main entrance, with eyes on the emergency exit on the opposite side of the room.

Sliding into the pool, she began her freestyle stroke; as she lapped, her mind was freed and her body relaxed.

After several laps, Detective Lemon waved at Kate to get her attention. "I'm going to the bathroom. I'll be right back."

Kate signaled her okay and kept on lapping, slowly relaxing into her workout.

Suddenly Bourbon Ball jumped off his chaise, barking and growling. Jarred back to reality, Kate stopped at the side of the pool, took off her goggles, and stared right into the muzzle of a gun.

"Don't yell for anyone. If that dog comes near me, I'll shoot it. Hell, I might shoot it anyway."

Liam O'Hara, dressed in a brown delivery man uniform, stood with his feet wide apart and his 9mm Glock trained on Kate.

She grabbed Bourbon Ball's collar, securing him beside her, but she did not get out of the pool. She took off her swim cap and stood in the water as if nothing were amiss. A stillness came over her.

So this is him, she thought. *After all these years, here he is—he's really not much.*

Even with the gun pointed at her, she noticed a serpent tattoo around his trigger finger and his smoldering black eyes, the same eyes she had seen the night he was at her condominium. He was about her height, with muscular arms and neck.

"Liam O'Hara, you changed your name. So did I. You became Hunter Lewis, and I became Kate Chambers," she said conversationally. "Now that you've found me, what do you want?"

"Isn't it obvious? I am my father's avenger. Remember him? The man you and your grandfather killed." Liam's mouth was half smile, half twisted grimace.

"Don't you have that backward? It was your father who killed my parents." Kate's adrenaline was pumping—her legs started to shake, but she continued the interchange, hoping to buy time to consider a way out of the situation.

"It was your father who stole your life, not me or my grandfather. Every time you visited him in prison, your father injected you with a little more of his poisonous, untrue story." Kate's heart pounded and raced. She feared she might faint.

"Shut up! Don't you find it poetic that I'm going to kill you, finally, in a swimming pool? All that red blood staining the water," Liam said in a bizarre whispery tone.

Kate watched him cock the gun. Out of the corner of her eye, she saw Annie Lemon, who growled, "Drop your gun. No one is dying here today."

"She will be dead before you can get off a shot," Liam countered, never lowering his arms nor taking his eyes off of Kate; his arms were absolutely steady even as Bourbon Ball started up his low, menacing growl.

"No, she won't." Jablonsky had crept up behind O'Hara and placed the barrel of his pistol firmly against the back of his head.

"Feel that? My bullet will blow your skull apart before you can pull the trigger. Now, drop your gun!"

"That's right, take care of poor little Kathleen, the little girl who lost her parents to that terrible drunk driver. Beautiful, desirable Kathleen, living the good life with old Grandpa Chambers, and romping around in bed with Indiana Jones Fitzroy. Yeah, let's all make sure she's protected," spat Liam.

Kate was stunned by the overtly sexual tone of his voice as he lingered over the word desirable—it was spine-chilling.

"Drop the gun, scumbag!" Jablonsky's commanding voice echoed in the pool room, the sound itself almost yanking the gun from Liam's hand. He finally opened his hand and let his gun fall. Jablonsky kept his pistol pressed against Liam's skull while Detective Lemon grabbed his arms, jerking them behind his back, securely cuffing him.

"Get on the deck, facedown," barked Jablonsky. Then, as if Liam had become nothing but a mat lying on the concrete, everyone holstered their gun, and the chief began to give orders.

"Lemon, get Coupe here. Then call the precinct and have them send a black-and-white for transport. I want a properly equipped police car to carry this piece of dirt to the precinct."

Suddenly, Liam started to seize, with legs flailing and torso violently contracting. Foam oozed out of his mouth, then blood. Liam O'Hara was dead.

"Can you beat that. He must have had a cyanide capsule in his mouth." Jablonsky looked as shocked as Kate and the detectives; Bourbon Ball lifted his nose to sniff the strange odor of the poison but remained by Kate's side.

"I've never seen anything like this in person," continued Jablonsky. "Bill Reeves said he was a talented forensics guy— he must have handmade the capsule just in case he was caught —an old British intelligence trick."

Everyone remained fixed, staring down at the contorted face smeared with blood and body fluids. Johnny arrived at the pool, thoughtfully carrying a fluffy, warm robe and slippers for Kate.

"I guess the only transport we'll need now is an ambulance to take the body to the morgue. This is one for the books," Jablonsky remarked, shaking his head.

Johnny put his arm around Kate, quietly saying, "It's finally over. You'll never have to worry about that crazy slimeball again."

"He *was* a slimeball. Now he's a dead fucking slimeball," Johnny and all the detectives burst out laughing at the emotional intensity behind her expletives.

Jablonsky responded, "That's the right attitude, Kate. Don't waste any tears on the likes of him."

Everyone in the pool room turned to practicalities—a large bath towel was found to cover the body, Lemon called for the ambulance, and Johnny rode up to the condo to start a fresh pot of coffee for everyone.

Still wrapped in her robe, Kate took Bourbon Ball outside, wanting to get some fresh air, but mostly wanting to avoid looking at Liam O'Hara's body.

Jablonsky followed her, just in case she had a delayed shock reaction to what had just happened. They leaned

against one of the low stone walls that surrounded the building, warming themselves in the sun.

"How did he get into the pool area?" she asked.

"The back service door to the pump room wasn't locked.
John saw it when he was collecting the lunch plates from our
outside security team, and when you weren't in the condo, he
became concerned and reported it to me."

"Oh," was all Kate could muster, still stroking Bourbon
Ball. "He was so filled with venom, and he said those
personal, kind-of sexual things about me."

"That's right, Kate. Not unusual for deranged stalkers—
they can both love and hate their prey, particularly pretty
women. He kept those letters of yours, still wrapped with the
ribbon." Jablonsky stood and took her by the arm.

"Let's go upstairs. You need to get out of your wet suit and
into a hot shower." The chief's manner comforted Kate, who
was happy to have someone tell her what to do.

The ambulance arrived and the EMTs loaded the body for
transport to the morgue. Everyone gathered on the deck
talking about what had just happened.

Kate took her time before joining them. A hot shower,
using Marco's almond scrub and moisturizer, helped calm her
nerves.

After changing into comfy leggings and an oversized
cotton shirt, she called Joan to let her know what happened.
Joan would give Marco the details after his surgeries, so there
would be no surprises when he came home. Kate finally felt
ready to join everyone.

"The nerves of steel on that guy—making his move with
three armed detectives around. Kate, that was quick thinking
—you keeping him talking. It gave us time to move into position. His plan was to step into the room, take the shot, and get
away. After eluding the police for years, he thought he could
just continue doing it. He thought he was the smartest person
in the room," said Jablonsky.

"Thank you all so much. Antoine, Annie, Chief, Johnny—you all saved my life. And, really, set me free from the years of feeling that there was someone in the world who wanted to hurt me."

Interrupting the murmurs of "only doing our job," she added, "Kathleen Byrne and Kate Chambers can finally become one."

Jablonsky offered her a stick of cinnamon gum. Kate looked at it with speculation, unwrapped it, chewed, then commented, "You know, that's surprisingly good."

Jablonsky shrugged his shoulders and replied, "Of course. I'm heading back to the precinct—I have to call Bill Reeves and give him the report."

Dry humor still intact, Kate remarked, "Tell him he should rethink how he does employee background checks."

EPILOGUE

Johnny came in through Kate's kitchen door, announcing his news as he entered.

"André Trembly has invited us to dinner at the bistro. I'm pretty sure it has to do with the Arceneau case. He's invited you and me, Antoine and Annie, Joan, Chief Jablonsky, Dr. Patel, and Marco. The dinner is this weekend—Friday night, seven o'clock. Sorry, Bourbon Ball, canines are not invited."

"It's fitting that he is holding it at George's," remarked Kate, who liked Trembly's idea of closure.

Everyone arrived at the bistro in high spirits, glad to reconnect with the detectives and the chief. No one seemed bothered by the fact that the table setting mirrored the one that had been arranged for Celine Arceneau's farewell party.

Once again, George's staff had set up a screened area in the back of the restaurant, placing a table long enough to accommodate the group, plus one; Carly Jablonsky walked in, smiling conspiratorially as she slipped into the chair next to her father. André clinked the side of his champagne glass to get everyone's attention.

"I have taken the liberty of ordering for us this evening. I think we should start with a taste of champagne." André remained standing while the waiters poured everyone a generous glass of Dom Pérignon.

"A toast to Detective Stefan Jablonsky and his team, who brought justice to Celine Arceneau."

"Hear, hear!" cheered everyone as they turned toward the chief with raised glasses. Jablonsky was taken aback by both the toast and the affection that flowed his way.

"Here is something for you, sent to me through the embassy." André produced an official-looking piece of parchment paper decorated with delicately tinted maple leaves.

Using an official tone, he read, "The Service de Police de la Ville de Montreal recognizes Chief Detective Stefan Jablonsky of the Pittsburgh City Police Department for his courage in the face of danger in bringing justice to Celine Arceneau, a daughter of Montreal."

André opened a small navy-colored box, which held a round, shiny medallion hung on a grosgrain ribbon; he walked over to Chief Jablonsky, who was now standing, bowed slightly, and pinned the medal on his lapel.

Brimming with excitement over this recognition of Jablonsky's work, the group clapped and whistled. French-Canadian born George hustled over to kiss him on both cheeks, amidst cries of "Bravo! Bravo!" It was a thrilling moment—it dawned on everyone why André had secretly invited Jablonsky's daughter.

Jablonsky's eyes shone as he thanked André and, through him, the Montreal Police. "I really was just doing my job," he remarked modestly.

Johnny spoke up. "Well, I'm glad my job doesn't require me to run headlong toward a crazed person wielding a loaded gun!" While everyone laughed, the chief sat down, keeping his sport coat on so that the group had a view of the medallion.

He and Carly leaned in together for pictures of them pointing to the medal. As a father, Jablonsky was thrilled that Carly had been invited—this was a memory the two would always cherish.

Of course, for this set of friends, the food served was equal in status to the award ceremony. The meal began with potato leek soup, toasted slices of a perfectly baked French baguette, paired with a buttery chardonnay. The entrée of beef tenderloin in a mushroom pan sauce, yellow squash, and oven-browned fingerling potatoes was served next, accompanied by a rich cabernet.

Since she wasn't scheduled to operate the next day, Joan was able to enjoy the wine; but even as she chatted and ate, everyone knew her left earbud was quietly feeding her the play-by-play of how the pitcher, Cheeks, was doing in the Pirates baseball game.

Johnny and Coupe were deep in an exchange about which mushrooms and wine were best for a pan sauce. Kate was happy to see that a friendship continued to grow between them.

When the forks were down, everyone pushed back their chairs in order to move around and visit with Jablonsky, Carly, and André. The table was cleared, and on cue, hot coffee, brandy snifters, and a selection of pastries arrived. André had brought three bottles of Martell XO, which the staff poured for anyone in the mood for cognac.

Kate wore a dark purple, long-sleeved knit dress with a modern silver necklace and matching earrings; the emerald engagement ring Eddie Fitzroy had given her was home, nesting in her jewelry box.

Johnny noticed that Marco couldn't keep his eyes off of her, so he leaned in and whispered, "You know, she might be too much horsepower for you."

"Man, that's true, but I'm committed to the race." They laughed together like brothers.

"What are the two of you laughing about? Whatever it is, I'm changing the subject. I visited Ellen yesterday, and she told me that she and Patricia are going to Poland to help with the Ukrainian war effort, and, that you, Marco, helped set it up."

"Guilty as charged. Ellen actually had been talking with me about this for over a year. She calls it her 'next chapter.' She'll be working with Doctors Without Borders, using her considerable medical skills for a good cause. And we are always in need of more anesthesiologists. Patricia, is a huge bonus for us."

Under the table, Kate linked her fingers with Marco's. "It's a great idea and important humanitarian work. It gives them both a needed radical change and keeps them close together."

"Marco, did you tell her how much cash you and I found in your parent's books?" remarked Johnny.

"No. Kate, I took your suggestion and went through my parent's books and found quite a stash. That was a great tip!"

"What are you going to do with the cash?" asked Kate. Clearly he didn't need the money; the important thing was that he and Johnny had a great time searching for it.

"I gave some of the money to Andrea and Renata, my mom's friends. And the rest, well, I think my parents would be happy to know that I'm going to use it to woo a very special woman."

THE END

ACKNOWLEDGMENTS

I'd like to thank Heath Fallin, MD, for his careful reading of this manuscript; he ensured that my use of medical terms and diagnoses, medical technology, and hospital procedures were true and accurate. I'm so grateful that he took time from his busy practice to help me bring authenticity to this novel.

My brother, Jeffrey J. Stepek, spent his career in the nuclear business, first with Westinghouse Nuclear, then at Master-Lee, another firm specializing in nuclear energy. His expertise in the area of radiation and gadgets used in nuclear reactors was essential to this book. And, how often do a brother and sister get to bond over how to commit a murder with radioactive material!?

Wally and Betty Turnbull, owners of Torchflame Books, continued their support of my writing. They are a unique treasure.

Finally, heartfelt thanks to my husband David, my close friends, and my two pups, all of whom provide laughs and a listening ear.

ABOUT THE AUTHOR

Rebecca A. Miles (Stepek) was raised, educated, and established her first career in the city of Pittsburgh, Pennsylvania. From her work in Behavioral Medicine in Oncology, she became a recognized expert and presenter on grief, the grieving process, and the psychology of dealing with loss.

Throughout the successful Pittsburgh Murder Mystery trilogy, *Ground Truth, Broken Glass, Locked Box,* she explores the themes of love and loss, two states that she considers to be universal in human experience. As the series unfolds, her main characters are revealed to be people who are psychologically flawed, literate, funny, and often courageous in their search for the murderer.

Miles portrays deep and lasting friendships as the healing salve for the personal and public losses that are visited on the victims of crime, and especially on amateur sleuth Kate Chambers and Chief Detective Stefan Jablonsky. Her readers close the last page of each novel satisfied that Kate, Johnny, Joan, Jablonsky, Patel, and Antoine DeVille have meted out justice and continue to thrive through their collaboration and friendship.

When not writing, you will find Rebecca knee-deep in research for her next book. She enjoys introducing her readers to the well-known public spaces of Pittsburgh and to the small secret places about which only locals know. Her mystery novels are book club picks; she provides a discussion guide posted on the Torchflame Books site.

Rebecca A. Miles holds a doctorate in psychology from Duquesne University. Connect with her at rebeccaamile sauthor.com.

facebook.com/rebeccaamilesauthor

instagram.com/rebeccaamystery

amazon.com/Rebecca-Miles/e/B06Y4ZJPJ2

bookbub.com/authors/rebecca-a-miles

youtube.com/@rebeccamiles-se5yh

THE PITTSBURGH MURDER MYSTERIES

Ground Truth

With a cold case reopened by two uncovered skeletons and witnesses dying soon after coming forward, Kate Chambers and Detective Jablonsky must work together to guarantee that whoever killed these people doesn't get away with murder a second time.

Broken Glass

When a fellow student in a local glass-blowing class suddenly drops dead, Dr. Kate Chambers can't help but get involved. With the victim's family heirloom missing, Kate must determine how the necklace drew enough attention to drive someone to kill.

A Pittsburgh Murder Mystery

LOCKED BOX

Rebecca A. Miles

Locked Box

When a Canadian law professor dies suddenly, Chief Detective
Stefan Jablonsky suspects foul play. Determined to prove her friend's
innocence, amateur sleuth Dr. Kate Chambers joins an investigation
that leads from Pittsburgh to Montreal.